SWEET, SMART, AND STRUGGLING

DOES A DUMPSTER HOLD THE SECRET TO SUCCESS?

CARMEN KLASSEN

By Carmen Klassen

Copyright © Carmen Klassen 2019

All rights reserved. No part of this book may be reproduced in any form or by any electronic or mechanical means, including information storage and retrieval systems, without permission in writing from the author, except by reviewers, who may quote brief passages in a review.

All characters and events in this book are fictitious. Any similarity to real persons, living or dead, is coincidental and not intended by the author.

ALSO BY CARMEN KLASSEN

SUCCESS ON HER TERMS SERIES

Book 1: Sweet, Smart, and Struggling

Book 2: The Cost of Caring

Book 3: Life Upcycled

Book 4: Heartwarming Designs

Book 5: A Roof Over Their Heads (Preorder)

Success on Her Terms: Boxed Set 1 to 3

***

NON-FICTION TITLES

Love Your Clutter Away

Before Your Parents Move In

CONTENTS

Chapter 1	1
Chapter 2	9
Chapter 3	16
Chapter 4	20
Chapter 5	23
Chapter 6	26
Chapter 7	30
Chapter 8	38
Chapter 9	44
Chapter 10	52
Chapter 11	56
Chapter 12	65
Chapter 13	69
Chapter 14	78
Chapter 15	87
Chapter 16	99
Chapter 17	105
Chapter 18	111
Chapter 19	116
Chapter 20	121
Chapter 21	125
Chapter 22	133
Chapter 23	139
Chapter 24	145
Chapter 25	149
Chapter 26	157
Chapter 27	164
Chapter 28	173
Chapter 29	177
Chapter 30	184
Chapter 31	190
Chapter 32	194
Chapter 33	201

Chapter 34	205
Chapter 35	209
Chapter 36	213
Chapter 37	219
Chapter 38	223
A note from the author	231
Sneak Preview	232
Also by Carmen Klassen	235

CHAPTER 1

Carrie fought back tears as she walked through the parking lot. *Stupid, stupid, stupid* she repeated in her head. She knew she should only spend $40 in the grocery store. That was the budget for the week. But she couldn't face the thought of not bringing anything fun back for the kids, so she had grabbed a frozen pizza and ice cream bars for supper. Not on the list, and now she had blown the budget.

Well, crying and getting mad wouldn't help anything. And she wasn't about to go back into the store and try to return any food. So she'd have to figure things out. Again. At 31 years old she was tired of making every decision based on money, and always worrying about money. Her idiot jackass of an ex-husband was no help. He had cleaned out their meager savings and racked up over $8,000 in 'joint' credit card debt on who knows what before she moved out. At least she had been able to charge a rental truck on the card to move some furniture. Small blessings. Very, very, small. Especially since she was also on the hook for the balance of the card when Don stopped making the minimum payments.

Now she was the proverbial broke single mom. With a nine year old son, a four year old daughter, a chip on her shoulder, and a net worth so far down the toilet she'd probably never see a positive number. Carrie fantasized about one day having enough money to take her little family on a vacation. Then she could prove to herself that she wasn't a loser with no money skills. But that's all it was, fantasies. Right now, reality demanded she get the groceries home and in the freezer before her 'big splurge' turned into a big mess.

Fingers crossed, she put the key in the ignition of her 1994 Ford Taurus. With only a small cough, the car started and she drove home. She had just enough time to put away the groceries and lay on the couch for 15 minutes before picking up Katie from preschool.

Pulling into her parking spot at home, Carrie tried not to let her mood get worse. She knew she should be grateful—at least she had a home. But it was so depressing. As a single parent with barely an income, she qualified for subsidized housing. But when she could finally leave her marriage, she didn't have much time or money to find something decent and affordable that kept the kids in the same school. So she settled for the first thing she found within walking distance.

Set in a block of brown townhouses, it was the worst looking area in a very average neighborhood. Her two bedroom unit was at least at the end of a row, so she only had to deal with noisy neighbors on one side. The family of six that lived there were often yelling, slamming doors, and leaving their bikes and scooters across the common area. Carrie tried to be friendly when she first moved in, but soon realized that avoiding them (and keeping her kids out of range of their crazy activities) was the best for all three of them.

The industrial looking brown front door made her want to turn around and leave. She had put up a fall wreath to add some color (a house warming gift from her parents), but it had blown off the door a few nights earlier, and the damage left it sitting in the dumpster. The area in front of her entrance was tidy. *That* at least she could do with no money. But with cheap, faded blinds showing through the windows, and nothing decorative or colorful, there wasn't anything to smile at.

Carrie grabbed the two bags of groceries and let herself into the house. Inside wasn't much better than outside. On the main level, the beige walls were scuffed and stained from years of abuse. The carpet was brown, with a path worn through the small living room to the kitchen. Built in 1980, the kitchen had never been updated. Even the stove was 'original' and as hard as Carrie tried, she couldn't make the stove, fridge, or sink look any cleaner than the day she moved in. Years of neglect had seeped into the appliances that no amount of elbow grease could undo.

She put away the groceries, set a timer on the oven for 15 minutes, and went to lie down on the couch. Sleep was the only escape she had from her life, but the easy, deep sleep of her early 20s was much harder to find now. The habit of laying down was still strong though, and it's not like she had anything else to do.

Carrie would turn 32 in January. Most of the time she was happy to be older. The torment of her marriage was a big part of her 20s and something she never wanted to go back to. She had tried her best to be a good wife, to support her husband, and to make him happy. It had never been enough. But it had taken years to realize that his problems weren't her fault. At that point she had worked hard to get herself and the kids out.

Most of the people around her were unsupportive at first. Without seeing her life behind closed doors, they assumed she had a good marriage, or at least one she could make better if she really wanted. She lost a few friends that she sometimes missed. But she had gained peace, freedom, and absolute poverty. So, if having no money was the price to pay for not spending the rest of her life feeling like a horrible wife, then no money it would be.

The timer jolted Carrie out of her dozing. It was loud, insistent, and in another room; forcing her to get up and get going. She slipped on the boots she wore everywhere in the fall, pulled on her jacket, and grabbed her trusty reusable grocery bag with a snap closure, along with her purse. That bag had helped put food on the table more than once. A great thing about living in a neighborhood like hers were all the empty cans and bottles people dropped. So, whenever she was out, she collected them, cashed them in at the recycling center, and used the money to help keep her head above water. She felt embarrassed sometimes to be so desperate, but she had no choice.

As she approached the preschool, she mentally straightened her shoulders and pasted on a smile. Other moms were already there, looking perfectly stylish. Clearly they didn't have the type of worries she did. They were polite enough, and included her in their conversations, but she never felt she had much to offer. Talking about how long the painter was taking to re-paint the house, or how tiring it was to take the kids to Disneyland didn't fit with Carrie's reality. So, she did a lot of standing and smiling until the kids were let out.

Carrie's daughter Katie was almost always one of the first to be ready for home time. Bright, energetic, and excited about everything, she couldn't wait to tell her mom everything she had accomplished in the 2.5 hours she'd been at school. With slightly curly light brown hair, a small frame, and an eclectic style, she was a miniature version of Carrie—although Carrie usually wore plain clothes that didn't attract attention.

"Hi Katie-girl," she said as she was engulfed with a fast and furious hug.

"Mom! We got to play outside today and Miss Tara gave me a star because I helped Jennifer with her shoes and I didn't eat my snack 'cause I didn't like it." At this Katie turned to look for Magnus, the little boy Carrie watched after school. Carrie had learned that Katie didn't often need a reply to her statements, and smiled as Katie ran back to get Magnus. He was the opposite of Katie—quiet, hesitant, and slow. Carrie was grateful to have a playmate for Katie, and for the generous rate his parents paid her every month. Magnus' mom was one of the few people who supported her when she ended her marriage, and she often told Carrie that *she* was the one who gained the most from the after school care, not Carrie's budget.

Walking home with the two children, they all played a game to see who could spot empty bottles and cans first. When they walked by the dumpster for the townhouse complex Carrie grabbed a six pack of empty bottles sitting beside a coffee table someone had discarded. Must be nice to be able to just throw things out like that, she thought.

By the time they got back to the townhouse Carrie's bag was almost full, and she added it to the growing collection in their tiny backyard. Once inside the kids quickly dropped their outer clothes and ran up to the bedroom where the small collection of Katie's toys lived. Carrie and Katie shared a bedroom, but when Katie was home it was always her space to play in.

Carrie made a simple lunch of pasta with butter and carrot sticks. At least the kids loved simple food, and Carrie was used to eating whatever the kids preferred. The time passed pleasantly with the two children playing well for the most part. Sometimes Katie needed to be reined in a bit, but she was learning to pay attention to what Magnus was saying with his body language, even when he wasn't using his words to say what he wanted.

At 3 pm Carrie braced herself for the rest of the afternoon. As much as she loved watching Magnus, his siblings were another story. Twin 11-year-olds Justin and Calvin were a force to be reckoned with. They walked home from school with Carrie's son, Matthew. At least, they were supposed to walk home together. But often they tore off without him or lagged behind so much that Matthew just walked home alone.

Today they arrived together, and Carrie served juice, cookies, and apple slices to all the kids. Justin was the only one to spill his juice today, which wasn't a surprise. His arms and legs often seemed to move independently from his body, and he created disasters wherever he went. Compared to Matthew, who was deliberate and careful in everything he did, the twins ran fast and hard through everything without worrying about consequences.

Fortunately, they brought their Nintendo Switch with them now, and often played on that together after the requisite 45 minutes outside that Carrie insisted on for all the kids. Katie was always happy to run around and play at the playground across the street, and Magnus was always happy to be near Katie. But Matthew wasn't as athletic and was always asking Carrie how much longer until they could go back inside. The older boys generally kicked a soccer ball around or tried to climb the trees. Carrie was silently very thankful for the maintenance crew that trimmed the lower branches on the trees. Eventually the twins would be tall enough to catch the bottom branches and pull themselves up, but for now they still had their feet on the ground.

By 5:30 Carrie was more than happy to see Kara at the door ready to take her boys home. Kara had just started a new job as a physician's assistant which gave her the need and the resources to hire Carrie for childcare five days a week. Although the twins would be 12 next year, Kara already said that there was no way she'd be leaving them home alone, and Carrie was grateful for the job security no matter how challenging the twins could be. Kara's husband Ken worked long hours as a sales manager for a car dealership, but Kara seemed to cope with all the family and work responsibilities without batting an eye. Carrie felt grateful to call such a competent couple her friends.

Once the boys left, Carrie and Matthew breathed a sigh of relief. It was Friday, so no sharing space and toys now until Monday. Both kids were excited about the special treat of pizza and ice cream for supper, and Carrie felt a lot better about her splurge. As long as she found another good bagful or so of empty drink containers to return, she'd be able to make up the difference in time to cover her electric bill before it was overdue.

After supper, the three of them watched *Underdog* together. Cable TV was not in the budget, so they were limited to watching DVDs that they borrowed from the library. At least Carrie made sure to take the TV and DVD player that was in Matthew's room when she moved out. Matthew still complained sometimes about not having it in his room, but Carrie now had the authority to keep screens out of the bedrooms and she planned to keep it that way. Of course, her ex found the money to buy a huge TV and entertainment center for his place almost before Carrie had moved out. But that was his issue, and not hers.

Carrie went upstairs with Katie to get her ready for bed, leaving Matthew to re-watch the ending to the movie. After all, happy endings were the best part, and she wanted him to have as many bits of happy as he could. Katie was quite willing to tuck into bed. At some point she wouldn't be so excited to share a room with her mom, but for now she still loved it. Carrie's ex had never allowed the kids to share their bed—no matter what. She had quickly learned to do whatever she needed to keep the kids from disturbing him, but she always missed being able to snuggle in bed with the kids. Now, she and Katie slept on mattresses just a few inches apart, and she was always there to comfort Katie in the middle of the night if needed.

She made it back downstairs for the last few minutes of the movie and turned a bit to watch Matthew without being too obvious about it. Although she knew all parents thought their kids were the sweetest, she was convinced Matthew really was the sweetest kid she knew. His kind heart almost always shone through his dark brown eyes. He liked to keep his short brown hair tidy, and it suited his thin frame. He was also the type of kid to tuck in his shirt and tie up his shoes whenever he went outside. Carrie suspected Matthew could be quite the smart dresser if given a chance but right now he had to wear whatever she could find cheap at the thrift stores.

When the movie ended Matthew asked her to play UNO with him. This was another nice change that came with single parenthood. There was no nighttime stress. She could devote as much time and energy to the kids as she wanted, without having to brace herself for the berating and complaints that used to lie behind closed doors at night. Now, in the middle of their bare, old townhouse, they could be a peaceful little family.

Later that night, Carrie lay in bed listening to the even sounds of her daughter's breathing. This was worth it, she knew. But she wanted more. Not a lot more, just enough money to buy whatever groceries she wanted, and get the kids some nice clothes. Maybe plan a trip to the coast to see her sister. And some furniture. She smiled wryly to herself—at least her body was young enough to tolerate a mattress on the floor every night!

CHAPTER 2

The next morning Carrie woke up feeling happy. She liked weekend mornings. No rush to get kids out the door to school, or even to get dressed for that matter. She quietly grabbed her well-worn robe after taking a quick peek at Katie sleeping. Like her mom, Katie loved sleep. She was sprawled at an angle across her mattress with her feet over on one side and her arms and head over on the other side. Her blanket was only half covering her, but Carrie knew that wouldn't bother her one bit. With her cheeks rosy and her hair mussed around her face, she looked positively angelic. Carrie held the image in her heart as she walked downstairs.

Matthew was already up and watching another one of the DVDs they had borrowed from the library. She felt guilty that he couldn't enjoy Saturday morning cartoons like other boys his age or get lost in video games for that matter. They did have an old laptop that worked well enough for doing homework and checking emails but it would never hold up to gaming standards. After a quick kiss on his head, she went into the kitchen. Both her and Matthew were not big talkers in the morning, but Katie would more than make up for that when she woke up!

Carrie flicked the switch for the coffee maker she set up the night before. She believed the less thinking she had to do first thing in the morning, the better. Even if the thinking involved setting up the coffee maker. She briefly thought about the fancy coffee maker she had left at the old house. It was one of her big treats back when there was a bit more room in her budget. But she couldn't afford the individual coffee pods now, so it was just as good there was an old-fashioned coffee maker hiding in the back of the cupboard that she knew Don wouldn't miss when she left him. Sure, it wasn't the kind of coffee she loved, but coffee was coffee and she needed that small indulgence every morning.

While she waited for the coffee to brew, she quickly checked her text messages. Speak of the devil, Don had texted late at night. He was supposed to have the kids Saturday until Sunday afternoon, but had a job opportunity come up and wouldn't be able to take them. She supposed that meant he wouldn't be at Katie's soccer game that morning either. Well, it wasn't like she had any big plans he'd ruined. But she knew the kids would be disappointed. Nothing new there. She tried to make Don tell the kids in person when anything changed since she really didn't trust herself to pass on messages without adding her own two cents about what she thought. Which is probably why he waited until he knew she'd be in bed before texting. Typical.

Matthew looked half asleep on the couch, but she knew he'd need time to get over the disappointment of not going to his dad's. Katie could be appeased with the promise of any activity, even going to the playground. But Matthew was different. Looking at him, she felt her heart squeeze with sadness. No matter how hard she tried to be reliable and consistent, there were other people in his life that would let him down. And there was nothing she could do about that.

"Hey bud," she said quietly. He looked up and gave her a half smile. His hair was about as messy as he would let it get, which wasn't much. His eyes were only half open, but they were clear and thoughtful. Carrie looked down at the faded pajamas that were starting to creep up beyond his wrists and ankles, and he adjusted them as he turned to her.

"Mom," he answered sleepily "what's up?"

"Your dad sent a text late last night. He has a job for today, so you won't be going over to his house."

"Does that mean we'll have some more money for groceries?" Matthew had overheard a friend's dad complaining about paying child support. Quick thinker that he was, he asked Carrie how much child support *she* got. He was too aware of how tight things were for their little family. Carrie explained to him that his dad didn't have a steady job, and so he couldn't pay any child support. She carefully omitted the parts about him always quitting or getting fired, and how he still seemed to have money for things he should have long since grown out of.

"No, one day of work isn't enough for child support. But I guess we can be happy for him that he has some work, right?"

"Can I stay home when you take Katie to her soccer game then? Please?" Carrie had planned to walk the kids over to Don's house after the game if he didn't show up. But now there really was no reason for Matthew to come along. He was responsible enough to stay home for an hour on his own. So she agreed. Plus, she didn't want to insist he come right after disappointing him with the change in the days' plans. She gave him a quick hug and went to get her coffee. So much for starting the day on a good note.

By the time Katie bounced down the stairs, everyone else was awake and ready for her. Together they sat at the table for breakfast. The weekends were the only time the kids were allowed sugar cereal. They could each have one bowl, and that was it. Carrie had quickly figured out that cereal cut into the grocery budget pretty fast, so on weekdays she made oatmeal every morning. Some days it was only the threat of taking away their weekend breakfast that convinced them to eat their oatmeal!

Breakfast done and cleaned up, Katie was raring to get to her soccer game. Carrie was grateful for the community league that kept the costs down. Really, she could put Katie in a lot more activities and Katie would love it, but there wasn't money. So, she 'played' soccer, or whatever you called a group of four year olds all running together after one ball for an hour. Carrie told Katie at the last minute that she wouldn't be going to her dad's. Katie had a moment of sadness, and then remembered her soccer game and cheered herself up. Carrie breathed a quick sigh of relief that she didn't have two disappointed kids to deal with.

After reviewing all the safety rules with Matthew and making him promise to stay in the house with the doors looked, Carrie and Katie walked down the road to the soccer field. It was right beside Matthew's school and Carrie tried to walk everywhere possible to save on gas. She was finding that her new life as a broke single mom was great for losing weight. Between the walking everywhere, feeling too stressed to eat, and never having extra money for snacks or wine, she was down at least an inch or two in her waist.

The game was a great success, with both teams feeling certain they won. The league didn't keep score for the small kids' games, and the atmosphere was always fun and relaxed. Katie's enthusiasm for everything—including her teammates—made her a favorite with everyone, and Carrie felt herself pulled into the main group of parents in an attempt to keep eyes on Katie. One of the other parents whom Carrie had chatted with a few times before came up beside her.

"We're going to take the kids out for ice cream to celebrate their win." She said with a big smile. "Can you and Katie join us?"

At this Katie spun around and added an excited squeal to the conversation. "Yay Mommy! Let's go have ice cream!" Carrie felt her heart sink. Unless it was McDonald's, there was no way she could afford ice cream for Katie and Matthew, even if she pretended she didn't want any herself. And she needed to watch the gas level in the car so she couldn't drive far.

"Um, where were you thinking?" The mom (Carrie remembered her name was Heather) listed the most overpriced ice cream shop in the area. Quickly Carrie tried to make an out… "Oh, I don't think we'll be able to. I've left Matthew home on his own and we really need to get back."

But Heather was not put off. "Oh, why don't we just take Katie with us? I've got an extra booster seat. And it wouldn't be a celebration without the team's most enthusiastic player!"

Katie chimed in with begging and puppy eyes. "Please Mommy please!"

"Well, if you're sure it wouldn't be too much…" She could tell that Heather genuinely wanted to include Katie, and didn't seem concerned about an extra child. But she felt uncomfortable having someone else spend money on her daughter. She did have one ten-dollar bill tucked into her wallet for emergencies. "Here, let me give you some money for her ice cream," she started to say.

But Heather brushed her hand away. "Are you kidding? She's so entertaining I should pay you to spend time with her!" Carrie tried to hide her relief.

After exchanging phone numbers, Carrie gave her daughter a hug in between jumps up and down. Katie was beside herself with excitement. They walked to their minivan and Carrie turned to walk home.

Matthew was in the same place she had left him and was re-watching the movie. He was clearly upset to hear his sister got to go out for ice cream while he was stuck at home. "Hey, why don't we go see if Boris wants to go for a walk?" Carrie asked, trying to give him something else to do. Boris was the neighbor's dog back at their old place, and Matthew had often taken him out for walks when they lived there. He loved dogs, and his biggest request every year was for a dog of his own. Fortunately, Boris' owners were a bit older, and loved having Matthew come and take him for walks. The only drawback would be walking past Don's house. But since he was working, there was no chance of running into him. She tried to avoid the area if she thought he might be around.

"OK!" Matthew answered. He was already perking up at the thought of spending time with his furry friend. In five minutes they were almost there, just a few houses away from Don's place, and Boris'. And then the world dropped out from under both of them. A strange minivan pulled into Don's driveway. For some reason, both Carrie and Matthew took a step back where the driver couldn't see them.

Don was in the passenger seat, and a tall blonde woman was driving. The sliding door opened, and two girls, about six and eight years old jumped out. They both had shopping bags with the LEGO logo on them and they raced to the front door. Don and the woman followed behind, with him grabbing her butt and whispering in her ear before unlocking the door and letting everyone in.

Carrie's shock turned to total devastation when she looked at Matthew. His eyes were glistening, and his hands were clenched into two white fists. "Mom," he whispered. And then he turned and ran back towards their townhouse. Carrie tried to catch up to him, but he was too fast.

Back at the house he ran to his room and curled up in a ball in the corner. Carrie just squeezed up beside him and scooped him into her lap. She had no words to say. Well, none that a nine year old should hear. How could Don do that? How could he lie, bail on his own kids, and then play happy family with someone else's kids? And LEGO? The one thing (besides a dog) that Matthew always wished for? The thing he always told Matthew was a waste of money? She knew Don would happily throw her under a bus and walk away, but she wanted to believe he would treat his kids better than that.

The rest of the weekend dragged on. Matthew was grumpy and rude to his sister. Carrie let it go, and just tried to keep the kids busy and apart from each other. She tried a few times to get Matthew to talk but he wouldn't. He was letting the hurt churn inside him. Carrie made sure he heard her tell him that this was not about him, and that any other parent would have done whatever it took to spend time with their own kids. But it felt like her words hit a wall. Matthew just looked at her, and then went to his room and closed the door.

CHAPTER 3

After Matthew fell asleep on Sunday night, she stood in his doorway and watched him for a few minutes. He looked so peaceful, and she needed to believe he was getting a break from the pain he had felt all weekend. Don hadn't tried to see the kids on Sunday, and she hadn't asked. He obviously had other priorities.

She lay in bed for a long time, thinking. While she knew she couldn't change Don, she felt like she had failed her kids. If she had money, she could have taken both kids for ice cream and spent time with other parents like normal people do. And they could have spent their weekend having fun, going to the pool, buying LEGO, and watching cartoons in the morning. She could have protected Matthew from that scene this morning if she had more money.

Only she had no idea how to fix that. Years ago, her plan was to become a psychologist. She was in her third year of university when she met Don. He was so charming she quickly found reasons to spend time with him instead of studying, and she let him convince her that the stress of her studies was too much. At the time it seemed like he was the only one who supported her when she chose not to go back for her fourth year. Years later she realized he was setting her up to rely on him and keep her accomplishments small.

When Matthew, and then Katie came along, she felt like her time was always full with trying to take care of them while unsuccessfully being married to Don. She did what she could to pick up part-time work, but only when it didn't interfere with Don's schedule. Even after school childcare was a challenge because Don hated coming home to other people's children in the house. That was when she started hiding cash until she had enough to get herself and the kids out of the toxic life Don tried to keep them in.

Student loans still took up a big part of her budget. They were a regular reminder of her failures. If she had a good job now, she could take care of her kids properly. Collecting pop cans wasn't exactly pulling her out of the red but she didn't know what else to do. Even if she could handle having more kids to watch after school, the tiny townhouse couldn't.

Her parents had no idea how much she struggled, and she planned to keep it that way. Her dad recently retired from his job as a mechanic, working until he was 72 so they'd have enough saved to live on. They lived just over an hour's drive away. Mom had always dreamed of going back to work when the kids went to school, but a devastating injury from a car accident when Carrie was ten and her little sister Jessica was four left her in chronic pain and unable to work.

Carrie had done as much as she could to help despite her young age, and she was grateful she could come home to her mom, rather than an empty house like many of her friends. It's part of the reason she accepted the after school childcare opportunities now, so she could always be home when her own kids came home from school.

It was just over a month ago that Carrie's dad helped her move out, taking the few pieces of furniture she knew Don wouldn't care about. Her mom hadn't come because she couldn't carry anything, and Carrie breathed a sigh of relief for that. Mom would have seen how dire Carrie's position was and tried to step in and fix things. She knew they would help financially if she asked, but they didn't really have any money to spare. Money. She should be helping them and making their lives easier in retirement! She kept claiming she would visit her parents for a weekend with the kids soon but needed to have money for extra gas to drive there, first.

Jessica was a different challenge. Just graduated from law school, she was now trying to work her way up the ladder while buried by even more student debt than Carrie. She had no doubt her sister would one day be a successful lawyer with a big house and a fancy car. And if she caught a glimpse of Carrie's life right now, she'd drain her meager funds to help out. That was the last thing Carrie wanted.

Don, of course, would be no help now or in the future. He always spent everything he made, even when he was in a steady job. His focused on his own needs, and refused to deny himself anything, even if it meant his family went without. There wasn't anything about him that she missed.

After Matthew was born, he quit trying to do anything nice for Carrie and that included making himself presentable if he was at home. Often, he smelled bad, his greasy brown hair stuck up everywhere, and he parked himself on the couch in torn sweatpants and stained shirts that Carrie hated. Going out was a different matter. Whenever he thought he might be seen he made the effort to look his best and put on a good show. People who just met him always talked about how charming he was. But Carrie knew that he used charm to manipulate people.

Behind the closed doors of their house he would shift back to complaining to Carrie about how she looked, the way she talked (especially if she accidently used a word he didn't understand), and how much of 'his' money she wasted. His last words to her as she left the house with the kids were "Don't you ever think I'll give you a penny. You're on your own now bitch!"

So, it was up to her. But there was no way she could keep going like this. The kid's needs would get more expensive as they got older.

And if anything happened to her and she couldn't make money they'd be in big trouble. She had to figure out something, and fast. And in the meantime, she still had a very sad little boy who believed his dad would rather spend time and money on someone else's kids.

CHAPTER 4

Monday started off cold and slow. Neither of the kids wanted to get out of their warm beds, and Carrie didn't dare turn up the heat past 19 degrees because her bill was already challenging her careful budgeting. Finally Matthew was off to school, and Carrie quickly tidied up the house before it was time to take Katie to preschool. Monday was always laundry day, so she braved the horrid basement to get the first load in the wash. She was going to spend the morning at the library after dropping Katie off, hopefully finding out some way to bring in some extra money.

As they started off to school, Carrie noticed the dumpster was overflowing again with other people's cast-offs. Right beside the coffee table she'd seen on the weekend was a decent sized plant, already starting to wilt in the crisp fall air. She sympathized with the poor plant. Some days you just felt like garbage.

By the time Katie was running off to join her school friends, Carrie decided she couldn't bear to leave the plant to die. So instead of going to the library, she headed back home. The plant was still there, along with the coffee table and a few other bits and pieces. She took everything she could and made a few trips back to the house. It was OK to help keep things out of the landfill, right?

Her dad was always one to 'rescue' something before it went to the dump. One time he even found a canopy bed in pieces at the side of the road, and he had lovingly repaired it and painted it before putting it up in Carrie's room when she was eight years old. It was the envy of all her friends for many years! Carrie hoped she could channel a bit of her dad's optimism for what other people saw as trash.

Once inside, Carrie was surprised to find the quality of the furniture was high. This wasn't some crappy particleboard. It was solid wood furniture that had been neglected for a long time. She started by gently cleaning the plant and watering it. Setting it beside her threadbare couch she smiled for the first time that day. It was the nicest thing in her living room. And it was free!

Next, she turned her attention to the coffee table. It had a mid-century modern look to it, with clean lines and a trendy oval shape. She tackled the layers of grime until the table looked beautiful. Although part of her wanted to keep it, she had a feeling she could actually sell it for a little bit of money. Getting out her digital camera, she took a few pictures and started up her laptop so she could download them. Twenty minutes later she had a listing up for sale on a Buy and Sell page that she sometimes used to find cheap clothes and toys for the kids. The listing was for $35, but she'd happily take $20 if anyone would buy it. That was more money than she could collect in drinks containers in a week!

The rest of her time she spent cleaning up a child's table and chairs she had also rescued from the dumpster. Again, the quality was good, but it was covered in scribbles and stickers that would take a while to remove. But she figured Katie would love it for now, even though she was almost too big for it. Just before it was time to get Katie and Magnus, Carrie went to the basement to switch over the laundry and start a new load. She always tried to get in and out of there as quick as possible. It was cold and dirty, and there was a pile of paint cans and junk that the last renters left. The landlord had offered to come back and clean it out after Carrie moved in, but he gave her the creeps and she didn't want him anywhere near her when she was alone in the house, so she told him she'd take care of it.

Now, she realized there might be something in the pile that she could try to sell. For the first time, she felt a tiny glimmer of hope. She'd definitely be coming back down here once the kids were settled after lunch.

CHAPTER 5

As she predicted, Katie was delighted with the little table and chairs, and immediately set up her coloring book and crayons. Magnus was more than happy to sit and color with her—it required much less interaction than some of Katie's other ideas. Carrie went to make lunch and decided to quickly check her email on her laptop. Her old cell phone was really only good for limited calling and texting, and she didn't want to miss an email if someone was interested in the coffee table. She was surprised to find three responses.

The first one asked if she could deliver it, and there was no offer to pay more for delivery. Yeah right, she thought. But the next email had someone asking if they could take a look at it that evening! She quickly replied with a positive response and the neighborhood she lived in, and then emailed the first person saying she couldn't deliver. The third email asked if the price was negotiable, so she decided to wait before she replied.

That evening, a very stylish lady knocked on her door, and Carrie felt a bit embarrassed to let her into her shabby home. But the lady only had eyes for the coffee table. She quickly took out $40, and Carrie had to admit she didn't have any change.

"Oh, not to worry, it's a bargain at forty." Carrie bit back a polite refusal. She could really use the extra $5. After Carrie helped her load it into her SUV and watched her drive away, she dashed inside. Both kids were jumping up and down.

"Forty dollars Mom!" Matthew shouted. "That's a lot of money!"

"I know, and it came from nothing! That table's been sitting in the dumpster since Saturday."

"Can I have the money?" Katie asked. Ever an optimist, she wasn't afraid to ask for things.

"Tell you what Katie, I'll put some of it aside so we can have pizza for supper again on Friday, OK?"

"Yes!" both kids answered.

That evening, after Katie fell asleep, Carrie remembered the pile of stuff in the basement. And her laundry. In the excitement of selling something, she had completely forgotten. She asked Matthew if he'd go on a treasure hunt with her. His whole body perked up a little bit, and they put on their shoes and ventured into the basement to see what they could find.

There was a side table, a broken chair, and a lamp without a shade. Carrie wasn't sure she could do anything with those. But there was quite a variety of paint colors, some brushes, and some empty cans and bottles they could add to their pile of returns. And some trash of course. Carrie was more than happy to put that aside to take out in the morning. She already had an idea for painting the child's table and chairs with a seafoam green paint they found and adding some decorative touches with a bit of white paint and a little brush she found that was still in its packaging. They agreed to leave everything in the basement for now and together brought the clean laundry upstairs to fold.

That night, Carrie lay in bed and dreamed about the future. It had been a long time since she had cash in her wallet that wasn't destined for a bill or groceries. Of course, she'd use some to buy a frozen pizza again on Friday, and not walk out of the grocery store in tears. That would be nice. And she'd put a few dollars aside to start replenishing her emergency fund. That cash saved her once when she needed to leave her marriage and starting to build it up again would feel so good.

In the perfect world she dreamed about, there was always a little extra in the bank account for when a bill was higher than expected, she could buy groceries based on a list not a budget, and she took the kids out once in a while to swim at the pool and eat supper at a restaurant. Granted, her dreams weren't exactly reaching for the stars, but they still felt pretty far out of reach.

She wondered where else she could find things for free to turn around and sell. Without a truck (and some more muscle) she'd have to stick to smaller items. But maybe one day she could turn it into something bigger...

CHAPTER 6

The next day Carrie still felt hopeful and happy. The kids seemed happier too. She tried not to think about what a big deal they had all just made over $40. There were probably kids in their complex who got more than that for spending money. But it was new to them, and it felt good.

After dropping off Katie she walked home to get the car and drove to the library. She wasn't sure where to start. Too bad there wasn't a section for *I have no skills or money and I need an easy way to get rich*. She took out a few books on small businesses and entrepreneurship but nothing seemed like the break she needed. Well, maybe there was a way to just sell things she found for free. There were a few other apartment complexes nearby that would have dumpsters. Maybe she could find something there.

Carrie checked out a few books and decided to take a detour on the way home to see if she could find some things to sell. At the first dumpster, she parked and took a deep breath. It was surprising she had any pride left after being Don's wife, but she did, and she felt embarrassed to be digging through a dumpster. But she'd feel even worse if she didn't try. So she put her car keys in her jacket pocket and zipped it up so they wouldn't fall out, and then went to dumpster dive.

Ignoring the smell, Carrie climbed up on the side just enough to look in. There were a few picture frames and some clothes within reach, so she grabbed them and put them in her trunk. It was possible they'd smell, and she tried to keep her car as clean as possible. She also grabbed a stool from the other side of the dumpster. Tempted to drive home as fast as possible, Carrie forced herself to stop at three other dumpsters before going home.

By the time she pulled up at her place, she had a trunk full of various home décor and clothes. Everything went straight to the basement until she could check and see what she could really sell. Plus, it felt a bit gross to be bringing things from the garbage into the house.

Carrie had just enough time to wash up and head back to the school to pick up Katie and Magnus. For the rest of the week she made it a habit to check the dumpsters in her own complex daily, and slowly the pile in the basement grew.

In the evenings Carrie worked on the little table and chairs. She got out the old shower curtain she used to keep under Katie's mattress when she was wetting the bed. Probably just from the stress of moving, because after a few weeks she stopped, and just last week Carrie had taken away the plastic protection, certain Katie would be fine. Now the shower curtain would have a third life as a drop sheet. After hot water and scrubbing removed the rest of the stickers on the table and chairs, Carrie was pleased to see the surface looked pretty good.

She found a quarter can of primer in the pile in the basement and a small roller and brush. If she was careful, she could reuse the same roller and brush to put the finishing paint on after priming. Soon, the bright red and blue paint was covered by a smooth coat of white primer. It looked like it would need another coat, but she was sure she could make it stretch enough to cover it nicely.

While the primer was drying on the little table she was working on, she started up her laptop. It occurred to her that she might find some free things on the Buy and Sell site that she could fix up and make a little money on. Plus, she had a few things from the dumpster to list. She had quickly removed the posting for the coffee table after the lady left, so she wouldn't have to deal with more unnecessary emails about it. Besides some end tables and a small shelf she had rescued and cleaned up in preparation for painting, she had also found a men's ski jacket in excellent condition. It sold for $20 to a lady who wanted it for her grown son. Carrie put the cash in her purse and planned to use it to buy more primer. She had already learned that a quality primer lasted longer and gave a better finish than the cheaper ones.

Sure enough, on the site she found a mirror that had potential, and another coffee table for free. She sent off an email to each asking about location. While she'd have to drive to pick them up, she wasn't going to lose any potential profit on paying for gas if it was too far away.

The next day Carrie bought more primer and worked as best she could in the small corner of the living room that was now her 'work' area. It was a bit of a challenge to get things done in between picking the younger kids up from preschool and keeping them busy. Sometimes she had to wait until the evening so she could start and finish something and not have to clean up halfway through.

She had just enough time to make up a plate of apples and celery with peanut butter before the older boys came in from school. With a little complaining from Justin about vegetables, the kids all ate up, and then she herded them outside for some fresh air and exercise.

Once they were back inside, Carrie checked her emails and was happy to see replies about both pieces of furniture. The person with the coffee table lived too far out of the city to make it worth it, but the lady with the mirror was close enough to collect from.

Tuesday evenings Matthew had Boys' Club at the church nearby. It was the perfect price for Carrie (free), and Matthew really enjoyed his time there. After dropping him off, she headed out with Katie to the mirror lady. It occurred to her as she drove that she really shouldn't be going to people's places alone. Next time she'd try to meet somewhere. But for tonight she was determined to pick up the mirror.

When they arrived a very interesting looking lady met them at the door. Her hair was tied up in a fluorescent scarf, she had on at least four different necklaces, her peasant-style blouse had tiny mirrors in it that reflected the light in the entryway, and her loose flowing pants were an emerald green.

Katie took one look and said "WOW! You're the most beautiful lady ever!" And with that, Carrie and her so honest daughter were invited in with a laugh. The mirror was a free standing, full length mirror. Carrie hadn't quite thought through getting it into her car, and she was struggling to get it into the front seat, since it was the only place it would fit and still leave room for Katie.

Suddenly the front door of the house opened and the lady came back out. "I couldn't let my new favorite person leave without a gift!" she said. Handing Carrie a rather large grocery bag, she said "Your daughter made my day. I hope she likes these little bits!"

Once they were back home with Matthew, Katie reverently began taking things out of the bag. Carrie had never seen her move so carefully. Apparently the 'beautiful' lady had made an impression. In the bag were enough scarves, necklaces, and little skirts to keep Katie in bright colors for weeks. At the bottom was a scarf holder that could hang in the closet and keep things relatively organized. Carrie had no idea how the lady could have grabbed so many things in such a short time.

After Katie was in bed, Carrie sat down and sent a Thank You email to the kind lady. Having something 'new' for Katie was beyond wonderful, and she struggled to find the right words for such a generous act. Matthew was happy too, having started a woodworking project at Boys' Club that they would continue for the next few weeks.

CHAPTER 7

The rest of the week went by quicker than usual. In between caring for the kids, Carrie finished painting the little table and chairs. During their weekly trip to the library on Thursday evening she returned the entrepreneurship books that failed to inspire her, and checked out an armful of DIY books about restoring furniture. She used some of the hints to add simple white accents to the table and the back of the chairs. The finished result was adorable, and Carrie wished she could do something like this for Katie while she was still small. She was quite sure some little girl would love it, if she could find someone to buy it.

The mirror was finished too, and ready to sell. Carrie used white paint to create a shabby chic look and her tiny set of tools to tighten all the connections so it stood sturdy and would hold up to years of use. The set had been a gift from her dad when she started university. "Every girl needs to be able to do basic repairs," he claimed, and she frequently used the tools for little DIY jobs.

She left the mirror in her bedroom for a few days, so Katie could enjoy trying on a new treasure each morning and seeing how it looked. She was careful to only use one item each day at first—

stretching her new wardrobe to really last! Carrie loved seeing these bits of her daughter's exuberant personality shine through her choice of clothes.

By Friday she had listed both items on the Buy and Sell site, and Carrie had to resist checking her emails every hour. Her weekly grocery trip took up a bit of her time, and she added a frozen pizza and a bottle of Orange Crush to her basket without feeling guilty. She also put aside $5 from her first sale in her secret savings spot. It was a pocket inside her Bible that was almost hidden. During her marriage, Don had often rifled through her things to make sure she wasn't lying to him. About what, she was never sure. But he always left her Bible alone, so it had been her secret stash of security.

The other $30 she had put in her bank account. After she paid her bills, she would have $32.41 remaining in her account. Carrie always budgeted to the penny.

Friday night, the kids were excited about their 'weekly' pizza night. Carrie had to smile—she loved her kids who were so delighted by any surprise and yet wanted their days to have predictable (but fun!) routines. She was happy to be able to give that to them, and answer 'probably' when they asked if they could always have pizza on Fridays.

Saturday was cold and rainy, and Katie's soccer game was canceled. Secretly Carrie was a little bit relieved to not have to stand in the rain for an hour, nor to deal with any after game plans that involved money. If all went well, they'd soon be able to start going to those activities as a family once in a while.

It took a few no-shows before buyers came for the furniture over the weekend, but again, people were really happy when they did actually arrive. The table and chairs sold for $50, and the mirror sold for $40. Carrie was happy to have cash in her wallet, and a little sad to see the furniture go. They were things she would love to have in her own home.

The first thing she did with the money was take the kids to the pool to go swimming. Although they had survived many boring weekends at home before, this time she would give them something fun to do. She ignored the guilt about spending money. It was almost like she could hear Don's voice in her head telling her all she did was blow money. But of course, *he* had only spent money on the kids if it made him personally look good.

They stayed until the last swimmers exited the pool and came home happy and tired. Carrie heated up the leftover soup from the night before for supper. Soup was a budget saver that she often made for at least two meals a week. After supper she scrolled through the Buy and Sell site for anything free she could re-sell, but nothing had potential. She'd check again the next day. Now that she had this chance, she was determined to make it work.

Six weeks later, Carrie had made enough extra money to buy Halloween costumes for each of the kids, put $70 into her secret cash savings, keep an extra $50 in her bank account, and buy Matthew and Katie brand new winter boots. She looked at the thrift store and the Buy and Sell site for boots, but in the end, there was nothing that would work well. While Carrie was relieved to have them both in nice boots that would keep their feet warm and dry, it cost her more than a week's worth of furniture sales. She had to remind herself that they would have been stuck wearing runners to school in the snow if it wasn't for that, instead of worrying about the cost.

Her days were usually divided between keeping the kids busy, reading through the DIY books from the library, and working on any project she thought she could sell. For once she was grateful for their tiny little house that took almost no time to clean. More time to spend with the kids and (hopefully) more time fixing things and making money. She realized she needed to get some money management books out as well. She didn't want to make money just to have it disappear. If she could figure out how to make the right decisions, maybe one day they'd get out of this hole they were in and she could actually plan for the future.

For the time being, she would put some cash in her emergency fund and bank the rest once her expenses were covered. Turns out that was easier said than done as it always seemed like there were extra things that cost money. Matthew came home with a field trip form for his class to go to the science center. He had already missed one field trip because Carrie didn't have the money. Being able to say yes right away to this one felt good. Immediately she filled out the form and included the $10. Matthew's smile made it all worth it.

They had dreamed of going to the science center since it opened earlier in the year, but admission and parking were way beyond Carrie's budget. "You'll have to pay attention to everything you see so you can come home and tell me all about it."

Still smiling he said "I will Mom. It's so cool you're making this money!" Carrie agreed. Her emergency savings was up to $80 and her bank account would have an extra $142 plus change in it when she deposited the $50 left over from the weekend sales. With getting paid from Kara for childcare, and careful budgeting, Carrie could cover rent and all her bills and it would still be another week before they were all due.

She had planned to use some of the money for gas so she could take the kids to visit her parents, but her mom had taken a bad fall and was back in bed full time recovering. Carrie wished she could be there to help her dad take care of her mom, but she couldn't do that with the kids, and she didn't feel comfortable leaving town for the weekend when Don was supposed to have them.

Without saying anything about having someone else's kids over, he had demanded Carrie bring the kids over on his next weekend as if nothing had happened. But by Sunday morning he brought them back with no warning, saying he had to get some things done and they'd be in the way. Carrie was relieved that she was home. That night Katie wet the bed. Without the plastic sheet under, it took Carrie the whole time the kids were at preschool the next day to clean everything and dry it.

After they ate lunch, Carrie checked her emails, and was happy to see that one person had responded and would hold some items for her to pick up the next evening. It included a box of knick-knacks, two lamps, and an end table. Like the first coffee table she sold, this end table had a unique shape, and Carrie was sure she could make it into something special. She thought longingly about the tools and supplies her dad had in the garage at home. He never threw anything away, and she knew he'd have everything from sandpaper to wood filler and furniture gloss. She couldn't wait for her mom to feel better so they could visit. That would be good for all of them.

When the boys arrived after school it felt like total chaos. She couldn't get the twins to sit down to eat their snack, which led to a spill, and crumbs scattered over the floor. Matthew uncharacteristically yelled at them that they were "stupid idiots" and Carrie had to be quite firm with him before he apologized to them. The whole incident hardly phased the older boys, and she was relieved to get them all out the door to play. She'd have to wash the floor later since the juice had spilled across the floor and sprayed up the wall a bit, but she didn't dare leave the kids to their own devices so she could clean it up right away.

At the park the twins ran off to throw a football they brought with them, Katie and Magnus ran to the play set, and Matthew slumped on a swing, barely moving it. Standing where she could watch all the kids, Carrie gave Matthew some space while being close enough that he could talk if he wanted to.

After a few minutes, he looked up at her with tears in his eyes. Carrie waited while he struggled to talk. Slowly he told her what was bothering him. The two little girls they saw at Don's house a few weeks ago had come up to Matthew in school. They recognized him from the kid's school pictures that were still on the wall at the old house. The girls told him that their mom was dating his dad, and that meant he had to be their brother and be nice to them. They also told him he didn't have a bedroom anymore since he didn't actually live at the house and he wasn't allowed to touch their stuff if he came over.

Carrie needed to focus on calming her own emotions before she could speak. She could feel the depths of betrayal that Matthew felt, and the agony of being replaced by two strange kids, even if all of what they told him wasn't true.

"Bud, the way those girls treated you was really mean, and it's not OK. I know that, and I can see how much it's hurt you to be talked to like that." He looked up at her with tears streaming down his cheeks, and she struggled to not go wrap her arms around him. At nine years old he didn't like showing affection in public. She knew that later on he'd let her hug him and try to make some of the pain go away.

"But remember, you're not responsible for the choices other people make. That includes the choices these girls made and the choices your dad has made. You are in total control of you, and you get to decide what to do next."

"I want to go to dad's house and kick those girls and their mom out and make them go away forever!" He spat out angrily.

"Yeah, it can feel good in the moment to imagine making people pay for hurting us. But it doesn't actually fix anything. You know that, right?" He nodded. "Can you spend some time thinking about what you want to do next? And then we'll talk about it?" He nodded again and wiped away his tears. "You're a really brave kid to think about this and talk about it. Sometimes people just fly off the handle and make things worse. It takes a strong person to stop and think about things. I'm really proud of you!"

He gave a half smile "Even when I call Justin and Calvin names?"

Carrie smiled back. "Shoot, if you didn't do something once in a while like that, I'd think there was something wrong with you. I need my nearly perfect boy to mess up a little once in a while!" Now his smile was full and genuine. Carrie was silently grateful for getting through that and reminded herself to take her own advice. She'd like nothing better than to force Don to be a real father to his own kids. But that was not something she could control.

The next night Carrie picked up the free items while Matthew was at Boys' Club. Katie was hoping for another generous gift from a stranger, but it wasn't to be. So they went back home to unload the things and look at them before it was time to pick up Matthew.

The box of knick-knacks had a variety of empty frames with interesting shapes. Carrie remembered seeing something in a design magazine at the doctor's office waiting room where an accent wall had a bunch of different picture frames all empty and painted gold. She figured she could pull that off if she could find some inexpensive gold paint and more frames.

The lamps needed new shades and something interesting done to the bases. And she figured the side table would look great with a distressed white paint finish and a floral decoupage on the drawer fronts.

So, she'd need to buy some supplies this round. As soon as she could get to her parent's she could check out her dad's garage for anything she might use. Again, she was getting excited about the potential these cast-offs had, and the chance to make some more cash. It was going to be a good week after all!

Once Katie was in bed Carrie got to work cleaning everything thoroughly. This was probably going to be the hardest part of every project—getting it ready. But it's not like her evening had anything else she needed to be doing. Matthew was on the couch, half watching a movie and half reading a book. After giving him some time, she asked him if he had thought about what to do next about the situation with the girls.

"I'm thinking about some things, Mom. If those girls have a mom who's dating, then maybe they don't have a dad. So, I should be OK about them spending time at Dad's house. But they're not my sisters and I don't need to take care of them like I take care of Katie. And I'm going to tell them that if they talk to me again. They're not in charge of me!"

"Wow, that's some pretty intense thoughts for a nine year old. I totally agree with what you're saying. It's fair, but firm. You're going to make an excellent dad one day!" she looked at him and winked. He gave a lopsided smile, and then got serious again.

"But I also don't like that Dad lied about work and that he's spending time with someone else's kids and not me. So I'm going to tell him that the next time I see him."

At this Carrie felt a pang of anxiety. Setting boundaries with two little girls was one thing, but trying to set boundaries with Don was another thing entirely. When he felt threatened, he was cruel and retaliatory, often throwing back an accusation or insult so he could try to demean the other person. She worried he'd do it to Matthew too.

"OK bud. But the thing is, your dad might not like it when you tell him that. It's really hard for him to take correction. I think the way you feel is right, but I don't want you to get your feelings hurt any more than they already are."

"It's OK Mom. I'll be nice about it." He clearly felt the discussion took care of everything, and ignored his movie and book so he could start his homework with full focus. Carrie couldn't shake the feeling that he was in for a harsh reality check. Aside from wishing she could make Don disappear, she figured all she could do now was be there for Matthew if it did go badly...

CHAPTER 8

After dropping off Katie at preschool, Carrie was keen to get home and working on her projects. Now that October was over, she was starting to think about Christmas. She planned to work really hard so the kids could have a nice Christmas.

She finished cleaning all the picture frames and started covering them with the rest of the primer she found in the basement. Her plan was to prime them, and then paint them black first, before covering them with gold paint and finally sanding away some of the gold so the black shone through. She had seen it done on a refinished table in one of the DIY books she got from the library and figured it would work well on the picture frames. Once the old shower curtain was covered with frames drying, she stopped to have a second cup of coffee.

Sitting at her table, she remembered that there was voicemail that she hadn't checked last night. She dialed in and waited for the message to play.

Young lady, you are not going to be the end of me! You might think you can take all poor Don's money, but you're not going to take retirement money from an innocent old man! You get the last three months' rent to me pronto or I'll have the courts after you!

Carrie's breath caught in her throat and she sat back hard. She'd recognize her old landlord's voice anywhere. Henry Morris was a grandfatherly type that had let them pay the damage deposit in installments when they first moved into the house after Katie was born. Carrie made sure after that to always pay him the rent on time, and she had enjoyed the monthly tradition of inviting him in for a cup of coffee when he came to collect the rent. He was always so kind and respectful to her, but the voicemail left her feeling threatened. If Don had convinced him of some lie about Carrie, how on earth could she change his mind?

One thing was for sure, the rent on that house wasn't supposed to be her problem anymore. When she moved out, Don was furious. He insisted on changing the lease so her name was off of it, claiming that otherwise Carrie would just try to take the house away from him. Carrie had been glad to change the lease and have one less obligation with Don. She didn't mind having her name taken off their joint bank account too, since she knew it would go back into overdraft when Don's car insurance payment came out. Actually, she had been eager to do anything Don asked as long as he didn't ask for full custody of the kids.

Checking the time, she sent her sister an email asking her to call her as soon as she could. Jessica was working as a rookie lawyer for a big law firm that specialized in personal injury claims, but Carrie figured she might be able to find out if there was anything to Henry's threat. Not sure whether her sister could take a call in the middle of the day, she figured an email was the best choice. A minute later her phone rang.

"Hey sis, what's up?"

"I have a question for you. Do you have a minute?"

"I'm in the office bathroom. I've got all the time in the world." Carrie couldn't help but smile. Jessica always found a way to get what she wanted, including talking to her sister in the middle of a working day. She explained the situation.

"I think the laws might be different where you are but there's a guy I graduated with who's doing property law there. I'll call him and get back to you as soon as I know, kay? Love ya, bye!"

Carrie hung up and said a little prayer of thanks for her sister. Once Jessica was onto something, she'd chase it till she got it. Whatever the answer was to this awful situation, Jessica would figure it out.

She left to get the kids from school with a heavy heart. Three month's rent on that house was $3,900. There was no way she could come up with that, or even a portion of it. It would take all the extra work she could find just to make a dent on it. And if he really did take her to court, she'd be devastated. Even getting the divorce process started had been stressful.

She hadn't stopped to think about Don not paying his bills since she had moved out. The last time she had bailed him out after he lost money on some business venture with a friend, she had borrowed $2,000 from her parents. Money she was sure they couldn't afford to lend her, but she didn't want Don to get in trouble. If she had that moment to live over again, she would have left Don to figure out his own problems. The problem now was that his problems might become hers again and there was probably nothing she could do about it. She felt powerless in the face of one man who would lie about anything and another man who seemed to believe the lies about her.

While they were finishing lunch, Jessica called back. "Do you have any proof that you're not on the lease anymore?"

Carrie remembered inviting Mr. Morris in for a final coffee before she moved out and explaining the situation to him. He was unimpressed about the divorce "You kids give up on marriage way too easily!" but he had no problem writing up a new lease just in Don's name. Don had signed the papers and then torn up the old lease as soon as Mr. Morris left. But Carrie hadn't thought to keep a copy of the new lease, and she wasn't sure if the landlord had a copy of the old lease with her name still on it.

Jessica explained that as long as there wasn't a lease with Carrie's name on it, he didn't have grounds to come after her for the money.

"God, I am so sick and tired of men ganging up against women and trying to force problems on them. Don's always been a lying piece of shit, but I would have expected any decent person to see through his lies and not try to go after you for the rent."

She used some more choice words to describe both men and advised Carrie to tell Mr. Morris to knock it off or she'd have him charged with harassment. Carrie was feeling worse and worse for the poor man and had no intention of lashing out at him. That might be her sister's style, but it wasn't hers. Jessica gave her a number to contact in the city that could help Mr. Morris with legal support in evicting Don. Since he was a pensioner, he might qualify for free help.

By the time the conversation was over, Carrie had a plan. She called Mr. Morris and asked if he could come over for a coffee. "You'd better have some money for me!" he growled. But even when she told him she didn't have any money he agreed to come over right away. She figured he was a good man who was in a bad spot and she was counting on the fact that Katie was home to help her cause. He always had a soft spot for Katie, since he had seen her grow up over the past four years. She gave him her address and went to put a fresh pot of coffee on.

When he arrived, she met him outside first. "We'll go inside for coffee in a minute, I just want to show you something." He followed her to her car. "This is my car. It's not worth much, but my dad's a retired mechanic and he helps keep it running." Then she turned and went back to the house.

Katie jumped up when they came in. "Mr. Morris!" she squealed, running over to hug him. "I haven't seen you in FOREVER!"

His face softened, and he hugged Katie back. "Well, you sure have grown in forever!" Looking at Magnus he said, "Hello young man."

Magnus shyly said hello back. Carrie let out a breath. This was going to work. She explained that she watched Magnus and his twin brothers after school and the money helped her cover her expenses. She pointed out the picture frames still drying and explained that she was finding free stuff in dumpsters and fixing it up to sell for a bit of extra cash.

Then Carrie asked him to follow her upstairs. She showed him the rooms with mattresses on the floor and cardboard boxes laid on their sides holding a few neatly stacked clothes. He didn't say anything, so Carrie led the way back downstairs to the kitchen.

"I'm afraid I don't have a fancy coffee maker anymore. Do you mind a cup of regular brewed coffee?"

"That's fine, thank you."

When they were each seated, Carrie looked him in the eye and told him that she hadn't received any money from Don for anything. The way they were living was proof of how tight things were. Then she reminded him that Don had insisted she be taken off the lease, so he had no legal grounds to come after her for any rent money.

He dropped his gaze. "I'm so sorry Carrie. Don made it sound like you had right cleaned him out and were living the high life. He started crying and saying how much it hurt to have you leave and take everything away from him. I just got caught up in it all. I didn't stop to think that you wouldn't do something like that."

"I forgive you. Don can be really convincing. Believe me, I know. And if I could help you, I would."

He held up his hands "No, no, this is not your problem."

"But you're my friend," Carrie replied, "and I want to help you. I called up my sister who's a lawyer on the coast. She's found this number that you can call, and they'll help you for free because you're a pensioner. You're going to have to evict Don, Mr. Morris. He'll try to give you another story, but I don't think he has any intention of paying you rent. You deserve much better than that."

"Thank you, dear. I'll go right home and call them. Looks like you and I are both in a bad money situation right now, but we'll get through it." He finished his coffee and stood up to go, and Carrie followed him to the front door.

"Don't be a stranger Mr. Morris. You know where we live now, and the coffee's on whenever you have time for a chat. Even if it is crappy coffee!"

He laughed. "It's the company that makes the coffee good. You take care and watch out for that snake of an ex-husband."

"You too Mr. Morris" she replied.

Closing the door, Carrie moved to the steps and sat down. That had gone as well as she hoped but she was still angry that Don had taken advantage of a senior like that. She hoped that one day he'd get what he deserved.

CHAPTER 9

At the preschool the next day she was surprised to see Kara bringing another little girl with Magnus. Kara was always adamant that she loved her kids, tolerated Carrie's kids, and that was enough for her. To see her bringing someone else's child was new. She gave Kara a questioning look, but Kara just gave a quick headshake before crouching down to talk to Katie.

"Hey Katie, this is Angela. It's her first day today so could you be her special friend and show her around?" Kara gently nudged the shy little girl forward, which was all the encouragement Katie needed.

"OK!" she said happily and reached out and grabbed Angela's hand. "Let's go play! Do you like to play house or store?" Angela simply smiled so Katie took her cue. "Let's do store first. You can come shopping and pick out anything you want OK?" Angela nodded and followed Katie and Magnus past the teacher and into the preschool.

Miss Tara gave Kara a sad smile after ushering the kids in. "How's her mom?" she asked.

"Not good," Kara replied. "I made it over a bit early to pick up Angela, and she could hardly get out of bed to answer the door. The chemo is really taking it out of her." She turned to Carrie. "I know it's totally last minute, but if she can't get here to pick up Angela can you walk her home? They live just down the street from us."

"Yeah, of course!" Carrie answered. "Do you want to let her know I can bring Angela home no matter what? Katie will be thrilled to have a few minutes extra with her newest friend!"

"That would be great, I knew you'd help. Tara, would that work even though Carrie's not on the pick-up list for Angela?"

"As long as Jenny can call me and confirm that's OK, we can do that. I think it's a time that requires a bit of flexibility."

Kara agreed to take care of sharing contact details and having Angela's mom call the preschool. As the two women walked towards Kara's car, she gave Carrie the sad story. Jenny was one of her patients and was struggling to cope with the devastation of a cancer diagnosis and the subsequent treatments. Her husband frequently traveled for work, and they didn't have any friends or family in the area because they had recently moved. Kara insisted on checking in on Jenny at home, which led to Angela being registered in the preschool, and Kara offering to help get her there in the morning.

That was one of the things Carrie loved about Kara. If she thought she should do something—like visiting a patient at home even when nobody did that anymore—she just went and did it. And she was always so good at connecting people with what they needed. Helping get Angela enrolled in the local preschool was no big deal for Kara, but probably a huge help to Angela's parents.

Carrie couldn't help thinking about the situation on the way home. Sure, things were tough, but she was healthy, and so were her kids. She still had a lot to be thankful for. She wished she had money to buy flowers or something to bring for Angela's mom when she dropped her off. At least she could help with *something* by walking Angela home.

A few of the moms were already waiting when she arrived back at school to pick up the kids, and she stood on the edge of the group so she could peak in through the front window. Katie looked to be in her glory, with Magnus on one side and Angela on the other. Angela looked a little less worried than when she first arrived, and Carrie hoped that she had enjoyed herself. Once the three kids were ready to go, Carrie sent a quick text to Angela's mom to let her know they'd be there shortly. She had never been around anyone during chemo treatments, but she figured she should give her time to get to the door if she was having trouble moving.

Sure enough, Jenny was already at the door when they arrived. Angela hung on to her mom tightly for a minute before she was ready to let go. Jenny was a tall lady, with a thin build. She was wearing pajamas that hung on her thin frame. The dark circles under her eyes gave away a hint of what she must be feeling physically. As she stood at the door, Carrie saw her hand suddenly grip tight to the doorknob and she just had enough time to brace Jenny before she stumbled.

"Oh, I'm so sorry," she said to Carrie shakily. "I guess it was a good idea for you to bring her home for me." She tried to turn towards the stairs leading up to the main level, but Carrie could feel her struggling.

"Angela, do you have any stuffed animals?"

Angela's face lit up. "Yep, I have a whole bunch!" Carrie placed the kids' backpacks down and put her free hand on Angela's shoulder. "Could you take Katie and Magnus up to see them?"

"Sure! Come on guys!" The kids ran off behind Angela, leaving Carrie room to close the door while still supporting Jenny with her other hand.

"Let's get you sitting down, OK? Which way?"

"Up the stairs and to the right. I'll be OK once I'm sitting. I was trying to get Angela's lunch ready before you got here, but I just can't seem to move very quickly."

"No problem. When you're ready, you start walking and I'll support you." Slowly the ladies made their way up the stairs. Carrie could see hints of a nice house, with beautiful furniture and décor, but it was hidden by evidence of illness. There was clean laundry piled on the couch beside an end table that had Kleenexes, water bottles, and a variety of pill bottles on it. The curtains were closed, and the room felt heavy and dark. To her left, Carrie could see the kitchen with dirty dishes and open containers on the counter.

They made it to a clear area of the couch, and Carrie gently helped Jenny sit down. She felt so frail she was worried she might hurt her if she wasn't careful. Jenny let out a sigh and brushed away a tear.

"Please don't mind me. I'm just so grateful you were here to help me up the stairs! We'll be OK now."

"I'm sure you will be. But the kids are happy for the minute so why don't I just grab Angela's lunch for her before we go. I think you need to stay sitting for a minute!"

Jenny gave a half smile. "I've never been so grateful to have a stranger in my house! I was just going to heat up a can of soup and make her a grilled cheese sandwich."

"I'll get that ready in a jiffy. You stay here, and I'll holler if I need anything." Carrie quickly moved to the kitchen, hoping to give Jenny a chance to catch her breath. She found the soup and a little pot already on the stove and got busy making lunch.

While the soup warmed up and the grilled cheese was cooking, she started to load the dirty dishes into the dishwasher. It looked like Jenny and Angela had been surviving on toast and soup. She turned the dishwasher on, and quickly wiped the counters and the table. A glance over at Jenny told her the woman was either sleeping or too tired to open her eyes. Carrie wished she had time to do more for her, but she knew Katie and Magnus would want their own lunch soon.

When everything was ready, she set a place for Angela at the table, and put a bit of soup into a mug for Jenny. Following the sound of the voices, she found the kids in what looked like the playroom of Katie's dreams. It was packed with stuffed animals, dolls, a play kitchen, and even a TV. In the middle of the chaos, the kids were happily setting up all the stuffed animals for what looked like a tea party.

"Well, this looks like a whole lot of fun! You're a lucky girl to have so many toys!"

"My Daddy bought them for me because Mommy's too tired to play with me. She's sick."

Carrie felt the little girl's sadness. "I know honey. Let's hope she feels better soon. Come on, I've got some soup and a sandwich for you so let's get you to the table."

She wanted to ask Katie and Magnus to clean up the toys, but it looked like there was nowhere to put anything away. So she called them to follow her out and left the toy room as it was.

The sound of the kids woke up Jenny, and she smiled wryly. "Sorry, I guess I had to sleep off my workout up the stairs."

"I've got Angela's lunch at the table, and I put some soup in a mug for you. Do you think you can try to drink it? I've heard chemo really messes with your appetite."

"Yeah, it's been way worse than I expected. But I'll have the soup. I can't thank you enough for all you've done."

"I wish I could do more. Is there anything else you need before I go?"

"No, my husband will be home tonight for a few nights so we'll be OK. If you don't mind letting yourself out, I don't really want to try the stairs again."

"Of course, not a problem. I'll make sure the door locks behind me. You take care, and the kids will look out for Angela tomorrow at school. Bye bye."

The kids all said their goodbyes to each other, and Carrie collected

Katie and Magnus and their backpacks before heading out the door. The walk home was a quiet one, which she was thankful for.

After lunch, Carrie set up the kids to watch a movie and took care of a little bit of housework before starting to prime an end table she brought up from the basement. She wondered how Jenny felt about her just barging in and taking over. Hopefully it made things a little easier, and she'd done the right thing.

Just before it was Matthew's bedtime, Carrie's phone rang and startled them both. She was tempted to ignore it but didn't.

"Is this Carrie, Katie's mom?" A man's voice was on the other end.

"Yes, this is Carrie…"

"I'm Max, Jenny's husband. Listen, I'm sorry to interrupt your evening, but what you did today for my wife today was a really big deal. I wanted to call you to thank you."

"Oh, you're very welcome Max. Your wife seems like an amazing lady, and Angela is such a sweet little girl. If I can help you with anything, please just let me know."

"Well, that's the other reason I called." There was a pause, and it sounded like Max was trying to clear his throat. "We just moved to this house in the middle of Jenny's treatment. She had a housekeeper who came highly recommended, but the first time Jenny couldn't get out of bed, the lady freaked out and said she'd never work for sick people. Jenny was so embarrassed she hasn't let anyone into the house since. And then you just came in today and made her feel like a decent person again." Again, he paused, and Carrie realized he was struggling to keep his composure. Immediately her heart was captured by this little family trying to survive a horrible experience. She knew what that was like.

After a moment, he continued. "I have a few days off now, but I was wondering if I could hire you to come over when I'm working and help Jenny out. Just during preschool hours. We could pay you $50 per day. Jenny really likes you, and she was happier when I came home today than I've seen her in weeks."

"Oh, well, it really wasn't much…" Carrie stalled. $50 per day, just to be nice?

"It was more than you think," Max replied. "Could you help us? Please?"

"So it's during the time the kids are at preschool?" Carrie confirmed.

"Yeah, that would be really great. You could start on Monday, that's when I have to be back at work. And we could pay you every Friday. Kara has offered to take Angela to school every morning when I'm gone, but I'd need you to bring her home until Jenny's feeling up to it."

"Well sure. I'd be happy to help." Carrie smiled. "Your wife and daughter are lovely; it would be a pleasure."

She heard Max release a big breath. "Thank you so much. I'll tell Jenny to expect you on Monday then. Thanks again."

Carrie ended the call and sat for a minute. Sometimes she forgot that she didn't need to 'get permission' from a husband to make choices, and there would be an automatic feeling of guilt before she remembered she was free from that. Yes, she could do this, and she was already looking forward to it!

"Mom?" Max called from the living room. "Who was that?"

She told him about the day, Jenny and Angela, and what she had been asked to do. Still a little shocked about the generous pay, she just mentioned that they would pay her to help out without giving too many details.

"Won't Dad be mad?" His eyes were wide with fear, and she could see his shoulders hunching up with tension.

"What do you mean?"

"You promised him you'd never go clean houses!"

Realization dawned on Carrie as her mind flashed back to two years ago. Don had lost his job—again—and Carrie was desperate to get enough money to buy some groceries. She had taken a job cleaning house for an elderly couple, and Don hit the roof when he found out. No wife of his would stoop so low as to be a house cleaner, and how dare she go behind his back like that!

She quickly apologized, canceled the job and promised him she would never do it again. That was the first week she used a food bank to take care of her family, but she had only gone when Don was out looking for a new job and was careful to not make it obvious the cupboards had a bit more food in them.

During that time, she thought Matthew was in his room. She had no idea he heard everything or that he had any memory of it still.

"Bud, sometimes, when you make a promise, you can't keep it. And that's OK. If you ever make a promise that goes against your values or could hurt someone, you don't need to keep it. This family needs my help, and the money I get paid will help us out too. So yes, I'm going to break that promise I made to your dad and take this opportunity. Are you alright with that?"

"Yeah Mom. I'm glad you can help them. And I'm glad you're not sick like that mom is. Do you think one day there will be someone like that dad who will fix everything if you get sick?"

"Tell you what. I'll stay good and strong and healthy and we'll never have to worry about that, OK? Now I think it's time for you to get ready for bed."

As Matthew walked upstairs, Carrie hoped that was one promise she could keep.

CHAPTER 10

Monday morning was gray, but at least the rain had stopped. The kids wore the best jackets she had found at the thrift store when they needed new clothes, but neither one was properly warm or dry. With Katie, she could carry an umbrella while walking to school, which kept them dry, but Matthew was not interested in being the only boy walking to school with an umbrella.

At the preschool later to drop off Katie, she was met by a beaming Kara. "I'm so excited you're going to help Jenny out! I've been so worried about her when her husband's gone, but now I know she'll be OK."

"I hope she's OK with it. And they're really paying me quite a bit. Do you think they can afford it?"

Kara rolled her eyes. "Not everyone's as cautious with money as you are! And they're fine for money from what I can tell. Jenny's some hot shot financial planner. She's hoping to be back at work in a month or so, but I think it will take longer for her to feel up to going. Now that you're there she'll be able to rest more and get well. I've offered to bring Angela to school for as long as they need, and with you or Max picking up that will help too. Oh, here's an extra house key. Jenny asked me to pass it on to you so you can let yourself in. Well, I'd better be off. I'm sure you'll do great with Jenny!"

She gave Carrie a quick hug and they went their separate ways. At Jenny's house, Carrie let herself in and went up the stairs. Jenny was on the same spot she had been on the couch Friday, looking worn out, but awake.

"Carrie, please come in. I'm so glad you're here! Could you make us a cup of tea, and we can have a little chat before I lay down again? Do you drink tea?"

Carrie didn't often drink tea, but she wanted to make Jenny feel comfortable, so she went ahead and made two cups. Everything in the kitchen was fairly easy to find, and she started doing a bit of tidying up while the water heated up. After clearing a spot on the couch near Jenny, she sat down with a cup of tea for each of them.

Jenny shared that she was normally a private person and wasn't used to people in the house. The housekeeper she hired had made that worse by releasing a horrible tirade on her when she found out she had cancer. Carrie was shocked how someone could act that way and could see how deeply it had hurt Jenny.

"Fighting cancer is something to be proud of Jenny. Getting sick was out of your control, but it won't last forever. And Angela will grow up knowing her mom is strong and brave. Be proud of that!" Jenny wiped tears away. "Thank you," she whispered. "I needed to hear that. For some reason, I felt so comfortable when you came in the door on Friday. I feel so much better about Max working away, knowing you'll be here."

Carrie could see Jenny was starting to fade, so she helped her up and back into bed. It wasn't until she was back in the kitchen that she realized she hadn't received any instructions about what to do. Thinking about what would make the biggest difference for Jenny, she decided to focus on what Jenny could see from her spot on the couch. The bedroom needed some cleaning and organizing too, but not while Jenny was sleeping.

She quickly got to work, rounding up all the dirty dishes to load in the dishwasher, folding clean laundry, and wiping down surfaces with the cleaning supplies she found in the hall closet. The dishwasher was full enough to start a load, but she didn't want to start the laundry because she'd have to leave things in the washing machine overnight. Carrie gave herself a mental reminder to start a load first thing when she came tomorrow so she could get it through in time. She opened the curtains in the living room and dining room once the area was clean.

A quick tour of the house showed her that the family hadn't had time to truly move in. There was still nearly a room full of boxes in the basement, just leaving a path to the washer and dryer. Carrie could see that someone—probably Max—was trying to keep up with the laundry, but with a sick person in the house, the laundry was piling up. She sorted everything and got a load of sheets and towels ready to go first thing the next day.

Back upstairs Carrie tidied up Angela's room and made her bed. She decided to leave the playroom alone, except for collecting dirty cups and plates. It was hard to tell if the room was in the midst of some imaginary game and she didn't want to upset Angela. She'd ask her on the way home what kind of food she liked for lunch, and then get that ready again while the kids had a few minutes to play.

Before leaving to pick up the kids, she popped her head into Jenny's room. She was starting to wake up, so Carrie let her know she was off to get the kids. Seeing a collection of glasses on the bedside table, she quickly cleared them to the kitchen and brought Jenny back a fresh glass of ice water. Jenny smiled her thanks and Carrie slipped out.

On the walk back home, Angela informed her that she liked to have soup and crackers every day for lunch, because "Sometimes Mommy can have some soup with me." Having grown up with a mom who wasn't well, Carrie could understand Angela's wish to do anything 'normal' with her mom. She had seen cans of soup in the cupboard, so it would be easy enough to make.

Back at the house, they let themselves in, and the kids immediately dropped their bags, shoes, and coats and ran to the playroom. Angela made a detour to her mom's room and Carrie gave them a minute together before going in. Satisfied her mom was OK, Angela went off to play.

"I'm just going to make Angela's lunch before I go. Did you want me to set up a tray in here so she can eat with you?"

"What a good idea! She always feels better when she sees me eating so I try to make sure I can when she's watching. I'm not feeling too sick right now, just really tired. There's a TV tray under that pile of clothes over there."

Carrie set the clothes to the side and cleared an area so she could bring over the TV tray. Then she went to make soup and crackers. Once she had Angela and Jenny set up with their little lunch in the bedroom, she gathered up Magnus and Katie and locked the door behind her as they headed home.

CHAPTER 11

Tuesday morning Carrie woke up before her alarm. The optimism she felt the night before had faded, and she was back to worrying about money. At this point, she should be used to not having money, but the worries were still there. The kids only had her to rely on, and if anything happened to her, they'd have nothing. She needed to get her feet under her and make some moves forward.

Not for the first time, she thought back to the past with regret. Going to university full time while working and dating had been hard. When she dropped out after third year, she was only thinking about how she could work full-time for a bit, maybe add in a part-time job, and save enough money to go back to school. She loved studying and wanted to be able to focus on learning without running off to work right after lectures and missing out on study groups because she needed to sleep before her next shift.

But life hadn't worked out like that. After leaving university, she first put all her earnings towards marrying Don. The simple ceremony she wanted was something her parents were happy to pay for. But Don wanted more, and she worked hard to make it something he could be proud of. Then, on the honeymoon, they both maxed out their credit cards, and had struggled financially ever since. He had often told her that if she hadn't racked up so much debt in student loans, then they could have had a better life.

Psychologists made good money, but she didn't have it in her to fight with Don about getting the three more years of school she needed so she could make a proper salary. And so she struggled, always trying to get ahead, and always coming up short. She still dreamed of going back to school and getting a good paying job. But she couldn't handle the idea of taking on more debt. Even if it got her ahead, eventually.

When the kids got up, she forced herself to put on a smile and get their day started pleasantly. It wasn't their fault she was in this situation and there was no way she would take out her feelings on her kids. She'd just have to be smarter with her money and figure out a way to bring in more of it. There was no way she could spend less, so making more was the only option.

Waiting for the preschool to open, she casually mentioned to Kara that she was getting into refinishing furniture for fun and was looking for some pieces to fix up and sell. "Why would you want more to do?" Kara asked. "I'd think after my boys are done with you in the afternoons you'd want to just sit and watch TV all night!" Carrie gave a vague answer about needing to do something with her hands, which Kara accepted.

Kara figured her parents had a bunch of furniture they'd love to get rid of, and she'd mention it to her dad the next time she talked to him. They lived out of town in the opposite direction from Carrie's parents. Carrie and Kara often joked about how lucky they were to have parents "close, but not too close!"

When she arrived later that morning, Jenny was waiting on the couch, and asked if they could have tea together again. Carrie delayed long enough to put a load of laundry in the washer and then made tea for them both.

"I was wondering," Carrie began, "I'd like to know how you're doing each day when I come, but I'm sure you have way too many people asking how you are. Would it be OK if I asked each morning what you wanted to do? That way, if you need to sleep you can tell me, but if you want to tackle something or have a hand getting dressed or anything, you don't have to always be talking about how you feel."

"So, kind of like the opposite of going to a counselor?" Jenny asked with a laugh. "Isn't that where you always have to talk about your feelings?"

"Not necessarily. But we can definitely avoid the subject if that's what works for you."

"That sounds perfect Carrie. Thank you for being so understanding! For today I'd like to be dressed and in the living room when Angela gets home from school. I think I was avoiding being in here because it was so messy. I'm OK with a bit of a messy bedroom, but it really bothered me to have the main areas looking the way they did. I don't know how you got so much done yesterday, but you're really amazing!"

Carrie let out a little sigh of relief. Compliments had been rare in her world when she was married, and it felt really good to know someone thought she was doing a good job now.

"That would be perfect! If you have an extra set of sheets, I could tidy up your room and change the bedding while you rest here on the couch."

"You'll have to find the box of linens downstairs. I have a few extra sets but didn't get around to unpacking them. It'll say 'Bedroom Linens' right on the box. We hired a moving company to pack up the house, and they did a great job of labeling everything. Unfortunately, I thought I'd have enough energy to unpack it all myself. That's why there are all those boxes still. I tried to focus on finding Angela's things first and that was all I could do."

"No problem. I'll just give the kitchen a tidy and then head downstairs to find the linens. And let me know if you need any help getting dressed when you're ready. My mom is disabled from a car accident a long time ago, so I'm used to helping with that sort of thing."

"I knew you'd have an interesting story! One day we'll just trade stories for the day and get to know each other."

"I'd like that." Carrie responded and was surprised to find she meant it.

After locating the box of linens, she carried it upstairs and got to work on Jenny's bedroom. She knew having the area feeling bright and clean would help Jenny feel a bit better about all the time she spent in bed. She quickly stripped the bed and gathered up everything that could be dirty laundry to take downstairs. Then she enjoyed picking out a bright yellow set of sheets, and a white duvet cover that was covered in colorful flowers.

She felt a bit amazed at the idea of having more than one set of bedding. In her world, one set was all that she could afford, and she had to be on the ball when she washed it, so it could be dry and back on the bed before the end of the day.

The fresh linens immediately brightened up the place, and Carrie got to work cleaning up the rest of the bedroom. Mostly it was a matter of folding and putting away clean clothes, gathering up garbage and old newspapers, and wiping down all the surfaces. When she finished, she grabbed the full laundry basket to take downstairs, and switched the load she started into the dryer. Jenny had fallen asleep on the couch, so Carrie took the time to clean the master bathroom next.

It was a beautiful bathroom with a deep soaker tub, separate shower, and two sinks with a beautiful marble countertop. There was lots of storage too, so Jenny put away the rest of the towels away after putting a fresh set out. Again she took pleasure in the thick, soft towels, all in matching sets of maroon, emerald green, or navy blue. She couldn't imagine what it must be like to be able to buy such beautiful things.

After cleaning the bathroom there was only about fifteen minutes left before she needed to go get the kids. She gently woke up Jenny and asked if she wanted to get dressed. Together they walked to the bedroom where Jenny stopped at the door and grabbed onto the frame. Carrie thought Jenny might be losing her balance and quickly put a supporting arm around her waist. But Jenny surprised her by turning around and enveloping her in a hug.

"Thank you so much!" she whispered. "That's my favorite set for the bed. It was my Grandma's before she passed away, but I didn't have the energy to get it out after we moved." Relieved that Jenny was OK, Carrie helped her into the room and got her dressed in a beautiful skirt and blouse with a cashmere cardigan over. Jenny had said she was tired of pajama bottoms and just needed to feel feminine for a few hours.

She walked Jenny back to the couch, and then quickly left to get the kids. It wasn't normal for her to be one of the last parents to show up, and Katie already looked worried when she arrived. Carrie made a mental note to plan more carefully. She didn't want her kids to ever wonder if she was going to show up.

Katie quickly recovered and regaled Carrie with everything that had happened at preschool until they got to Angela's house. After the kids had hung up their bags and coats and put their shoes away nicely (Carrie figured they could get in the habit of being tidy here too) they ran upstairs and Angela let out an excited squeal. "Mommy! You're up! And you're wearing a pretty skirt!" Carrie felt her heart expand to be a part of giving Angela a moment of happiness. Angela didn't want to leave her mom's side, so Carrie asked if the kids could watch a kid's TV show while she got lunch ready for mom and daughter.

With the kids happily settled, she quickly went downstairs to get the clothes out of the dryer and folded. She'd put them away tomorrow but didn't want them sitting in the dryer getting wrinkled overnight.

Jenny and Angela were both happy with soup again, and Carrie added some sliced French bread with melted cheese on it to hopefully give them a little more to eat. Both seemed quite thin, although

Carrie thought it might be natural, she wanted to give them as much as they could comfortably eat.

When Jenny had thanked her again for everything she had done, she left for home with Katie and Magnus. The kids were feeling silly, singing the theme song from the show they had watched, and adding nonsense words in between giggles. Carrie took a few big breaths and reminded herself to be grateful. These were priceless moments, and she wanted to file them in her memory.

The rest of the week went by quickly. Carrie was able to keep Jenny's house clean while starting to bring up boxes from the basement and unpack them. When Jenny was feeling up to it, they'd talk together about where things should go and how to organize them. And when Jenny needed to rest, Carrie felt comfortable continuing to unpack the things that clearly belonged in one room or another. She had always been good at figuring out people, knowing what made them tick, and what they would prefer. Because of that, she was still baffled at how she had missed all the signals about Don—it was easy to see them now looking back, but at the time he really had her convinced that she was the problem.

On Friday, Jenny wrote her a check for $250 for the five days of work. Even though she knew it was coming, Carrie was thrilled to receive it. She put it in her bank on the way back home with Magnus and Katie. The bank would hold the money for three business days, but Kara always paid her in cash, so she was happy to let the check stay safe in her bank account and use some of the cash from Kara for the weekend.

She didn't have time for her usual Friday morning grocery shopping, but she figured they'd be OK until Monday since she was hoping to visit her parents. It was hard to know when to let her parents know she was coming, since she didn't want to cancel on them if Don decided to take the kids. But by Friday morning she couldn't wait any longer, so she made a quick call to them on the way to Jenny's to say they were coming, and then turned off her phone. Maybe it wasn't the most mature thing to do, but she could always claim her battery had died if she missed Don's call.

As soon as Kara picked up the three boys, Carrie turned to her kids. "Are you ready for a surprise?" Katie immediately started jumping up and down, and Matthew got a big grin on his face. "We're going to Grandpa and Grandma's for the weekend!" They both cheered, and then Carrie had them carefully empty their school backpacks so they could pack them with clothes for the weekend. Grandpa and Grandma had cable TV, a big yard, *and* lots of games so there was no need to pack toys. Carrie guided Katie a little bit with her packing, and in less than fifteen minutes they were driving away from the house.

She drove until the next town where she got a full tank of gas and then pulled up at the MacDonald's. Even Katie was speechless with surprise. Carrie hadn't fully budgeted what to do with her extra money, but she would use some of it to make her kids' weekend special.

An hour later they were pulling into her parent's driveway. This was the house she had grown up in, and it always felt safe to come home. She was glad her parents were both around and able to enjoy time with their grandkids. Her mom was sitting at her place by the window, waving as they exited the car, and her dad was out the door and hugging the kids before Carrie had even gotten out. Then he enveloped her in a big bear hug and Carrie held on tight and felt all the stress and worry of the last few months fade away. Her dad always smelled a bit like Old Spice and a bit like engine oil. It was a smell that left her feeling like Daddy's little girl again, when she counted on him to protect her from everything bad in the world.

He had always seemed larger than life to her as a little girl, and sometimes it surprised her that they were both the same height now. Most of his hair was gone, and he carried around a belly that had gotten bigger since retirement, but his broad smile and brown eyes that had permanent laugh lines hadn't changed one bit.

"How's my little girl?" he asked.

"Better now Daddy," she said and gave his cheek a kiss before letting him go.

The kids had already run inside to snuggle up to Grandma. Carrie's dad took their backpacks, and they followed the kids inside. Her mom turned her wheelchair towards the door and opened her arms to Carrie. "Care Bear!" she exclaimed. "It is SO good to see you."

"Good to see you too Mom!" She was so pleased it was a good day for her mom and she felt up to meeting them. When the pain got too strong, she had to stay in bed, and couldn't move enough to get the hugs she loved so much from her daughter and grandkids. Her Mom's hair had gone white when Carrie was still a teenager, but she kept it lovely in a classic bob. Kindness and caring were always showing in her blue eyes that gave every person she was talking to her full attention.

They settled in the living room, the kids with a glass of chocolate milk each, and the grown-ups with a glass of red wine. Carrie couldn't remember a better tasting glass of wine. Going without for so many months sure did something for the taste buds!

They all brought each other up-to-date with news, and Matthew told them that Mommy was making lots of money for free. She loved his explanation because that was really what was happening. After explaining it to her parents (and being careful to talk about it as a hobby and not a desperate necessity) she mentioned that she was hoping she could use some of her dad's supplies.

"Of course you can, sweetheart! We'll go out to the garage tomorrow and see what you can use. But I'm pretty sure we've also got some things kicking around downstairs that you could fix up and sell. You know I'm not so good at getting rid of things when we don't need them!" They all laughed, but Carrie knew it was true. Especially since she had left to go to university, her dad had resorted to moving anything he didn't know what to do with down into the basement. She could only imagine what was down there!

That night Carrie lay in bed in the bedroom that had been hers since she was ten years old, still feeling the effects of the wine, and basking in her parent's love for her and her children. Katie was already asleep on the floor beside her, and Matthew was sleeping in her sister's old room. It was nice to know he could sleep on a proper bed for the next two nights. As she dozed off, the moonlight slipped through a gap in the curtains and highlighted her bookshelf of old psychology books. *I might as well bring those back with me too* she thought. Any evidence of her higher education threatened Don, so she had purposefully put everything from university back in her old bedroom before she got married. Now she could be as smart as she wanted whenever she wanted.

CHAPTER 12

Saturday morning dawned bright and crisp. Carrie was tempted to stay in bed longer, but the smell of coffee wafting into the room was enough to convince her to make the most of the day. Plus, if the kids kept sleeping she'd have a few treasured minutes alone with her dad.

Coffees in hand they both sat down at the dining room table. Carrie loved everything about her parent's house. It had been a godsend for them to buy shortly after her mom's accident with the help of an injury settlement. The ranch-style house gave room for her mom to maneuver her wheelchair almost everywhere, and her dad had slowly worked over the years to make it more accessible for her. The closest neighbors were almost out of sight, and the fields around them were still used by a local farmer to grow crops.

As they sat drinking their coffee, Carrie's dad reached over and gave her hand a squeeze. "You look good. Happier."

"I am Dad. Every day I feel like my heart heals a little. Some things are still hard. Don's been a total jerk to the kids. But at least they don't have to deal with him every day."

"You get any money out of him yet?"

"No. He's not working right now. I have no idea how he's managing. He never could stick to a budget. Not my problem anymore, thankfully."

She told him about her new job helping Jenny, and how much she could relate to their situation with a sick mom. "I'm so proud of you Carrie." Her dad held her hand for a minute before letting go and clearing his throat.

"Once the kids are up, we'll have breakfast and then we'll go downstairs and see what we can find for your little hobby." He gave her a careful look. Carrie figured he could see right through her story and knew things were tight. But he always seemed to know when to say something and when to be quiet. The years when she helped with caring for her mom and little sister had created a deep bond between her and her dad. Just one of the good things that came out of a bad situation.

Later on, Carrie and her dad ventured into the basement. Her mom was having another good day and suggested she play games with the kids while Saturday cartoons were on. The kids both decided that was much better than going in a smelly old basement.

Carrie was shocked at the volume of stuff her dad had squirreled away. It was obvious this was one area where no one could tell him what to do! She put aside an empty box to pack her psychology books in and then followed him in further. There was a bag of old picture frames she could add to the project she was already starting, and all sorts of smaller furniture pieces. Her dad was always going to yard sales to find something or other that might make mom's life easier. Apparently, little shelves and end tables were his go-to items.

Carrie was drawn to a little end table with curvy legs and a halfcircle shaped top. It was different than anything she had seen, although the dark wood stain didn't do it any favors. "I thought your mom could keep it beside her chair when she watches TV, but the drawer didn't open easily and I haven't got around to fixing it." Sure enough, the drawer didn't open all the way, but Carrie was confident she could fix it. Once they had everything her car could hold, they carried it all upstairs.

"Don't put it in the car yet." He called out from the stairs. "I want to change the oil and check things over this afternoon." Carrie smiled. She was hoping her dad would do his magic again on her car. He was the only reason she could afford to keep driving. "That would be great Dad. It sometimes doesn't start on the first try anymore. Hopefully, it's nothing major."

In the afternoon Carrie sat with her mom in the living room while Katie played in the leaves outside, and Matthew helped his Grandpa work on the car. Her dad loved doing manly stuff with his grandson after raising two daughters that had no interest in mechanics. Once he knew they could check the fluids and change a tire, he gave up teaching them anything else.

Over cups of tea, Carrie talked to her mom about Jenny, and Kara and the boys, and of course Matthew and Katie. Her mom had an amazing memory for all the people in her daughters' lives and loved to hear about them. On the days when she couldn't get out of bed, she'd pass the time thinking about each person and saying a prayer for them.

Carrie decided to head back home on Sunday afternoon, so she'd have time to get groceries before Monday. It was usually a 'rule' that she never shopped with the kids because it was too hard to say no to everything they wanted. But this time she'd bend the rules. Plus, she wanted the time on Monday to work on her projects. Jenny had said Max would be home all day Monday so Carrie wasn't needed there.

After driving, unpacking the car, and getting groceries, Carrie was exhausted. She made macaroni and cheese for supper, and then finally turned on her phone. After a few minutes, the voicemail icon flashed repeatedly. The first message was fine, just Kara saying her dad had some old furniture she could have, and he'd drop it off Monday afternoon. The next three messages were Don, getting angrier and angrier that she wasn't answering her phone. After calling Don back and listening to him blast on and on about how much of a failure she was, she finally got a word in, "What do you want?" It was always easiest to try to get to the bottom of things with him before he remembered even more things about her that he hated.

"I want the kids to come to my place from school on Friday. Get Matthew to walk Katie over, you don't need to come." Usually, Carrie walked them over after breakfast on the Saturday they were scheduled, since Don claimed it was too expensive to feed them if they came on Friday.

"That's fine." She answered quickly. "They'll see you on Friday then. Bye." She breathed a sigh of relief. That wasn't so bad. And there was no way she was letting the kids walk to his house unsupervised. She'd just follow a little behind and make sure they got there safely.

CHAPTER 13

Monday after the kids were all at school, Carrie was happy to have a few hours home to work on her projects. She started with the picture frames, so she could have a whole set of them ready to go by the end of the week. Her goal was to sell $150 worth of things this week.

After getting Katie and Magnus home and having lunch, she sat for a minute with a cup of reheated coffee while the kids watched TV.

The doorbell rang, startling Carrie. She opened it, and there was Kara's dad standing there. "Stan! I'm sorry, I forgot Kara said you'd be coming this afternoon. I can make a fresh pot of coffee; do you want to come in for a cup?" Magnus jumped up and ran to his Grandpa for a hug, and Katie followed suit.

"No time Carrie, I just wanted to drop off this furniture. Looks like you don't really have any more room. I brought along a tarp. Can I put the things in your backyard and cover them up until you're ready for them?"

"That's a great idea. It's small, but there's nothing there except for the recycling. Katie and Magnus, I need you to stay here while I help unload things."

"Oh, that's OK" Stan interrupted her "I'll bring these things around myself. You stay inside with the kids, and I'll come say goodbye before I leave." With that, he turned around and walked to the truck. Carrie went to the backyard anyway and moved the two bags of recycling that were still waiting to be returned. In all the busyness of the last two weeks, she had totally forgotten about collecting and returning the cans and bottles. Maybe now that she had other ways of making money, the refunds from recycling could be Matthew and Katie's spending money. She wanted them to get used to having money and hopefully they'd grow up to be better at managing it than she was.

When Stan left she took a quick, excited look at everything he had brought. There was a little bit of everything and Carrie couldn't wait to get started on making these things beautiful so she could turn them into cash.

Carrie went to Jenny's in the mornings for the next three days and still kept busy with the kids and repainting the picture frames the rest of the time. With her lack of space, she really needed to finish one thing and sell it before moving on to another. Even though she didn't want to, she could turn the basement into a work area. It was silly to not be using that space when it was there.

She finally braced herself on Wednesday evening to go down and try to clean an area so she could have a workspace. The floor needed vacuuming and she needed to get more light down there, and a heater. It was just too cold to work without gloves on right now, and anything she painted would probably take forever to dry. The lamps left in the basement by the previous tenant still worked, but she needed a table to put them on. It felt like one step forward one step back. But once she vacuumed, the floor was cleaner, and she also used the vacuum to suck up the worst of the spider webs from the walls and ceiling even though it really wasn't enough to make real progress. She quickly ran upstairs, chiding herself for being a sissy while gladly closing the door to the basement and putting an old towel back in front of the door to help stop the cold air from coming into the kitchen.

Thursday evening they went to the library as usual. Carrie made sure to check out a few books on personal finances, and some décor magazines. She quit looking at magazines a long time ago because it always reminded her of everything she couldn't have. But now she was ready for some inspiration. And maybe soon she could start making her own home a little nicer.

They took longer than usual since the kids had trouble picking some more DVDs. They had watched so many in the last few months that there weren't many options left. Carrie wondered how irresponsible it would be to get cable TV...

Before Matthew went to bed, she reminded him about going to his dad's after school the next day. She made it sound like a big deal that he would walk his sister over there and told him she'd stay a bit behind until they were in the door because she was a silly mom who was overprotective. Matthew laughed and told her it was fine.

Friday! Carrie was looking forward to a few free hours after she dropped off the kids to list the picture frames for sale, and finish repainting a shelf so she could list it too. Max met her after the kids were let into the preschool and gave her a check for the three days. He had such an easy way about him, she wondered how good of a salesman he was. All the salesmen she knew were pushy, but she couldn't imagine Max being pushy. Maybe he was just easy to trust and gained business because of that. At any rate, there weren't many men she felt comfortable talking to, so it was nice to have someone to have a quick chat with. Kara had run off right away for work and Carrie realized how much she valued having any brief 'grown-up' interactions.

She stopped at the bank to deposit the check and got a quick printout of her account activities. It was still amazing to have a three-digit balance, and she was going to make a plan this weekend for how to make the most of her new earnings.

Back at home she cleared a space on the floor of her bedroom and set up the finished picture frames in a few different ways to take pictures. The carpet in the living room had too many stains and worn spots to make a decent backdrop. Satisfied with the results she cleaned up the frames and straightened out the bedding again before going downstairs to put up the posting for sale. Taking a big breath, she set the price at $125. She had spent almost $20 on paint and more brushes, and she really wanted to make at least $100 profit.

Then she finished painting the shelf. She'd wait for it to dry before setting it up to take pictures. Happy to have another project for sale, she turned her attention to the side table her dad gave her. She figured she should fix the drawer first, in case she had to take some of it apart. Then she couldn't wait to cover up that horrible brown wood stain with something bright and cheerful. It deserved a chance to shine after being such a depressing color for so long!

It sure seemed like something was stuck and stopping the drawer from opening. She could only get part of her hand in and felt something plastic inside. After some twisting and pulling it released, and the drawer popped open. There in Carrie's hand was part of an old grocery bag, with $100 bills spilling out. It had been a long time since Carrie had seen a $100 bill, especially the old kind. They were fake, right? It wasn't possible for money to just fall into her lap!

Carrie had spent so many years lowering her expectations again and again. To suddenly be faced with something *better* than she expected was just too impossible to believe. And yet she really wanted to believe that things had just changed for the better.

She took one bill out and put it in her purse, and then ran up to her room and tucked the rest under her mattress. Maybe not the most creative place to stash money, but if it was fake it didn't matter. There wasn't time to count it. After she picked up Magnus and Katie from school, she'd stop at the bank and see if it was real. Until then she'd try not to get her hopes up.

But as Carrie quickly walked to the preschool, she could only think about the money. *If* it was real, she needed to keep it away from

Don. Since her divorce wasn't final, she worried that he may have some sort of claim to this money, and she had to make sure that didn't happen.

At the bank, Katie and Magnus ran to the kids' table where there were always coloring books and LEGO. There was no line, so Carrie went up to the first teller. "Um, my dad found this old bill and gave it to me, but he wasn't even sure if it was real or not. Can you tell?" The teller looked it over carefully before putting it down. "I'll have to get my supervisor. Just a minute please." She left Carrie standing there feeling worried. She hadn't done anything wrong, had she?

The supervisor arrived and looked over the bill. "It's been a while since I've seen one of these! It actually makes me feel nostalgic if you can believe it. Yes, these are still good, although if you want to spend it you should exchange it here for one of the new ones. People don't like to take the old ones anymore."

"Oh, thanks. Maybe I'll do that now if that's OK?" The teller gave her five $20s, and Carrie walked the kids home with her mind spinning. After lunch, when she was sure they were happily settled watching a movie, she went to her room and took out the bag. In all, there was now $8,900 in old hundred dollar bills. She called her dad.

"Carrie? Is everything OK?"

"Yeah Dad, we're fine, don't worry. So, remember that side table I got from you? The one with the drawer that didn't open?"

"My memory's not that short Carrie! Of course, I do. Why? Did you find a dead mouse in it or something?"

"No, nothing like that. But there was something in it. Do you remember where you got it from?"

"It was a house in town. The family had a garage sale before they moved. I think the dad got some job overseas so they had to clear everything out before they moved."

"Dad, there was a bag full of money stuck inside the drawer. It's real. And there's $9,000!"

Her dad let out a long whistle. "Then you're now $9,000 richer young lady!"

"Are you sure Dad? Shouldn't we try to give it back?"

"Honey, that was years ago. Those people are long gone. It was meant for you, and it couldn't go to someone who needs it more. This will really help you out, won't it?"

"I can't even think it through right now Dad! What should I do?"

"Absolutely nothing. You put that money somewhere safe until you're ready to make a plan. You're smart, you'll figure it out!"

"Thanks Dad, what would I do without you?"

"You'd miss out on the big money, that's what!" Laughing, they said their goodbyes. Carrie tucked the money on the top shelf of her closet behind a box until she knew what to do next. That kind of stash wouldn't exactly fit in her Bible!

Before it was time to meet Matthew at school, Carrie packed each child two changes of clothes and pajamas to take to their dad's. She had learned to send their worst clothes to Don's. Although they had agreed to leave clothes and toys at his house for the kids when she moved out, he always seemed to leave their nicer clothes there and send them home in stained or torn clothes. So she did what she could to not lose the few nicer clothes the kids still had.

On the way to school that afternoon, she told Katie and Magnus that Katie and Matthew would be walking to their dad's ahead of them, and she, Magnus, and his brothers would follow behind like secret spies to protect them. She hoped she'd be able to pull it off without Don noticing.

Matthew looked so terribly small walking alone with his sister. Carrie hoped with all her heart that they'd be OK for the weekend. When they got to the door, they hesitated for a minute before walking in. Matthew looked like he wasn't sure whether to knock or not, and Carrie wondered if the horrible words those girls had said were echoing in his mind.

There was some notice flapping on the front door, but Carrie couldn't read what it said. Once Katie and Matthew were inside, she turned to walk back with Kara's boys. She stopped at the park with them for as long as she could before heading home. Although she was looking forward to the boys going home, she wasn't looking forward to not having her kids around for the weekend. She'd keep herself busy and hopefully the time would pass quickly.

Kara tried to convince her to come over for a glass of wine that night, but Carrie declined. She wanted to get the shelf listed and start on her next project. And she needed some time to think about the stash of money hiding in her closet. She promised to come the next night instead. It would be nice to get out for a bit.

After heating up some leftovers for supper, Carrie went and double-checked the money. It was still there. She counted it again. Yep. All of it was there, minus the one bill she had exchanged at the bank. She tucked it back away and went downstairs. No matter if she suddenly had a windfall, she needed to get that shelf listed and check her emails.

She was surprised to see that the lady who bought the first coffee table from her wanted to see the picture frames. Either she loved to shop, or she had some sort of decorating business. Both would be just fine for Carrie. She replied that she would be home all day tomorrow, and then set up a new listing for the shelf. Keeping her goal of $150 in sales, she listed the shelf for $30, and then she opened the spreadsheet she kept her budget on.

Carrie's monthly expenses were pretty basic. $550 for rent, $150 for heat and electricity, $50 for her cell phone, $30 for basic internet, $80 for car insurance, $160 for groceries, $110 for gas, $150 for student loans and $67 minimum payment on the old joint credit card. That was a grand total of $1,197. With the money she got paid for watching Kara's boys, this left $3 remaining to pay for anything else that might happen in the month. The extra $20 to $30 she got from recycling cans and bottles made the difference between eating and going hungry when there was an unexpected expense.

The furniture sales and working for Jenny had already made a huge difference to her bottom line. She had $110 in her emergency savings, and $355 in her bank account plus whatever she made selling things this weekend. It was more money than Carrie had in years. Oh, and then there was that crazy stash of cash upstairs. Carrie felt that this could be a turning point for her if only she could be smart enough with it and not screw everything up. The pressure was enormous, and she didn't know who to talk to about it.

She worried that if Don got wind that she was doing OK he'd figure out a way to get her money. For one thing, she couldn't tell her kids. She never wanted them to feel they had to keep secrets, and this would be a pretty big secret to keep. Her parents were always careful with their money, but they still had to be careful now and Carrie didn't want to live with money worries for the rest of her life so maybe they weren't the best people for advice. Maybe she could ask Jenny about it without being too obvious.

At least she could make a list of possible things to do with it:

- *More in emergency fund*
- *Christmas gifts*
- *Winter jackets for the kids*
- *Cable TV*
- *Guitar lessons for Matthew*
- *Swimming lessons for Katie*

It felt surreal to even be thinking about this. After sitting for almost ten minutes, just looking at the words and numbers on her computer screen, Carrie saved it and turned off her computer. She figured the only certain thing was that she needed to keep her hands busy or she'd go crazy, so she went into her living room and started cleaning the little side table that had changed her life. One thing for sure, she would never sell this table! It would get a makeover and then sit in her bedroom as a reminder that miracles happened.

Later, Carrie lay in bed, still thinking about the money. Beds for the kids got added to her mental wish list, and then suddenly her eyes flew open. Pay back her parents! How could she have not thought about that until now? Top priority was giving them back the $2,000 they loaned her. With a sigh of happiness, she fell asleep.

CHAPTER 14

A pounding at the front door woke Carrie up with a start. Looking at her alarm clock she saw it was 8:30 am. What on earth was going on? She grabbed her robe and ran downstairs. Opening the door, she was faced with a very angry ex-husband, and two terrified looking kids. Katie had tears streaming down her face. They were both still in their pajamas.

"I'm done with you using these little brats to screw up my life! You're turning them into bitches just like you are!"

Carrie quickly reached for the kids and pulled them into the house. Katie cowered behind her and started saying "I'm sorry Mommy" over and over. But Matthew stood beside her, trying to look defiant. Carrie could feel him shaking as she put her arm around him.

"Don, these are your kids! They haven't done anything to you!"

"No? What about using Katie to get that asshole Morris to evict me? And Matthew flipping off to my girlfriend's kids and acting like he's so much better than them? I'm finished with you! All of you!" He turned around and stormed over to the minivan Carrie and Matthew had seen the other month. The woman driving leaned forward and held up her middle finger to them before driving away.

Carrie closed the front door and locked it and then walked the kids to the couch. Both were crying now. She sat and held them, tears streaming down her own face. Her heart broke for them, but felt cold and angry against the man who did so much harm with his words.

Eventually they all calmed down, and Carrie spoke. "That man's words are *not* true, OK? You are both wonderful gifts from God to this earth and every day I think about how lucky I am that I get to have you as my kids." Matthew looked up at her with tear filled eyes before wrapping his arms around her waist and hugging her tightly.

"What happened, bud?"

"Everything was OK yesterday. It was just us and Dad. We had leftover pizza for supper and watched TV, and when Katie went to bed, we played Xbox. And then this morning that lady came over with her kids, and they came into my room and told me to get out and said it wasn't my room. I kinda yelled back at them. And then Dad came in and grabbed me and pulled me out of the room and…" his voice got much quieter "he called me bad names… Then Katie came in and yelled at him that he was a big meanie and told him to leave me alone."

"Yeah Mommy, Daddy was being really bad!" Katie's eyes were wide with the shock of what she had heard and seen.

"And then there was this banging on the door and Dad went to get it and it was these two men in uniforms and they said he had thirty minutes to get some things and he had to leave the house. Dad started yelling lots of bad words and called Mr. Morris some bad names."

Katie interrupted, "And then I kicked Daddy in the leg and told him to stop it because Mr. Morris was the nicest man in the whole world and he was your friend. And then Daddy said this was all my fault and he said to go home and never come back."

Matthew took over talking, "I said she wasn't leaving without me and I went outside with Katie, and then the men said they would report Dad if he let us go alone, and Dad's girlfriend said she'd be happy to drive us out of her life and said we were crap. Well, she didn't say crap..."

"I'm sorry Mommy! I didn't mean to make Daddy mad. I just didn't want him saying stuff about Mr. Morris or yelling at Matthew anymore." Katie's lip trembled.

"You didn't do anything wrong, Katie. In fact, you were very very right because you stood up to a bully and told him to stop! I'm so proud of you! And I'm so proud of you too Matthew for sticking with your sister! None of this is your fault, OK? None of this!"

They sat together in silence for a while, except for Katie's occasional dry sob as she tried to recover from crying so hard. Carrie thought about reporting Don to the police, but it wasn't like he had broken any laws. Using all her cash to pay someone to break a bone or two also crossed her mind. But she had to focus on getting the kids through this with as little damage as possible. It was tempting to tell them about the stash of money so they could have something happy to think about, but she still feared it might get back to Don. If he really was getting evicted today, he'd be even more desperate than usual for money. At least she had sent the kids with their worst clothes, because it looked like she wouldn't be getting them back.

"Let's all get dressed and have breakfast, and then we'll go get groceries, OK?"

"Sugar cereal!" Katie cheered. Carrie wished everything could be fixed with sugar cereal.

Just before they left to get groceries, Carrie remembered about the things she had listed for sale. She checked her emails, and the lady who was interested in the picture frames wanted to come over later. Carrie replied that she'd be home all afternoon, and she was welcome to come anytime to look at the frames.

SWEET, SMART, AND STRUGGLING

At the grocery store, Carrie told them they could each pick two treats. Katie spent the whole time putting things in and out of the buggy as she constantly changed her mind about what to choose. Matthew waited until he could look down every aisle before making his choices. Carrie splurged too, adding ingredients for homemade cookies, strawberries, and a loaf of garlic bread to go with their spaghetti tomorrow night. Tonight, they would have pizza and ice cream and keep the weekend tradition going. She knew she couldn't do this every time, but just this time she'd give herself a little treat. Pausing for a minute, she texted Kara:

Change of plans. Don made kids come home this morning. Nasty stuff. Will talk on Monday.

Seconds later Kara replied:

Glad the kids are away from the asshole. Sad you can't come drink tonight. Love you!

She smiled and answered:

Love you too!

After letting the kids decide which ice cream to buy (and reassuring Matthew that it did *not* count as one of his treats), she headed to the checkout. Impulsively, she grabbed the latest Marvel superhero movie that was on display by the cashier. Matthew's eye widened in surprise. She whispered to him, "We'll have a special movie night when Katie goes to bed, OK?" He smiled a huge smile and nodded his agreement. Katie was so busy waiting to put her two treats on the conveyer belt that she missed the whole thing. Carrie made a mental note to do something special with her before bedtime.

Once they were home Carrie happily put the groceries away. It felt like so long ago when she had left the grocery store in tears because she spent over her $40 budget. Today she spent just over $80 and she still felt great. Then she remembered the incident that morning with

Don. It dampened her joy a little bit but she refused to let it totally ruin her day.

In the afternoon the lady came to look at the picture frames. She introduced herself as Eleanor, and said she ran a décor company. Carrie wasn't sure what that meant aside from the fact that she wanted to buy things and didn't care that they came from a rundown townhouse. Eleanor was thrilled with the picture frames and planned to use them just the way Carrie imagined.

It was a huge boost to her confidence that someone with her own successful business thought Carrie had good taste! Then she asked if Carrie could do more. Taking a quick mental inventory, Carrie figured she could do at least another five with what she had, and she could probably pick up more frames from the thrift store. She answered that she thought that she could. "Could you have 18 more ready by the end of the month?" Eleanor asked, interrupting her thoughts. "I'll pay you $140 for these seven, and another $360 for the next group."

Carrie was shocked at the price. "Are you sure? That's really very generous."

Eleanor smiled "I'll let you in on a little secret. My clients will pay me more than double that when I install them, so I think the price is just fine. I'm all for helping you out, but it'll benefit me just as much!"

Carrie was more than happy to agree to her first order and wrapped up the frames in some leftover tissue paper before packing them in two bags for her new client. "I'll email you as soon as they're ready to pick up then."

"Wonderful! And I have to say, your daughter has a fantastic sense of style." She looked over at Katie who was sitting on the floor coloring. She had a scarf wrapped around her head, a scarf and a long necklace over a pink t-shirt with a purple skirt and long red socks. Carrie bit back a smile—those were her socks! "Maybe you'll come work for me one day young lady, and you can help me make rich people's houses look beautiful."

Katie looked at her in shock. "You can get paid to make things beautiful?"

"Oh yes, they pay me very well!"

"OK," Katie agreed "But I have to go to big kid school and university first. That's what Mommy said."

"It's a deal!" Eleanor laughed. "I'll see you all in a few weeks then."

Carrie thanked her once more after accepting the $140 and then let her out. "What do you think Katie? Are you going to be a fancy designer when you grow up?"

Katie smiled big and went back to her coloring. Carrie didn't mention the socks, but she'd try to get Katie more colorful socks sometime soon, so she didn't feel the need to take her mom's clothes. There'd be time enough for that in her teens, if Carrie ever got herself some nice clothes.

She went upstairs and tucked $40 into her 'Bible savings plan', put the rest in her wallet, and then braved the basement to gather up all the picture frames she had. Sooner than later she needed to finish making the basement into some sort of work area. She already had a table and a portable heater on her wish list.

After supper, Carrie and Katie worked on using one of the scarves that Katie had accidently torn to be turned into a cheerful wall hanging. They chose a frame that still had a good backing inside it, cleaned it, and then painting it a bright pink color that they found in the basement. Carrie wondered who on earth had chosen such a vibrant color — most of the can had been used somewhere! They mounted the scarf on top of the backing and used some duct tape Carrie's dad gave her to secure the fabric to the back. He had insisted "You always need duct tape around the house!" but Carrie was pretty sure he hadn't been thinking about securing fabric!

When the frame was dry tomorrow, they'd put it together and hang it on Katie's side of the room. It looked surprisingly professional, and Carrie wondered if she could do more of something similar and sell it. Transporting picture frames around would be much easier than furniture.

Once Katie fell asleep, Carrie made popcorn on the stove and settled in with Matthew to watch the new movie. She kind of liked superhero movies and was grateful she had a boy so she could watch them once in a while. And she knew Matthew would be happy to watch it on his own lots too.

Her mind briefly went back to what she would have been doing tonight if the kids weren't home. She did miss the idea of hanging out with Kara for a bit of girl talk. Maybe they could figure something out for tomorrow with the kids.

After Matthew was in bed, Carrie texted Kara again:

> *Need girl talk! Any chance you want to meet at the new indoor play area sometime tomorrow? The kids could burn off steam while we chat...*

Kara didn't reply right away, so she turned off her phone and went to bed.

Sunday morning they woke up to snow falling. Katie was thrilled and eager to get outside and play. Matthew and Carrie could have stayed inside all day and been perfectly happy. Her boots weren't warm or waterproof, so time outside with Katie always meant time with freezing cold, wet feet.

Fortunately, Kara had replied:

> *Yes!!! Hubby is taking the twins to their hockey game, and now you've given Magnus and me an excuse to skip it. Thank you!! Can you do 10, or is that too early?*

Carrie was happy to get the kids occupied as soon as possible.

10 is perfect. Now I can delay taking Katie out to play in the snow!

LOL! I know how much you hate the snow. Glad to help.

Carrie smiled at Kara's response. It was nice to have a friend that knew her so well!

Later, as the three kids climbed through the play area, Carrie and Kara grabbed coffees and found a table with a decent view of the kids. Carrie brought Kara up to date on everything that had happened with Don. Just telling someone else about it brought up the anger again, but also somehow made it easier to face. Kara let out a stream of choice words about Don, and Carrie enjoyed every minute of it. She was terrible at putting more than one swear word in a sentence, so Kara's rant helped put into words exactly what she wished she could say.

They both agreed that having Don out of the picture was a good thing. Kara suggested that Carrie report the incident to her family doctor so there was a record of it. Then, if Don tried to spend time with the kids again, Carrie could try to insist that he take an anger management course first. Carrie hadn't thought that far in advance, but it was a good idea. She'd email her doctor's office as soon as she got home and request an appointment.

"Can't you email from your phone?" Kara asked.

"Nope, not on this antique! I'm limited to texts and phone calls!"

"Carrie, honey, you need to get with the program! How are your kids ever going to keep up their high scores on games if they can't play them on your phone?"

Carrie hadn't really thought about upgrading her phone. It would be nice to email and keep her Buy and Sell listings up to date if she had a new phone. But it really seemed too extravagant. Especially when her kids were still sleeping on thin mattresses on the floor. Beds! She made another mental note to put those beds on her wish list.

"Earth to Carrie!" Kara called out. Carrie gave herself a shake. "Sorry! Got a little lost in my thoughts there."

"When was the last time you had a break?"

"Every day's a break when you don't live with a jerk anymore!"

"Girl, you need to raise the bar! Please do some nice things for yourself, and let's go out for fun sometime, OK?"

Carrie smiled. "I'll try!"

After two hours the kids had worn themselves out and worked up a sweat. The two moms said their goodbyes and headed home. Carrie figured the kids had earned a break and could each choose a DVD to take turns watching for the afternoon. And she decided to take a break from the furniture business and read a novel she had picked up on impulse at the library. It was nice, this new life they had with a little bit of fun money!

CHAPTER 15

On Monday morning Carrie was surprised to see Max walking Angela to school. She said hello and asked if he still needed her today. He smacked his forehead. "I'm so sorry! They changed my work schedule on the weekend and I totally forgot about updating you! Is that OK? I can pay you for today anyways since you made plans to come?"

"Not at all! It was a crazy weekend, so it works out perfect that you're home today. When would you like me to come again?"

He booked her for Wednesday to Friday, and Carrie walked home wondering if she had enough time to get a coat of primer on the lucky end table from her dad. When she was almost home her phone rang.

"Carrie? This is Henry Morris. Can you meet me at your old house right away? It's important."

Carrie changed her path and headed towards the house. She hoped he wasn't going to try to get money from her again. Their visit a few weeks ago seemed to go so well!

As she got close to the house, she saw a rental moving truck backed into the driveway. Mr. Morris was nowhere to be seen, but his car was on the road in front of the house. She cautiously walked to the door and knocked. The eviction notice was still on the door.

Suddenly the door swung open, and Mr. Morris was standing there with the biggest smile she had ever seen. "Hello! Come in come in!"

She stepped in and he closed the door. "So, you managed to get Don out?"

"Yep! The bugger, excuse my language, left me a threatening voice-mail on Wednesday so I was able to escalate the eviction and kick him out Saturday morning! The bailiffs came and everything, and they brought me the keys after the locks got changed. I might never get all of my money from him, but I'm sure going to try. And now, young lady, would you like to be my next tenant here?"

Carrie was stunned. She hadn't even considered that possibility. But she knew what her answer was right away. "That's so very kind of you, and I would love nothing better than to have you for a landlord. But this house has some pretty rough memories for me and the kids, and it wouldn't be good for us to live here again." She didn't add that it was also way out of her budget.

"I thought you might say no. It's too bad, because you're the perfect tenant. I just need one more thing from you then…" His eyes twinkled "Do you know anyone who could use a bed? I've suddenly got a few that I need to get rid of."

Carrie gasped, and then shocked herself by starting to cry. "Are you serious?"

"It isn't right that you've all been sleeping on the floor. I've got moving men upstairs taking the beds apart right now. They'll take them to your place, along with anything else you want from here. Legally it's all mine now and I want you to take everything you need. According to the court order, I can sell everything to get back some of the money he owes me, but he already took the expensive stuff—except one thing: I checked, your fancy coffee maker is still here."

SWEET, SMART, AND STRUGGLING

She reached out and hugged her new angel of mercy. "Thank you!" she managed to croak out through the tears. Awkwardly he hugged her back and then she stepped back to dig for a Kleenex in her purse.

"There, there young lady. It's just the things that are rightfully yours. And I wouldn't have gotten that man out of the house without your help! My son, the one in Australia, sent me some money so I can get the house cleaned out and ready to rent again. We're all going to be OK."

"We really are, aren't we? The kids are going to be so surprised!"

"Let's go look at the bedrooms first, and then you can decide what else you want."

Upstairs, the movers had almost finished taking Matthew's bed apart. She decided to take everything from both the kid's bedrooms — beds, linens, night tables, dressers, toys, and books. A quick look didn't show many clothes. She wondered where they were.

Carrie declined the master bed and everything else in the master bedroom. It wouldn't fit in the room with Katie's bed, and everything in there held bad memories. Even if there were things she could sell, she didn't want them in her own home.

Back downstairs, she wasn't surprised to see that the Xbox and all the games and controllers were gone, along with the TV. How on earth Don managed to move it out she didn't know, and quite frankly didn't care.

She smiled to see her favorite chair and footrest pushed into the corner of the living room. It was a tropical floral pattern that Don had always hated, but she got it for $20 at a yard sale and loved the bright colors. It would fit in her living room, but then she'd lose more work space...

In the kitchen, Carrie took a quick mental inventory and an idea began to form. The table wasn't very nice looking, but it was sturdy. Now that there were some strong men to help, she could get the table moved into her basement. She was going to have a full, functioning house soon with a separate work space!

Mr. Morris came in after taking a phone call outside. Carrie noticed that even he had the latest smartphone! He repeated to her that she was to take everything in the house she could use. What she didn't take he'd have to donate to the thrift store or take to the dump. Grabbing some loose paper and a pen from the counter, Carrie wrote down all the big things she wanted so the movers would know what to load first:

- Beds and furniture from kids' rooms
- Flowered chair and footstool in living room
- Floor lamps in living room
- Kitchen table and chairs

She was getting part of her wish list delivered to her door for free! Grabbing some garbage bags, she went back upstairs to pack the smaller items in her kids' rooms. They were going to be so excited to have all their things back!

Everything fit into a few bags that she took straight to the mover's truck. Stopping for a minute to set an alarm on the oven so she wouldn't be late to pick up the kids from preschool, she ran back upstairs and took the best linens from the upstairs closet. Then, she went to the basement to look for some boxes for the kid's books.

As if everything wasn't working out good enough already, she turned around and saw a portable heater. It would be perfect for taking the icy cold out of the basement when she was working down there! And, piled in front of the washing machine were the kid's clothes she had been looking for. She filled another garbage bag with them and grabbed a few empty boxes.

By the time she needed to go get the kids, Carrie was completely out of breath. She felt like she had been on one of those game shows where you ran through the grocery store grabbing all the best groceries before the clock ran out.

The movers were just finishing loading the truck and would meet her at her house shortly. In addition to all the kids' things and furniture there was the heater, coffee maker, DVDs, and board games, bags with clothes and linens, all of her baking trays and her mixer, the kids' school pictures, her sewing machine, the Christmas decorations, and all the unopened food she had found in the cupboards.

Mr. Morris was sitting on the couch, beaming. "You make me tired just watching you! Today has been the most fun I've had in a long time."

"I think it's time you found some hobbies then," Carrie laughed. "Evicting people doesn't pay very well!"

"Just knowing your little ones will be sleeping on their beds tonight is worth a lot. You three are going to be just fine."

"Thank you, I'm starting to think so myself but it's only because people like you are looking out for us. It's going to be so good to get this all set up at our place. We always have pizza for supper on Friday night. Could you join us this week?"

"I'd love to dear! I can bring dessert from the bakery near my place. I usually can't go there because I just end up eating everything myself!"

"Perfect, come on over for six and we'll show you our new and improved house before we eat. Thank you again for everything." She reached over and gave him another hug before leaving. He had an appointment and wouldn't be following the movers to her place.

Carrie couldn't help but skip down the street for joy for a block. Her kids were going to sleep on beds tonight! It was too good to be true, and she could hardly wait to pick up Magnus and Katie and get back home.

As the three of them walked into the parking lot of the townhouse complex, Carrie was happy to see the moving truck backed up to the door and ready to unload everything. On the walk home from preschool, she told Katie that there was a wonderful surprise waiting for them at their house. Katie tried to guess everything under the sun, but even in her optimistic imagination she hadn't thought of a bed.

"Katie, do you remember how your dad had to leave his house because he hadn't paid Mr. Morris the rent in a long time?" Katie nodded sadly. "Well, Mr. Morris got to keep everything in the house, and he's giving ALL your things back to you! They're all in that truck, ready to unload!"

"YAAAAAAYYYY" Katie cheered, bouncing up and down. When they reached the truck, she ran over to one of the movers and wrapped her arms around his legs. "You brought my room back!!! You're the bestest!!" Carrie loved that Katie was so fearless and open with people. The surprised young man patted her on the shoulder awkwardly but couldn't hide his own big smile. "Will you show me where your room is then?"

"Yep, I share a room with Mommy. Come on!" He looked over at Carrie in surprise before following her into the house. Katie ran upstairs to show the mover where things should go. Carrie quickly moved her furniture repair project onto the kitchen table so it would be mostly out of the way, and got Magnus settled on the couch with a few of the kid's books Katie had chosen from the library. When she was sure he was feeling secure in the middle of the craziness that was happening, she ran upstairs.

"I'll just move these mattresses out of the way and you can bring the beds and bedroom furniture up. Maybe we'll put everything else in the living room for now so I've got some room to put the beds together. Oh, but the table and chairs need to go down in the basement please."

"Mr. Morris is paying us to stay here until the beds are set up. You don't need to worry about that."

"That man is an angel," she said with a smile. "I'll happily let you set up those beds!" She went downstairs and insisted Katie stay with her now so she wouldn't interrupt the movers working. There soon wouldn't be room in the kitchen so she quickly made peanut butter and jam sandwiches for herself and the kids. She offered the movers lunch as well, but they declined. They did each take a cup of coffee when they finished setting up the beds. By 1:30 everything was in the house, and the beds and furniture were set up upstairs.

Carrie sat in her armchair in the living room, suddenly feeling quite overwhelmed. She had a reheated cup of coffee in her hand that was much needed. There were lots of bags and boxes that needed unpacking, and she wanted to wash the kid's bedding before making their beds. She figured it would be a few days before she could get back to her furniture projects. Thank goodness she had the morning free tomorrow before being at Jenny's for the rest of the week.

She never did well when the house was messy, and she needed to focus on priorities so everything would get done in the right order. Finishing her coffee, she found the bag with the dirty kids bedding in it and went downstairs to start a load of laundry. It looked like they hadn't been washed since she moved out, so she decided to run them through a hot water wash. Normally she washed everything in cold to save money, but today would be an exception.

Magnus and Katie were now watching one of the DVDs she had grabbed from the old house. Katie was raring to get at her things in the bedroom, but Carrie knew it was better to get it all organized first. Katie could make a small hurricane in a short amount of time, and Carrie couldn't deal with hurricanes right now. She moved things around in the living room so there would be room for everyone to sit when the older boys came in, and then did the same in the kitchen. Riffling through the boxes of food she had taken, she found a box of granola bars and a case of fruit cups. That would do for snack for everyone.

Then she went back upstairs to get Matthew's room looking better. Like his mom, he didn't like it when things were messy. He also didn't like surprises, so Carrie planned to meet him outside the house before he came in and explain what was going on before he stepped in and saw things everywhere.

She was so grateful Mr. Morris had asked the movers to put the beds together. It would have been hard to do alone. The bed, night table, dresser, and bookshelf were easy enough to arrange, since there was really only one way to make them fit in the small room. Carrie quickly wiped everything down, and then moved Matthew's clothes from the cardboard boxes they were using for storage into his dresser. She put the one LEGO set he had on top of the dresser and moved his library books onto the shelf. The rest of the bags and boxes she moved to the side where they weren't the first thing you'd see when you walked in the room. That would have to do for Matthew.

There was just enough time to set up Magnus and Katie with the Guess Who game on the couch, put the kid's bedding into the dryer, and start a new load with their clothes before stepping outside to wait for Matthew.

He walked up with Justin and Calvin, and Carrie was grateful they hadn't run ahead of him this time. She explained that things were a little crazy in the house, because Mr. Morris had delivered all of their things to them. Matthew looked confused, "Aren't those Dad's things?"

"No bud, they were all given to Mr. Morris. I can explain more about that later. The important thing for now is that your bed is all set up in your room, and we have a bunch of bags and boxes in the house that we get to unpack. You OK with that?"

"My bed is here?"

"Your bed, your night table, your dresser, and your shelf! And my favorite chair and footstool, and Katie's bed too!"

"Awesome!" He turned to Justin and Calvin "Wanna see?" They all ran into the house, with Carrie hollering behind them to take off their boots and hang up their coats. She had been lucky to find a decent wall-mounted coat hanger in a box of free things she had picked up, but it was taking a while to train the twins to hang up their jackets instead of dropping them on the floor like they used to do at her house.

After the boys checked out the room (and Calvin expressed how lucky Matthew was to not have to share a room with his brother), Carrie got everyone settled for snack and then out the door for some fresh air. She would have loved to start organizing things right away, but that would have to wait. The snow had melted a bit, leaving everything slippery and messy. The twins were happy to practice sliding across the ice under the basketball nets, and Matthew sort of joined them, while taking much more care to not fall.

Katie and Magnus chose the swings, allowing Carrie to zone out while she pushed them. It was all a bit much to take in. This morning she had been dreaming about all the things she might do with the money she found, and suddenly now she had a much more pressing opportunity to deal with. Even if she didn't sell a single thing all week, having beds, furniture, some extra sheets, and food that she hadn't needed to pay for set her way ahead.

She thought about Mr. Morris and hoped he'd find the good tenants he deserved. It occurred to her that she should get some sort of copy of the threatening voicemail Don had left him. It might help if she needed to prove he had an anger problem. Stepping away from the swings, she called Mr. Morris. She didn't want that message being erased, if it wasn't already.

Mr. Morris told her he'd ask his lawyer to send her a copy of the voicemail. They had used it as evidence, so it was saved. "I hope you don't have to deal with him again, Carrie. He's a bad man." Carrie agreed, but reassured him that Don was out of the picture. She hoped she was right.

By the time Kara came to pick up the boys, Carrie had made a small dent on the things in the house. The bedding was almost dry (the old dryer took forever to dry anything), and Carrie had set up Katie's things as best she could, leaving room for her own mattress on the floor still. She'd heat up some of the spaghetti for supper that she made yesterday. It was the kind of day when she wished she could order take-out, but after all the extra spending she had done over the weekend she needed to go back to being careful so she didn't blow it all.

Kara was momentarily speechless when Carrie told her what happened. But it wasn't about getting things from Mr. Morris. "You guys have been sleeping on the floor this whole time? Why didn't you tell me Carrie? We could have helped you out!"

"I didn't want to be a freeloader. And look at how amazing it's turned out!"

"But still Carrie, you've gotta ask for help when you need it. That's not being a freeloader, OK?"

Carrie smiled. She was determined to stand on her own two feet. Even though she knew that nobody was an island, and life was better when everyone helped each other out, she still wanted to feel like she had gotten somewhere on her own steam.

She managed to move her furniture project back into the living room and they ate supper squeezed onto the edges of the table because it was full of things she had grabbed from the kitchen at the old house. Carrie informed the kids that they would just call it the old house, and not Dad's house, since it really had belonged to Mr. Morris the whole time. She explained a little bit about renting, eviction, and people's rights. They were both suitably impressed with the importance of paying their bills and not causing harm to others by being irresponsible with money.

It was Matthew's turn to clean up supper, so she left him to it and went downstairs to get the dry bedding and transfer the kid's clothes into the dryer. There were some nice clothes in there that she had forgotten about. Hopefully they'd still fit and the kids could feel a little better about what they wore—especially Matthew who wasn't interested in spicing up a dull outfit with a bright scarf or two!

Then they all went upstairs to make their 'new' beds. Carrie was just as excited as they were. Tonight would feel like a fancy resort for the kids after sleeping on the floor for months! At some point, she should get herself a bed too. Maybe she'd put that on her wish list. She decided to let Katie help put her things away while Matthew unpacked his things.

She brought out the CD player and radio that had been in the kitchen at the old house, and they found an oldies radio station to listen to while they worked. Katie wanted to play with or try on everything that came out of the bags, but Carrie was firm that this was 'putting away' time not play time. She needed the bedroom to feel peaceful for sleeping and they didn't have much time before Katie needed to go to bed.

Once Katie was cozily tucked in her bed with clean sheets and all her favorite stuffed animals, Carrie moved to Matthew's bedroom to help him finish setting up. She realized she had failed to take the posters off his walls at the old house. That would be something to spend a little bit of money on so he could be proud of his room. It didn't take much longer to set everything up. Matthew said it almost made him want to go to bed early, but he'd wait till his bedtime. Carrie reached and gave him a hug and ruffled his hair. "I love you so much, son!"

"Love you too Mom! Thanks for getting all this stuff back."

"You can thank Mr. Morris yourself when he comes to dinner on Friday, OK?" Matthew nodded and they headed downstairs.

Carrie figured the next most important thing was making sure she'd get her morning coffee. She cleared a spot on the counter for the nice coffee maker and moved the old one into the basement. There might be a time when she'd need to save money on coffee again and then she'd be glad she kept it. In the meantime, she'd enjoy the good stuff. She had found quite a few boxes of coffee pods in the old house, but it took a while to dig them out from the bags of food. Since cupboard space was tight, she'd have to keep them on the counter, but she stacked them neatly. Just seeing all that coffee there made her feel better. Tomorrow would definitely be starting on a good note!

While Matthew watched a DVD from the old house, Carrie worked on unpacking the food, and fitting it as best she could into the cupboards. A little burst of inspiration had her scooting into the basement and bringing up a small shelf. It fit quite well between the table and the back door and would give her a little extra storage space. After cleaning it, it gave her just enough room to unpack the rest of the food. She decided to re-paint it when she had time, and maybe even put up a little curtain so it was nicer to look at. For now, it would have to do, and she was pretty happy to have found a solution right in her own house.

The last thing Carrie did was set the table for breakfast and put two boxes of sugar cereal on the table. There were four boxes of cereal that were opened but almost full that Carrie had grabbed. She figured they'd be fine to still eat, and they wouldn't keep forever, so the kids could enjoy some unhealthy (but fun!) breakfasts until the cereal ran out.

CHAPTER 16

Tuesday morning Carrie struggled to wake up, and only the thought of a decent cup of coffee got her out of bed. Her muscles were really letting her know that she had been running up and down the stairs the day before! While she thought she was in pretty good shape from all the walking she did, it was clearly not the same as a few hours running up and down stairs.

While she enjoyed her coffee, she started up her computer and looked at her money list again.

- $110 in emergency savings
- $355 in bank
- $8,900 put aside (***Give $2000 to Dad and Mom)
- $1,197 monthly expenses
- Extra money from Jenny
- Extra money from furniture

The curser flashed at her from the screen as she stared at the numbers. They should make her feel good, but instead she felt confused. What did she do next? Buy the things she needed? Put more money in her bank account? Start investing?

She heard Matthew up in the bathroom and closed down her computer. He didn't need those sorts of grown-up worries on his little mind! When he came downstairs, he was thrilled to see the breakfast choices, and decided to have a half a bowl of each cereal since they were both his favorites. Carrie waited to wake up Katie until she finished her coffee. Then she went to get her daughter up and get them both ready for the day.

It was wonderful to sit on the side of Katie's bed to wake her up, instead of kneeling on the floor. And Katie was in no hurry to get out of her comfortable bed. Carrie left her there waking up while she had a quick shower and got dressed. Then she bribed Katie out of bed with the promise of sugar cereal for breakfast.

Before the kids left for school Carrie had just enough time to bring up the laundry from the dryer and unpack one of the bags in the living room. It had DVDs and games and Carrie found another little shelf from the basement to hold them. The living room was feeling a little crowded, but it was nice to have some things around them today. Carrie couldn't wait to put everything away and arrange the extra furniture nicely. She was going to enjoy having her chair and footstool and some decent lighting in that room!

After Katie ran off into the preschool with Magnus and Angela, Carrie had a quick chat with Kara, and then walked straight back home. She needed to have her house in order and the basement set up so she could get back to the furniture business. With her first order on the books for 18 picture frames, she needed to keep going. The paint needed almost a day to dry between coats, and with her work moved to the cold basement, it might take even longer.

In the rest of the time that the kids were at preschool, Carrie moved everything else that had been dropped in the living room to its new places, centered the table in the basement, and ran the heater for a while to take the edge off. She realized she'd still have to do some work upstairs since she didn't want to be away from the kids when they were home. The shower curtain could go on the table in the kitchen to protect it while she put a coat of paint on some picture frames. She could probably do five a night, leave them on the table overnight to dry, and then move them to the basement in the morning so the kids could have room to eat breakfast. It would work even though it wasn't ideal.

When she went to pick up the kids from preschool, she made sure to grab the bag for collecting cans and bottles. Most of the snow had melted, so they should be able to find them again. Carrie wanted to keep doing everything she could to get ahead. She had forgotten about the drink containers for a week or so and it was time to get back at it.

They didn't find too many, but everything helped. Carrie put them with the others in the backyard right away since they were a bit dirty from the slush. Then she made the kids' favorite plain pasta for lunch and sent them to pick out a DVD. That job took longer now with all the new arrivals!

While they were occupied, Carrie gathered up all the picture frames that would work for her order. In all there were seven, so she'd have to find eleven more in the next few days. She also brought up the fun framed scarf that she had been working on with Katie on the weekend. That felt like a lifetime ago now. Putting the frame on made the project look surprisingly good and got Carrie to thinking again that this might be another way to make money. Picture frames were a lot easier to work with than shelves and side tables and if she could make things that someone like Eleanor was willing to buy, she could make more money than the bigger items seemed to get.

Katie was delighted with the finished project and they hung it above her bed. It was nice to have something on the walls! They spend the rest of the time before the big boys arrived from school playing games with the alphabet flash cards Carrie brought from the old house. Both Katie and Magnus had picked up most of the letters simply from watching their older siblings so she focused on learning the letters they weren't familiar with.

Carrie noticed that Katie liked to hold the flash cards herself. At first, she thought Katie was just trying to be in control, but after watching her for a bit it seemed like Katie might have trouble seeing the letters if they were further away. That would have to be checked—and soon. She didn't want Katie missing out on anything just because she needed glasses!

Before the older boys got in, Carrie put out strawberries and the Oreos she had brought from the old house. She made them all have a serving of fruit first before getting Oreos. Matthew was the only one to ask for more strawberries, which didn't surprise Carrie at all.

When the kids were back inside again after some fresh air, Carrie started up her computer. She was hoping to find more picture frames for free. Otherwise, she'd have to start looking at the thrift stores. A search for 'picture frame' didn't bring up anything, and Carrie was feeling discouraged. Finding things for free was an important part of making money on these projects. Then, she remembered that the other frames had been in a box of knick knacks. So, she started again, scrolling through all the postings and looking for ones that might include picture frames.

This time, she had better luck. She found three postings with promise, although two of them were from months ago. After sending off an inquiry to each one, she started supper. It was too bad she hadn't checked out the fridge and freezer at the old house. There might have been some usable food there. As it was, she'd have to get a little creative to use up the cans and boxes of food she had brought over. Determined to stretch her grocery budget, she pulled out a can of some sort of stew. Served with some fresh homemade biscuits she figured it would be all right.

Katie and Magnus helped her mix up biscuits while the twins played on their Nintendo Switch, and Matthew watched a DVD. Carrie could have made the biscuits a lot faster on her own, but the kids had so much fun squishing the dough together while they mixed it. She had just enough time to get them in the oven before Kara arrived to pick up her boys.

Kara was amazed at all Carrie had accomplished since the day before. Carrie was so proud of how things were coming together, she took Kara for a quick whole-house tour. When they got to the basement, Kara picked up one of the frames that Carrie had already cleaned and primed. "Is this the kind of stuff you're doing?" She asked. "These look amazing!"

"Yeah, that's actually my first real order! After the frames are primed, I paint them black, and then gold. Then I sand off a bit of the gold so the black shows through, and it looks a bit antiquey. I made seven that this designer lady bought, and now she's ordered eighteen more!"

"Well shoot, I'm pretty sure I've got a box of old frames downstairs that I took down when we re-did our family pictures a couple of years ago. Can you use them?"

"Seriously? That's perfect timing! I was just trying to find enough on the Buy and Sell site without much luck. Thank you!!"

"Great! I'll bring them tomorrow."

A loud thump from above interrupted their conversation. "Sounds like my elephants! I'd better get going. Carrie, I'm so happy for you, and so amazed with all you're doing. You've really turned things around since leaving the asshole!" And with that, Kara jogged up the stairs to rescue Carrie's house from the twins. Carrie basked in the compliment for a second before following her. It was like every time someone told her she was doing the right thing, a little bit of the luggage from Don fell off her shoulders.

It's a good thing her oven timer was so loud, or she would have burned the biscuits. Carrie quickly pulled them out of the oven before saying goodbye to Kara and the boys. Then she heated up the can of stew and cut some carrot sticks for supper. Carrie loved sitting with her little family at the table. It was the best time to hear about Matthew's day (Katie always covered everything about her day on the walk home from preschool), and to just enjoy casual conversation with the kids.

Matthew had taken a while to start talking at the table. Don had always used dinnertime to criticize, so Matthew had wisely stayed quiet. Now, he was coming out of his shell, and Carrie felt like she was getting to know her son better just by listening to him.

It was Katie's turn to clean up supper, which meant Carrie did her best to stop the kitchen from flooding with Katie's enthusiastic dishwashing. At least she was learning how to wash dishes! Carrie had grown up with a dishwasher, but this kitchen didn't have room for one, even if she had money to buy it. So they all took turns washing the days' dishes.

Carrie checked her email once more before they walked Matthew to Boys' Club. There were no responses, so hopefully she would get that box of frames from Kara tomorrow. They brought the bottle bag along, and both Matthew and Katie spotted cans and bottles that Carrie would have missed. Carrie wondered if this was a good life skill the kids were learning, or a completely useless one. She hoped with all her heart that her own kids wouldn't have to collect cans and bottles to earn money when they were adults.

CHAPTER 17

On the walk to Jenny's the next morning, Carrie tried to practice ways to ask for financial advice without sounding silly, or like a freeloader. By the time she arrived, she still had no idea what to say.

She needn't have worried. Jenny was in her bed sleeping, so Carrie quietly closed the door and got to work. It was easy to fall into the routine she had started. Put a load of laundry on, take anything in the dryer out and bring it upstairs to fold it (Jenny's basement was nicer than hers, but it was still a basement and the less time spent down there the better!). Then she'd make her way through the kitchen, dining room, and living room, cleaning as she went.

It took a while to wake up Jenny. She looked like she had lost even more weight since last week. Carefully, Carrie helped her put on a clean set of pajamas. Max had bought her six new pairs of beautiful pajamas so that Jenny could have some nice things to wear. Carrie thought that was one of the sweetest things she ever heard of a man doing for his wife. "He learned it from his dad." Jenny explained. "The Halden men are a rare breed! I thank God every day for Max."

Carrie agreed, Jenny was a lucky lady and it made her feel good to know there were still good men out there.

It wasn't until Friday that Carrie had an opportunity to talk to Jenny about finances. Jenny was having a good day and was dressed and at the table when Carrie arrived. There were two cups of tea there, waiting. Carrie was delighted to sit and chat with her newest friend. She was always careful not to ask too much of Jenny because it was obvious that some days even talking was exhausting.

Jenny mentioned that she thought her office should have a dusting and a vacuum. Carrie had peeked her head into the office the first week she was there, but it looked pristine so she had closed the door and left it alone. The ladies went now to look together. It was a very professional looking office, with a stunning walnut desk covered by a glass protector, a flat screen monitor, and a gorgeous Robert Bateman painting behind the desk. It was one Carrie hadn't seen before, of an orange-breasted bird sitting amongst white blossoms.

Carrie had to get a closer look at the painting. It was beautiful. "Are you a fan of Robert Bateman?" Jenny asked.

"Love him! But I haven't seen this one before. It's so pretty and delicate, and yet you get the feeling that bird can handle anything."

"That's exactly the impression I want to make with my clients! The painting is called Baltimore Oriole and Plum Blossoms."

"Wait, your clients come here? How does that work?" The desk took up most of the small room, and the wall opposite the desk was floor to ceiling shelving. There was no room for chairs, or clients.

"I do all my work online. Most of my clients are people overseas, so I have web conferences with them. Well, I used to. Right now, I'd just fall asleep at my desk, so I've had to take leave from my work. I miss it terribly."

Carrie was amazed. Here was this obviously very successful lady, who could work from home and support her family. It was everything Carrie dreamed of! She said as much to Jenny, who had taken a seat in the desk chair. "It really has been great." Jenny agreed. "I love what I do, but I refused to go sit in an office building downtown and pay a ridiculous amount of rent, just so I could put a fancy address on my business cards. And that wouldn't have worked with my hours anyways."

"You must be really good at what you do, to have clients from all over the world!"

"I am! I was determined when I was a teenager to learn everything I could about money because my parents were so terrible with it. We were always having to move because they didn't keep up with rent payments, and I could never just go to the store and buy things, even though my dad had a good job. When I was getting my degree in finance, I helped my parents get their own finances in order. It was the most empowering thing I had ever done, and I was hooked. They bought their first house two years ago and are on-track to retire at 70."

"You're exactly what I need!" Carrie exclaimed. And then put her hand up. "That's not what I meant! I just mean that it's amazing that you can do that for people!"

Jenny gazed at her for a minute. "Could I really help you Carrie?"

"Oh Jenny, you've already helped me so much! Having this extra income and getting to know you and Angela and Max is wonderful! I couldn't ask for anything more!"

Jenny groaned. "You're killing me Carrie! I'm dying to do something useful here! Do you know how discouraging it is to lie in bed everyday doing nothing? It would be so fantastic if I could do something for you. Honestly, please tell me I can use my real skills for a change!"

Carrie couldn't tell if Jenny really wanted to help her, but she seemed sincere. Taking a breath, she smiled and nodded her head. "If you could give me some guidance, I'd appreciate it. Actually, I have a really hard time managing money. Could we exchange my housecleaning for your advice? I'm sure it's way less than what you charge your real clients, though."

"Carrie, you're way more than a housecleaner, and worth way more than one! Everything you've done for our family has made it possible for us to get through these last few weeks, and that's worth more than anything I can pay you. So let's call it even. But if it's not too weird, could we go to my bedroom so I can lie down, and you can tell me about your situation?"

"What, now? Oh, no. Let me get your office dusted and vacuumed, and go start a load of laundry, and then we'll see how you feel."

"Nope, I've got my heart set on it. I'm OK with you starting a load of laundry but that's it. Meeting in my bedroom in ten minutes!" Jenny smiled, but her tone of voice was firm and not to be messed with.

Carrie laughed. "All right, all right! I'll go start the laundry and then come up. But be prepared, my story is totally depressing!"

"Perfect!" Jenny exclaimed. "I love the depressing ones!"

Ten minutes later, Carrie was sitting on the bed facing Jenny, who was propped up by pillows. Jenny asked her to talk about money and what it meant to her. Carrie started with her parents, and how hard her dad worked to make sure her mom had the best care and therapy. She talked about Don, and never having enough money and how he always blamed her for their situation but discouraged her from doing anything about it. She even told Jenny exactly how much her monthly expenses were, how she was paying her bills, her little furniture business, and what a big difference working for Jenny had made. At this point, she was feeling completely comfortable with Jenny so she also told her about finding the $9,000.

Jenny didn't say much while she was talking, except to occasionally clarify things. When Carrie finished talking, she looked at Jenny and smiled. "That's the very first time I've told anybody all of that. You're really easy to talk to!"

"Well, I always find it fascinating to hear people's money stories, and yours is quite something. Can you tell me what your biggest fears are about money?"

"I'm afraid I'll screw it all up. That I'll make some stupid choices about what to do with the extra money, or that I'll stop sticking to my budget and start wasting money. I'm afraid of being worse off at the end of it all. Plus, I'm the only parent my kids have, and I'm afraid that if I ever got sick that we'd lose everything."

"Oh Carrie. I can tell you first off that you are definitely not going to screw this up! You've been disciplined, smart, and really creative about solving your money problems. Those are all qualities that people need in order to succeed financially and you've got them! My goal is to help you make a plan that keeps you on the right track and addresses those fears."

"You can do that? I'm sorry, I don't mean to sound like you're not very good, I just mean can you really help me, so I don't worry about all this stuff?"

"Definitely! And it'll be fun, too!"

"Wow! OK, I'm in!" Carrie was flooded with a feeling of relief. She would do everything Jenny told her and get her finances fixed.

"I noticed you didn't mention life insurance in your budget. Do you have any?"

"No. I've always wanted to, but Don said it was a waste of money."

"Well, for people that have sufficient resources it's not necessary. But when you don't have hundreds of thousands of dollars set aside for your children's future, it's an important step. Life insurance and a will are things most people don't want to think about, but once they're set up, you can pretty much forget about them. Do you have a will?"

"No, I don't have that either. I think now, especially, I need something. But I always thought getting a will was expensive."

"At your income level you can use legal aid to write a will for free. It will be quite basic for now, since your financial situation isn't complicated. Later, when you have investments and savings, you can update your will to reflect your circumstances. Could you bring me the laptop that's in the desk in my office? It'll be in the middle drawer."

Carrie brought her the laptop. It was light and sleek—the opposite of Carrie's old beast at home. After it started up, Jenny pulled up links to legal aid and some good life insurance companies and emailed them all to Carrie. Then she had Carrie take the laptop back to the office. "I'm too tempted to start working when I have it!"

Carrie thought it would be wonderful to have a job you loved so much you still wanted to do it when you were fighting cancer and said as much to Jenny. "I know how lucky I am to be able to do what I love." Jenny replied. "To be honest, I'd like to help more people like you though. For the clients I have now it's more about wealth management than survival. Which is fine, and I charge high fees for what I do, but I miss the challenge of making things work in tough circumstances." Carrie promised she'd bring her all the tough circumstances Jenny wanted. After agreeing to look into life insurance and getting a will, she went down to put the laundry in the dryer and get lunch ready for Jenny and Angela.

In the fridge there was some leftover takeout food from a nearby Thai restaurant. Carrie checked that Jenny felt up to eating it and then got it ready to heat up when she came back with the kids.

Walking to the preschool she said a silent prayer of thanks for meeting Jenny. With her guidance Carrie felt like she had the best chance to make something of her life, and make sure her kids were taken care of no matter what.

That night the kids and Carrie enjoyed having Mr. Morris over for supper. He seemed to enjoy his time too and the tour of their 'new' house with the things in it that he had been such a big part of getting back to Carrie. They all thanked him again before he left.

CHAPTER 18

On Saturday, Carrie sent out requests for life insurance quotes to the three companies Jenny recommended. In her email, Jenny suggested she look for $250,000 in coverage. Carrie would never have chosen such a high amount, but she figured Jenny knew what she was doing. She'd ask her more about it on Monday if she had a chance.

The most recent check from Jenny was now in her bank account, bringing her total after she paid her bills and rent to $455. Plus, she still had her cash savings in her Bible. She was also allowing herself a little bit of cash to spend on the kids, and happily joined the other families at the ice cream shop after Katie's soccer game. For her and Matthew, it was their first time there, and they were suitably overwhelmed with the choices. Katie, of course, had the unicorn sundae with rainbow ice cream, strawberry syrup, whipping cream, and rainbow sprinkles. Carrie and Matthew shared a hot fudge sundae after seeing the portion sizes the people in front of them were getting.

It was nice to be out with other families. One reason Carrie was determined to stay in their neighborhood was because it was full of working class families who were friendly and approachable. No one looked down on her for being a single mom. One of the other moms asked if she was interested in the 'hottie' new teacher at the kids' school, but Carrie gently but firmly shut down that line of talk. She knew not every guy out there was like Don, but there was no way she was willing to try to find out. Her life was just fine without a man in it.

After stopping to buy groceries (and reminding Katie a few times that not every trip to the grocery store involved her being able to choose her own treats) they headed home. Carrie hoped to spend a few hours working on the picture frames Kara had brought earlier in the week. There were five in the box perfect for her project, so now she only needed six more. One person from the Buy and Sell site had replied, and Carrie would pick up a few boxes of things later on in the day. If there weren't enough frames there, she'd have to go to the thrift store on Monday with Katie and Magnus.

The kids seemed to sense that she had more money available than before and asked to do more activities. Swimming was always on the list, as was skating. Carrie decided to keep an eye out for good used skates for her and the kids. Renting them was too expensive, but if she knew they could get a lot of use out of them, it might be worth it to buy some. There was a cheap matinee one Sunday a month at the theater, so she promised they would go tomorrow.

She also told the kids they could keep the money from recycling the bottles and cans. Trying to make sure they learned some budgeting, she sat down and they talked about a plan. Although Matthew was just learning about percentages in school, he was quick to pick up on the concept as they talked. They agreed to put 10% of the total into their bank accounts (which meant Carrie needed to open some accounts), 10% they would give to charity, and the rest they would divide between Matthew and Katie—but with Matthew getting more because he was older.

They were both so excited with the thought of having their own spending money that they begged Carrie to go on a walk to look for more cans and then go to the recycling center right away to return them. She figured it was worth it to let them follow the idea through, even though they'd be waiting a while at the depot since it was always busy on Saturday.

After filling another bag during their walk, they put everything in the trunk and headed to the recycling center. It was less busy than Carrie expected, and not long after they were back in the car with an extra $34 in cash. Carrie asked for it in small bills and change so it would be easier to divide up. Back home they set aside $3.40 each for their bank accounts and charity, and then $20 for Matthew and $7.20 for Katie. Both were desperate to go shopping right away, but Carrie insisted they wait and calm down for a few days before spending any money.

They were quite happy to play on their own for a while, giving Carrie time to continue working on the picture frames. She had the coat of black paint finished, and the frames were left on the kitchen table to dry overnight. After eating grilled cheese sandwiches in the living room for supper, Carrie bundled up the kids to go pick up the things from the Buy and Sell. The boxes had good frames that would work well for her project.

Later that night after Katie was in bed Carrie got out the newest frames and started taking them apart for cleaning. Some of them had staples and hooks that needed removing when she took the backing off. She was saving everything in case it came in handy for other projects. Matthew helped with cleaning them, and after he went to bed, she braved the basement so she could get them primed. She planned to have them ready early for Eleanor as a thank you for giving her this chance.

Carrie woke up feeling excited and ready to go. Now that she had the frames for the order, and they were all in progress she could count on selling them. She set her coffee on the counter and started painting the frames on the kitchen table with the gold paint. They'd have to eat breakfast in the living room—and probably lunch, too—but she was still happy. By the time Matthew and Katie were up the frames were all drying, and both kids were suitably impressed with the transformation. It was nice to have them see her as capable.

Carrie sometimes wondered what the impact was on the kids who heard their dad say so many cruel things to their mom. Perhaps only time would tell, but she hoped that those memories would fade, and they could be proud of their mom.

On their way to the movie that afternoon, Carrie stopped to pick up some gum and candy at the dollar store. She would buy a popcorn and soda for the kids to share and give them the candy after. The gum would help her not eat too much of the popcorn. It was crazy how expensive popcorn was, but it really wasn't a movie out without it. The kids tried to remember the last time they went to a movie, until Carrie admitted that this was Katie's first movie. Katie thought about this for a moment before reluctantly believing her. Hopefully they'd be able to go to another one before this memory faded too much!

It was a perfect family movie. Funny, a little sad, and then the happy ending that everyone wanted. Katie ended up on Carrie's lap for the last half, and Carrie reveled in the moment of being able to cuddle with her two kids and forget about all their troubles for a while.

When they got home, the frames were dry enough to move downstairs, and Carrie got started on making soup for supper. That was definitely a meal to eat at the table! She had picked up all the ingredients to make a proper beef and barley soup. There had been many soup days without meat, so this became another treat to add to their weekend.

While Matthew cleaned up supper later, Katie carefully helped her mom bring up the last frames that needed to be painted. She watched in awe as Carrie covered each frame with black paint. It was satisfying to sit back and watch all the different frames become a group together. Carrie let her help clean the paintbrushes afterwards, and Katie talked about getting a turn at the painting easel tomorrow at school. Normally she liked the more active choices, and Carrie wondered how long this newfound interest in art would last.

After the kids were in bed, Carrie sat down and looked at her budget again. She could at least count on being able to get Christmas presents for the kids this year. And she felt confident enough in her added earnings to pay for a life insurance policy. But it was still hard to figure out what to do next. Twenty minutes of staring at the screen didn't help any, so she shut it down and went to the basement to choose her next furniture project. At least that was a decision she could make easily.

She chose a cute little corner shelf that had seen better days. The 'charming country' look seemed to get buyers quickly, so she painted it with the same colors she used for the kid's table and chairs. It was hard to believe that only six weeks ago she had been digging through dumpsters trying to find a way to make an extra $20. Now she had a back yard and a basement with lots of future projects, a client who was coming back for more, and a friend who was paying her to help out.

Tomorrow she'd spend the morning at Jenny's, and in the afternoon the frames should be ready for final touches. After a quick check to make sure the coffee maker had water for her morning coffee, she headed to bed with her heart full.

CHAPTER 19

Matthew left for school excited to tell his friends about the money he got over the weekend. Carrie wasn't sure how impressed his friends might be, but it was nice to see him smiling as he left the house. There was just enough time to tidy up before taking Katie to school.

Kara didn't have her first patient until later in the morning so the two moms enjoyed a quick catch-up before the preschool opened and Carrie left to go to Jenny's. Kara reminded her that they still needed to have a girls' night out. Carrie wasn't sure how that would work with the kids but promised to try to figure something out. She wondered if Jenny might feel up to getting out.

Jenny greeted her at the door looking noticeably better. She even felt up to eating breakfast and getting dressed, and the tea was waiting at the table for the two of them. Carrie was enjoying this second chance in a day to have a bit of adult conversation, especially after being with the kids for the whole weekend.

Jenny's husband had convinced her to try eating out, and over the weekend the three of them had enjoyed their first meal out together in months. She admitted she wasn't much of a cook and eating out had been a regular part of their week. Carrie used the chance to bring up the idea of a ladies night out, and was pleased to see Jenny's eyes light up. "That would be fun! I might only last for one drink, but I'd like to try sometime soon. You could leave your kids here with Max when he's home, I highly recommend him for childcare!"

Surprised that her babysitting challenge could be fixed so easily, Carrie sent off a quick text to Kara that they should go ahead and plan a (short) night out, and Jenny would come too. Having settled that, Jenny asked her about her finances. They talked about life insurance, and what types of things to put in a will. Jenny emailed the link to the free wills service and Carrie agreed it was a priority.

She insisted on starting a load of laundry, and then offered to give Jenny time to rest, but she declined. "This is far more interesting than lying in bed! Although I'll need to rest again before Angela gets home. Do you have any thoughts on long-term plans? I know you said you started university…"

"My plan was to become a psychologist—a counseling psychologist. I've always loved helping people work out their problems. I even volunteered as a student counselor at university before I started dating Don, and it was fantastic. I left after third year though, and now there's no way I could finish my degree with having the kids. Just getting into the city takes almost an hour each way, and it's really important to me to be there when they get off school. Plus, I can't bear the thought of student loans again."

Jenny thought for a moment, "You'd make an amazing psychologist. You're so easy to talk to, and you have such great insight. What about online school? You can pretty much do everything from home. Probably even your masters!"

"To be honest with you, I never even thought of that. The idea of getting my degree is fantastic. But I'm sure it's way out of my budget."

"Carrie, didn't you just get a little windfall?"

Carrie did a gentle face palm. "Do you know how many times I forget about that? I'm just so used to not having any money, it still doesn't feel real. Is that a good thing to spend money on? Shouldn't I be saving that in an emergency fund or something?"

"Oh, having a few months expenses in savings is smart. But your monthly expenses are pretty low, and it won't even nearly use all that money. Plus, getting yourself set up for a higher paying career is one of the best ways to prepare for your future. Why don't you think about it and do some research about online university? It's always easier to make decisions when you have the facts."

"I really need to thank Kara for connecting me with you! Between the advice and the inspiration you are with your own business I feel like I hit the jackpot meeting you!"

"Well, I kinda feel the same way. I think we'll both be toasting Kara when we make it out for an evening!"

Carrie got up to clean up the kitchen and enjoyed having Jenny to chat with while she worked. In the back of her mind she kept replaying the idea of finishing her degree and getting her masters. She wasn't *that* old, and she could still watch Kara's boys and fix up furniture, so she wouldn't be losing any income. The job with Jenny would eventually slow down as Jenny was able to do more herself, but Carrie was sure they'd stay friends, and that was worth a lot.

When Jenny went to lie down, Carrie switched over the laundry and brought up a few more boxes to unpack. It felt good to get everything organized for Jenny. When she was ready to start working again, she'd have her entire house set up, and wouldn't have that extra chore hanging over her head.

Seeing that Jenny had fallen asleep, Carrie slipped out to get the kids. It was gray, and almost cold enough for snow but at the moment the rain was winning out, making it a messy walk. That didn't dampen Carrie's spirits at all. She could hardly wait to get home, finish her projects, and look for online programs.

SWEET, SMART, AND STRUGGLING

Later that night after the kids were in bed Carrie called her sister. "Hey little sister!"

"Is everything OK?"

"Why, do I only call you when there's a problem?"

Jessica snorted, "Kind of!"

"Well there's no problem! I just wanted to call my little sister for some big girl advice." Carrie proceeded to explain about her windfall, and that she might use it to finish her degree and then get her masters. While Jessica couldn't understand why Carrie wouldn't just get student loans, she was ecstatic for Carrie.

"This is so cool! You ditch the loser husband, find cash, and then go back and do what you were always meant to do. Seriously Carrie, you need to get this stuff done as soon as possible. I know a TON of people who need your help!"

"Aw, thanks! Actually, the lady I do housecleaning for runs her whole financial planning business from her house with video calls. Can you imagine if I could do that, and never have to be away from the kids? Oh gee, Jessica I am seriously going to need a new laptop and better internet!"

They chatted a bit more about everything sisters love to talk about. Jessica was mourning the total loss of her social life as she worked 12-14 hour days in the law firm but was hoping she would move up the ranks soon. Carrie knew that Jessica's smarts plus her ability to get anybody on her side would serve her well as she navigated office politics. They'd both be going home for Christmas, and Carrie was looking forward to some real face-to-face time with her sister.

So far Carrie had filled out an application for life insurance from one of the companies Jenny recommended, sent a request for an appointment to get her will done, and found out that finishing the last year of her degree online would cost about $4,300. If she could find a laptop for $1,000 or less, she would have $1,600 remaining after paying back her parents and paying for a full year's tuition.

Getting her masters was a different story. At about $19,000 for the two-year program she had no idea how she could save that in time to start. She may have to take some time off after getting her undergrad degree to save up before she could get her master's and then meet the qualifications for a counseling psychologist. But if she was careful, she could probably have her own business set up by the time Matthew went to university. It wouldn't be easy, but at least it wasn't impossible...

CHAPTER 20

Carrie wasn't scheduled to help Jenny until Thursday and she was keen to get the picture frames finished. After seeing Matthew off, and then walking Katie to school, she was hurrying to get home and make more progress. She just had time to wave to Kara, who looked late for work. Carrie figured she should try to enjoy these days when she made her own schedule. One day, she'd have to meet with her own clients!

At home she spread out the final five frames on the kitchen table and put a coat of gold paint on each of them. As they dried, she went downstairs to the other frames to sand off some of the gold paint, leaving just a hint of black showing through. She was pleased with the final product. It was kind of like her life. She needed some cleaning up, and there were dark times that would always be part of her history, but the gold paint made everything shine, and somehow the hints of black just added to the effect. Rolling her eyes at her own sentimental state of mind, she carefully cleaned off the frames that had their final sanding and brought them upstairs. They really did look amazing. She set them up in two groups to photograph them and would add photos of the last frames still drying when she finished them the next day.

Looking up, she was surprised to see it was almost time to get the kids. Quickly she wrapped the finished frames in tissue paper and laid them in her closet for safe keeping before heading off to pick up the kids.

Max arrived at the preschool at the same time as Carrie, and he confirmed that Jenny was definitely feeling better. Last Christmas they had been reeling over her diagnosis, so he was looking forward to really celebrating Christmas this year. After they collected their kids, they all said good bye, and headed home. Katie was extra enthusiastic about collecting cans and bottles now that she knew she'd get her own cash out of it. Magnus got caught up in her excitement and they detoured by a few streets to add more chances to find containers.

By the time they were home the bag was nearly full and Katie was dreaming about all the things she could buy. Carrie was heading into the kitchen to make lunch when she heard Katie ask Magnus how much it cost to buy a 'Mommy's bed'. It was bittersweet to think of her four year old trying to save money to buy a bed for her mom.

In the afternoon, the frames had dried enough to move downstairs and Carrie got the first coat of paint on the corner shelf while the kids watched a DVD. Magnus fell asleep and Katie brought her coloring over to where Carrie was painting. It was nice when she was calm enough to be near Carrie without demanding her attention. The shelf was already turning out beautifully and Carrie couldn't wait to finish and list it. Realizing the boys would be home soon, she tucked it as far out of the way as possible in the tiny living room and went to get snacks ready for everyone.

Matthew came home from Boys' Club that night with his woodworking project finished. It was a small shelf that he sanded by hand and put together by himself. He was so proud of it, and carefully set up his best LEGO on it.

The next morning after the kids were all in school Carrie sent off an email to Eleanor to let her know the frames were ready. Then she got to work finishing the shelf. A little bit of sanding on the edges gave it the charming country look that Carrie was hoping for, and then she added some decorative accents with glossy white paint. Personally, she went for bolder look in décor, but she was already figuring out what things got the most attention when she listed them.

Her next job would be a rocking chair that Kara's dad had brought. He gave her the cushions that went with it to keep inside, and she had been looking at them in the basement for a few weeks, wanting to get working on them. It would make for a crowded living room, since she didn't think she and Matthew could carry it to and from the basement without damaging it, but she was confident it would sell quickly once she finished it.

Kara finally responded to her text about the girl's night:

> *Yes! This Friday PLEASE, Momma needs a break! If Max is watching your kids, then we can meet there and take a taxi to the restaurant and back so we can really enjoy the night. So FUN!!*

Smiling to herself, Carrie replied that she would confirm with Jenny on Thursday unless Kara talked with her earlier. Again, she was surprised at how quickly the morning passed. It seemed like the better her days got, the faster they went. Sometimes she just wanted to pause everything and think about everything good that was happening. She hoped her brain would soak up these good feelings and fade out the bad memories of past years.

When she picked up the kids, Magnus was looking decidedly under the weather, so she insisted they go straight home instead of wandering the streets looking for drink containers. It was a good thing the kitchen table was clear, so she could heat up some soup for lunch. Both kids fell asleep on the couch after lunch, and Carrie was happy to let them sleep. It wasn't quite December yet, but already there was a feeling of busyness and she figured the kids could both use some extra sleep.

She used the quiet afternoon to list the little corner shelf for $50 and reply to Eleanor who wanted to pick up the frames that night. At least this time Carrie was prepared and had bought some black tissue paper with gold flecks in it to wrap up the frames. She had also grabbed two empty boxes at the grocery store on Saturday to carry them all in once Eleanor had a chance to check them over.

By the time the boys arrived from school, Magnus and Katie were both up and looking more energetic. Carrie was relieved she could still take all of them outside to burn off steam. It would be a much longer afternoon without that break from their small home.

Just before Eleanor came, Carrie went upstairs and got the framed fabric picture she had made with Katie. She still wondered if she could focus more on picture frames and wall hangings, and wanted Eleanor's opinion on it. When she arrived, Carrie gave her time to look at all the frames from her order first. She was pleased and showed Carrie and the kids a picture on her phone of the first set of frames installed in a client's home. They were all amazed at how elegant they looked.

After she paid Carrie the $360 they had agreed on, and all the frames were carefully packed, Carrie showed her the colorful framed scarf. Eleanor looked it over carefully before suggesting she use something other than duct tape on the back (Carrie had forgotten about that part) and create sets of two and three coordinating frames. When Carrie asked what price range she should aim for, Eleanor paused before answering. "To be honest, I'd like you to give me one price, and everyone else another price! I'd pay $25 each for something like this, but you could probably get upwards of $40 each if they were in pairs. People are always looking for interesting ways to add color to their walls and I think this might really be popular."

They agreed that Carrie would give Eleanor the first chance to purchase anything she made at the reduced price before listing anything on the Buy and Sell site. Eleanor also suggested she look into setting up a website or using an online shopping platform. Carrie wasn't sure she could do that, but she agreed to consider it. She had a lot to think about.

CHAPTER 21

The next morning Carrie got up earlier than usual. She tucked $40 from the picture frame sales into her emergency cash savings, bringing the total to $150. The other $250 in earnings would go into her bank account tomorrow giving her over half a month's expenses as a back-up. *That* made her feel much better about her situation. The rest of the money from the frames was for her night out with the girls and buying more supplies.

As she sipped her coffee Carrie realized that she was in the best financial position she had ever been in as an adult, and she was feeling more confident that she could continue to do better. She could even allow herself the luxury of planning to buy Christmas presents. It would be the first year when she wasn't accountable to Don for what she bought the kids and she would enjoy every minute!

When it was time to wake up the kids, they picked up on her happy outlook. Together they talked about ideas for Carrie to do more frames and she promised to let them help her look for frames and fabric at the thrift stores in the area on Saturday. Katie was finished with soccer until March now, so there was a full day free to do what they wanted.

After Matthew left for school Carrie got Katie ready, and had to laugh at her non-stop chatter all the way to preschool. If she had even half of Katie's energy, she'd have all the furniture in her basement and backyard refinished already! While waiting for the doors to open Kara confirmed that Jenny was in for a girls' night on Friday. They smiled over what a big deal they were making over a few hours out without the kids. Carrie couldn't even remember the last time she went out on her own, so she was long overdue.

At Jenny's, she quickly started a load of laundry before sitting down for tea and a chat. Jenny was just as excited about getting out of the house for an evening. There was a trendy fusion restaurant that just opened that she suggested they try. Getting out her phone she made reservations online. Carrie realized a new phone might make her life a lot easier. Maybe if her furniture sales continued to do well, she could get herself one as a Christmas gift.

It was fun to talk to Jenny about her new plans for the future. She was already approved for a life insurance policy and agreed that the $24 per month was well worth the peace of mind that her kids would be taken care of if anything happened to her. And if she was accepted into the online program to finish her degree, she could pay for the tuition in full without taking out a loan. The challenge would be paying for grad school.

Jenny was thoughtful, "How much extra can you make in a month, I mean on top of paying all your expenses?"

"Right now, with working for you and selling things it's about $700. I've been trying to put most of it aside, but there's been some things I felt I needed to buy, like good winter boots for the kids, and we've spent money on some activities too. It gets a bit hard to have fun with the kids without spending any money, but I don't want to blow it all and then have no future."

"Carrie, I think it's really important to enjoy the fact that you're making more money. There's no point in being miserable just so you can save every penny. When were you thinking of starting school?"

"I'd like to start next September..."

"OK, that's nine months away. If you put $500 per month in savings for grad school and increased your spending by $200 per month so you could enjoy life you'd still have $4,500 saved by the time you started in September. Which is fantastic! And if you cut back a bit but still worked the business enough to continue to put, say, $250 in savings every month then by the time you were ready for grad school the following year you'd have an additional $3,000. Put those two amounts together, and that's close to your first year's tuition paid for already!"

"No way! Do you really think I could do that?"

"Absolutely! Oh, and I think you qualify for interest relief on your current student loan if you go to school full time. That means you wouldn't need to make payments, and you wouldn't be charged interest during that time. So, you'd have a bit more room in your budget."

Carrie sat back in her chair. Part of her mind kept saying this way too good to be true. But she *was* putting money in savings every week, plus being able to take care of the kids. And it was fun! She looked at Jenny. "So this is what you do. You somehow make it possible for people like me to have a future?"

Jenny smiled. "No, I don't make it possible. I just help you see what you are already capable of. Carrie, people like you who have watched every single penny and are determined to make the most of every opportunity have a huge advantage. You have everything you need to create the future you want. And I'm cheering for you, not just because you're my friend, but because I think you'll make a lot of lives better as a psychologist!"

"I can't thank you enough for your support. Seriously, Jenny, I couldn't even think about what to do with that money, even though I kept dreaming about finishing school. I just didn't see it as a real possibility. It's like the longer I struggled to make ends meet every month, the more I felt paralyzed by the whole situation. I felt like nothing would ever change, and it's only when I started to make a little extra that I could even start to think about new possibilities. Speaking of possibilities, do you think I'd be able to counsel people online, like you do with your clients?"

"Absolutely! There are still people who want face to face sessions, but more and more I'm seeing that people want the convenience of an online session. It saves them time and money because they don't need to come in to an office, and it gives you access to a much wider client list. As you build up a reputation, you can go as far as you want with this!"

"Wow. This leaves me feeling all tingly! Now, tell me what you'd like to do today."

"You turned that around on me pretty quick. I knew you'd make a great counselor! I'd like to get the bedding changed out on our bed and Angela's bed, and see if you have any ideas for setting up that room in the basement where the boxes used to be as a guest room. Max's brother will be coming in two weeks to stay until after Christmas and I'd like to have a comfortable place for him. I've got some client emails to take care of while I'm feeling good. Are you OK to get started on everything?"

Carrie was happy to have something physical to do. She felt like she had to get some of this excited energy out of her body. It was a strange feeling to think of her future in such bright terms. For such a long time her days had focused entirely on survival to the point that she had stopped hoping for a better future. Now that she was back to dreaming and planning, everything felt a bit strange.

By the time she had both beds stripped, the laundry was ready to switch over. Carrie decided that the first thing she would do when she was working as a psychologist was to buy herself a washer that could run a load in 45 minutes like Jenny's could. *That* was a luxury she could get used to!

Looking at the now empty spare room, she could see its potential. A typical basement room, it had two high, narrow windows but they did let in some natural light. And the room was nicely finished and carpeted. Really, all it needed was some furniture. There wasn't a closet, but Carrie figured for a guest room it probably just needed a few hooks on the wall for hanging clothes, plus a dresser, bed, and night table. A little bit of art on the walls, and it would feel quite cozy.

The bathroom downstairs was a basic three-piece bath. Nothing like the luxury in Jenny's bathroom, but it was functional and just needed a quick clean. Jenny was still working in her office, so Carrie got fresh sheets on both beds, vacuumed, and cleaned the kitchen before getting the last load of laundry in the dryer. Popping in to let Jenny know she was off to get the kids, Jenny looked up from her computer in surprise. "How did the time go so fast? Alright, I'll see you back here in a bit."

Walking back with the kids, Carrie kept running the numbers through her head. $150 in cash savings, $705 in her bank account, $60 in her wallet, $8,900 in her closet. A phone call to the Legal Aid center first thing in the morning put her mind at ease about the extra money. It was hers, and Don couldn't claim any of it. But it would feel much better to have it safe in the bank instead of hidden in her room! She really needed to get that money into her bank account!

Jenny had lunch started for her and Angela when they came in, so Carrie was soon walking back home with Katie and Magnus. After lunch she walked over to the bank with the kids to make a big deposit. She'd keep the $2,000 cash aside that she would give her parents to pay back the money they lent her when she was still with Don. It felt good to know she could do that, and since she'd be there in a few weeks for Christmas, it would make a nice extra gift for them.

The older lady at the bank who served her remembered when she had brought the first old $100 bill in a few weeks ago. She asked Carrie if she would be keeping the funds in her account for a while, in case there was an opportunity to earn some interest on it. It felt good to tell her that it would stay in the account to pay for finishing her degree next year. They agreed to put the money into Carrie's savings account, which would earn more interest than her checking account.

It had been a while since Carrie had money to put in a savings account. The last time she managed to save $400, Don had taken it out one night without explanation. Now she had total control of her money, and she knew the only way it was going anywhere was with her say so. The teller gave her some information on some short-term investment plans that started at $5,000, and also advised her to apply for a low-limit credit card. That was another thing Carrie was hesitant to do, since she would be paying off the joint card she held with Don for a few years to come. But the teller was supportive and seemed to understand that Carrie was trying to improve her financial situation. With brochures about the credit card and investment options in hand, Carrie thanked her for her help and promised to pop in if she had any questions or wanted to take further actions.

The walk back home was also productive, with Katie and Magnus finding almost another bag full of cans and bottles. When they got home, the kids choose their favorite DVD and were soon draped over the couch relaxing. Carrie put the receipts and brochures from the bank into a small file she kept on a shelf in her kitchen.

She couldn't stand having papers lying around and had set a routine of going through the things in her folder once a week in the morning before the kids woke up. It started because of fear that she might forget something important that Don would get angry about, but now she did it because she liked to know she was in control of everything that came through her house. Plus, keeping track of paperwork was a lot nicer now that the bills were always paid on time, and there weren't nasty surprises showing up in the mail.

Carrie's secret cash savings had been just enough to get started on her own without owing any money, and she had been determined to not get behind on anything since. Fortunately, Don had been so concerned about controlling everything that he had insisted all the household bills were in his name only, so Carrie walked away from amounts owing on nearly everything from the old house when she left. There *was* still the credit card she was paying on, even though she had tried desperately to only pay for half of it. The credit card policy was rock solid on that, and she had been left with the choice of paying it herself, or having the full amount owing reflected on her credit report. At least they canceled the card so Don couldn't charge anything further on it, but it annoyed Carrie every month when the bill came with her and Don's name on it.

She toyed with the idea of using the cash she found to pay off the credit card, but she knew the money would go much further if she invested it in her future, and in being able to earn a good salary.

Pulling herself away from her thoughts, Carrie went back to the living room where the rocking chair was waiting for her attention. She wasn't sure what to do with it yet, but it needed a good cleaning before anything else could happen. Again, she found that making it shine (and smell nice) was a nice reward for all the elbow grease she was putting into it.

Just before the boys came home, she remembered to check her email, and saw that someone was interested in the corner shelf. She sent off a reply and then started to get snacks ready for the kids.

Later that night after their weekly visit to the library, she sat with Matthew and Katie and wrote down ideas for Christmas. Now that she had some extra cash, she wanted to make sure they had a chance to give gifts to their teachers and friends. In the past, she made little packages of Christmas baking for their teachers, and both kids wanted to do the same this year. Matthew wanted to give chocolates to a few friends at school, and Katie wanted to give a big present to everyone at her school. Carrie convinced her that a handmade card and a candy cane would be a more reasonable plan, and they would find something special for Magnus and Angela at the dollar store.

They had lots of ideas for their Grandparents and Auntie Jessica but couldn't decide on anything. There was still time, though, even for a gift that needed some extra effort. Carrie also wanted to do something special for Kara and Jenny.

Katie was excited about spending Friday evening at Angela's place while Carrie went out with the other moms. Matthew was much more reluctant. He was often nervous around other men, and worried that they might get mad at him. When she tucked him into bed Carrie reassured him that Max was a kind man, and that she'd do her best to 'screen' people before Matthew had to spend time with them.

Just as she was about to leave his room, he asked her if he could earn some money by helping her with the furniture. He was still excited about the money from returning bottles, but he wanted to save enough to buy a Nintendo Switch, and it would take too long if he only had one way of getting money. Carrie promised to think about it. She wondered if there *was* a way for him to help...

CHAPTER 22

Carrie looked at the meager pickings in her closet. She wanted to dress up for going out with the girls, but she really didn't have much to choose from. Her best jeans fit much better with all the walking she was doing, and it was dry enough outside that she could pair them with her only heels. But she wanted to wear color for a change. The white blouse she was wearing was nice, but plain. Her eye caught Katie's collection of scarves and necklaces.

"Hey Katie, can I borrow your clothes?"

Katie and Matthew came running up the stairs. "Mommy! You're too big for my clothes!"

"I know, but I'm not too big for a pretty scarf and a necklace or two, right?"

"Oooohh, yes, you could wear my purple and green scarf. Then you'll be beautiful!"

"Thanks honey!" Wrapping the scarf around she turned and looked at her kids. "What do you think?"

"It's nice," Matthew said slowly. "I've never seen you wear anything colorful. You always wear brown stuff."

"Well, I used to wear lots of colors when I was younger. Maybe that's where Katie gets her love of colorful clothes from! Alright, it's about time for us to get going. Are you guys ready?"

"YES!" Katie shouted. Matthew tried to give Carrie a half smile, but she could see he'd much rather stay home. He'd find out soon enough that Max wasn't someone to be afraid of.

They walked to Angela's house, where Kara would meet them so they could take a taxi to the restaurant. Carrie was almost as excited as Katie about going somewhere new and hoped that Matthew would end up having a good night too.

When they arrived, Max let them in. "Jenny's just getting ready. Come on in! Hi Katie!" Katie gave him a quick hug before running after Angela to the playroom. Reaching out his hand to Matthew he smiled "Hello Matthew, I'm Max. Thanks a lot for coming along, I'm tired of being outnumbered by all the girls around here!"

Matthew shook his hand, trying to be grown-up about the greeting. "I know what you mean. I'm the only guy at my house too."

"I think we'll get along just fine then. Do you want to join me at the kitchen table? I was just going to order pizza for supper. Maybe you have a favorite?"

"OK. Katie likes cheese pizza, but I like that kind with all the kinds of meat on it."

"A man after my own heart!" Max exclaimed, leading them into the kitchen. There was a laptop on the table, and beside it was a chess set. "Do you know how to play chess Matthew?"

"Kind of. I'd like to get better."

"Excellent. Let's order pizza, and then we can play chess until it's time to eat. I think the girls are probably buried in stuffed animals and tea parties already so we have time."

Jenny came down the hallway, wearing dark leggings and a yellow tunic. "Looks like we both broke out the bright colors tonight! You look great!"

"You too, but the credit goes to Katie for lending me a scarf!"

They said good-bye to the kids and walked out just as Kara showed up. Her curvy figure looked amazing in tight leather pants, a shimmering silver top, and gorgeous black boots. They all climbed into the waiting taxi and headed out for a much-needed break.

The restaurant was in an area of the city that Carrie had never been to. Stylish shops sat next to a cozy looking coffee shop and an independent bookstore. It felt like a brand new world, and it was a boost to be walking down the street with such beautiful ladies as her friends. Inside they took a minute to adjust their eyes to the candlelit restaurant with colorful mosaics on the floor, mismatched tables and chairs, and exotic smells that Carrie couldn't quite identify. It was a good thing Jenny made reservations because the place was full. They were directed to a round table tucked into the corner where they settled in.

Kara remarked that she was glad the music wasn't too loud because she was dying for a long night of girl talk, which led to a mutual agreement that they must all be getting old because they all felt the same way. They all ordered girly cocktails — another first for Carrie — and toasted the growing friendship between the three of them. In between tiny courses full of surprising flavors, they shared more of their stories.

While Carrie knew that Kara came from a close family, she had no idea one of her brothers was autistic and had given them a lot of challenges before they found a group home that he loved. Her parents had not been able to take a holiday away until last year when they made up for lost time by taking a month-long cruise through the Mediterranean.

Jenny was an only child, and Carrie already knew a bit about her childhood living at the edge of poverty and always struggling to get

CARMEN KLASSEN

ahead. She had gone to university on a full scholarship and was completely dedicated to helping her clients avoid the financial challenges she lived through.

Carrie brought Kara up to date on her plans to go back to school, and how Jenny was helping her manage her own resources so she could do it without student loans. Kara was immediately on board with it all. "We are seriously in need of a good psychologist at the clinic. Even when people qualify for subsidized counseling, it's hard to find someone good. You've only told me a little bit about your marriage, but I think the crap you've been through will make you an excellent person to help others."

"Well, if it means anything, every time someone tells me something nice, or thinks I'll be good at something it's like a little piece of me gets put back together. Maybe that's just really lame, but it's where I'm at. You both have done tons for me by believing in me *and* by hiring me! I feel so fortunate!"

"To girlfriends!" Jenny raised her glass, and they all toasted their friendship. "By the way Carrie, there's a guy over there that can't seem to keep his eyes off you. Are you interested? He's not too bad on the eyes!"

"What? Oh, good Lord no! I'm afraid I'm destined for life as a single lady. You two are married to the nicest guys, and I love seeing you together as couples, but I'm really not interested in giving the whole relationship thing a go again."

"You sound like Max's brother Jonathan."

"Is that the one who's coming to visit for Christmas?"

"Yeah. He was engaged to this girl about six years ago now, totally head over heels for her. Then he got a call that she was in a serious car accident. He rushed to the hospital, only to find out that she had been out with another guy and they had both been drinking. She died the next day, and he said it will never be worth trying to have another relationship. He's super successful and really nice, but he just focuses on work and traveling. The past five years he's been in Singapore so it'll be nice to have him around for a while."

"I can't imagine how painful that would be. Betrayal is a cruel weapon."

Their quiet mood was broken with the arrival of dessert. Each plate had five miniature desserts on it, and they agreed sugar was probably the best way to feel better! They all laughed when they ordered decaf coffees afterward. Nobody would lose a good night's sleep just because of caffeine.

They chatted about everything and anything, learning more about each other, and finding an easy settling in with each other as they discovered the things they had in common. Kara had gone back to school to become a physician's assistant when the twins started school and had to take a year off when Magnus was born before finishing just last year. She had complete confidence that Carrie could pull off school, childcare, and her growing business and still be an amazing mom to her kids.

Carrie talked about her ideas for working more with picture frames than furniture. They all thought it made sense to focus on something smaller that she could charge more for. Jenny offered to place a set on the wall behind her desk for her clients to see, but Carrie was adamant she was not to replace Robert Bateman on anyone's wall!

Jenny talked about how frustrating it was to have spent so much time lying in bed the last few months, especially since she missed her job so much. Kara guessed that her clients were missing her as much as she was missing them. They all agreed they were lucky to be doing something they loved, but Carrie reminded them they could take the credit for where they were. All of them were on paths of their own choosing, and she was enjoying just spending time with people who were so positive about their lives. Even Jenny was focusing on how nice it would be to start work again, and how lucky she was to have been rescued by Kara and Carrie. They agreed that women needed to look out for each whenever they could.

Finally, Jenny admitted that she was running out of steam and needed to head home. They split the bill, and Carrie was more than pleased to be able to open up her wallet and pay her portion without worrying about spending money. The taxi dropped off Kara first before going to Jenny's house. Jenny insisted on paying for the fare, including driving Carrie and the kids home. After a quick thank you to Max, she picked up the sleeping Katie and the sleepy Matthew and buckled them in. She woke up Katie just enough for her to appreciate her first taxi ride. Matthew was quite impressed with having someone drive him the few blocks home.

He wanted to tell Carrie all about the night, but when she went to chat with him after tucking in Katie, he was fast asleep. She reminded herself to listen for him getting up in the morning so they could have some time to talk before Katie woke up. Hearing the even sounds of her sleeping kids breathing deeply, she said a little thank you for finding such wonderful friends. She hadn't enjoyed friendships since before she met Don and hadn't realized how much she had missed it.

CHAPTER 23

Despite the late night, Carrie was up early. She was grateful for a little bit of time with her coffee before Matthew came down. When he did wake up, he had lots to say. He almost beat Max at chess before the pizza came, and then they all played Candyland together before the girls got too tired. Then he and Max watched a movie until Carrie got back. "He's really nice Mom, and he even got Katie to try a piece of meat lover's pizza without her fussing at all. And when the girls came in and asked him to do their hair for something they were playing he totally knew how to do their hair! It was weird. But kinda cool I guess."

Carrie had wondered about the two Pippi Longstocking type braids in Katie's hair. She would never have guessed that a dad knew how to do that or would even want to. It just showed that there were a lot of decent guys out there. Matthew didn't actually say it, but she knew he was comparing Max to Don, and she hoped he realized that not all guys were like his dad. That would be a really good thing for him to learn.

"Hey bud, remember how you asked me about earning more money?" He nodded. "Well, I think we could go on more walks, especially on the weekend when we have more time. Hold on, that's not all! I'm going to try to do more picture frames like the one I did for Katie and the ones that lady bought. And if I do, I'd like to hire you to help me with them. It's kind of picky work, but it would help me get more done. I'll pay you $2 for every frame you clean up for me, and that might include sanding any rough bits like you learned to do at Boys' Club. Then, if you get good at that, you might be able to do the priming for me too—that's the coat of paint I put on each frame before the color goes on. And you can earn another $2 for that. Does that sound OK?"

"Really Mom? But what if I wreck it or something?"

"I don't think you *can* wreck it, but if you make a mistake, it's always something that can be fixed. I wouldn't ask you if I didn't think you could do it. I've seen how careful you are with every project you work on, and I think you can really help me out. Plus, I have a big plan for the future, and selling frames is an important part of it."

She went ahead and told him about going back to university and eventually becoming a psychologist so she could help other people *and* earn more money. Without telling him about the money she found, she explained that she was saving almost all the extra money she was making so that she could pay for university. He was excited to be a part of her plan and thought it was a little funny that they'd both be going to school at the same time.

Katie came down in time to hear about something funny, and Carrie caught her up on their new plans. After making sure her mommy could still take her to school and pick her up when Carrie started university, Katie was happy to go cuddle up on the couch to watch the DVD she had chosen from the library.

Carrie checked her emails while the kids watched TV and replied to one asking about the corner shelf. She was still online when an email came back asking if they could come right away. Sending the kids up to get dressed before strangers came, she moved the shelf near the door ready to go. It was another project she was quite proud of, even though the pastel colors weren't really her style.

She wondered if Jenny would be interested in having some furniture refinished for their basement room. It would be nice to do something for her, and Carrie knew there was a dresser under the tarp in the backyard that would fit nicely in the room. She sent off a quick text before the doorbell rang. For the first time, the person tried to get Carrie to lower her price. Knowing the shelf was well-built and would last for years, she tried to stay firm until they raised their offer to $45. That was more than enough for her, and only $5 less than what she was asking. Now she was well set to visit some of the thrift stores in town and maybe pick up some more paint and brushes too. She had spent less the night before than she expected and she was itching to get the rocking chair looking beautiful.

After breakfast the three of them headed out for a morning of shopping. Carrie had to shake her head. A night out with the girls, a morning of shopping, and she hardly recognized her life! At the first thrift store they went to she found an assortment of frames. Many of them didn't have any backings and were down to 50 cents each. Definitely in her budget! She also picked a few larger ones that had backings she could use with fabric inserts, and then went to look at the fabric and sheets.

There wasn't anything that caught her eye until Katie walked over. "Mommy, there's the softest blanket by the toys, come see!" It wasn't a blanket, it was a flannel sheet set that was clearly high end. Carrie had never felt something so soft. The gentle plaid pattern had pink, blue, green, and yellow, and she knew it would be perfect for covering the cushion and backing on the rocking chair.

"Katie, you just found the perfect fabric for fixing the rocking chair! We're going to make it wonderful for some mommy or daddy to buy for rocking their baby!" Katie cheered, and was clearly proud of being able to help. Before they left, Carrie took a quick look through the kids' clothes and found a bright red Christmas dress for Katie absolutely full of sparkles and ruffles. Last year Katie had worn her toddler Christmas dress as a top with leggings, so it was extra special to be able to get a proper one for her this year. Carrie's family always dressed up for church and dinner on Christmas Eve and she was hoping to have something nice for all of them to wear. She looked in the boys' and ladies' sections, but there was nothing else. Their grand total came to $14.

At the next thrift store, Carrie found more frames and some bright scarves that would be perfect for framing. Matthew found a dress shirt and tie all on his own, and assured Carrie that Max or Grandpa could teach him how to tie it properly. The shirt was blue with white pinstripes, and the tie was bright yellow with Christmas lights embroidered across it. Carrie loved the look and Matthew's bold choice. Again she looked through the ladies clothes, but nothing stood out. At least her kids were set! Matthew could get away with wearing jeans with his dress shirt, and she'd keep an eye out for dress shoes for both of them.

There was a hardware store right next to the thrift shop, so they put their purchases in the car and went to look at paints. Carrie knew that sometimes there were mis-tints that sold for a reduced rate. It took a while to find them, but finally Matthew noticed them in a corner on the floor. They found a light blue that would be perfect for the rocking chair, and a small can of bright orange that had Carrie eager to do some fun, colorful picture frames. After the second thrift store and the hardware store Carrie had only spent $36, so she surprised the kids by suggesting they eat lunch out.

There was a café known for gourmet hot dogs in the next block, so they walked there and all had hot dogs for lunch. Carrie let Matthew and Katie split a soda but stuck to water for herself. She had enjoyed her own overpriced drinks the night before. Happy and feeling quite spoiled, they made one more stop to get groceries before going home. Katie was getting whiny, and Carrie figured that Friday's late night was catching up to her. She set her up in her bed with some new library books before putting away the groceries.

Matthew was excited to get started on the picture frames. Carrie chose two larger frames that were similar for him to clean and sand. She had grabbed some fine sandpaper at the hardware store, and he diligently got to work on the frames. Carrie did her best to make

SWEET, SMART, AND STRUGGLING

space in the living room to start priming the rocking chair. She planned on using all her spare time to get it done quickly, since it was just too big to work around for very long. Matthew found a footstool downstairs that almost matched, and she was pleased it would make the perfect setup for a new parent.

Katie came down a little while later, content to color while Carrie painted and Matthew worked on the frames in the kitchen. They had the radio on playing classical music. The following week she'd be sure to pick out some Christmas CDs from the library, so they weren't stuck only listening to the few radio stations that were available. By the time they were getting hungry, the primer was drying on the chair, and Matthew was carefully wiping down the newly sanded frames. Supper was eaten with all three of them cuddled on the couch and watching a DVD. It was another perfect little family moment, and Carrie tried to capture it in her memory. She was thinking more and more about getting a better cell phone that could take decent pictures as well. Right now would have been an ideal selfie moment if she could have taken one.

After Katie was in bed, Matthew asked Carrie if she could show him how to prime the picture frames. She was tired, and ready to call it a day, but decided that the more work they did the more she could sell, so it was worth it. They covered the kitchen table with the old shower curtain, and she poured some primer into an empty yogurt container for Matthew to use. Together they painted the frames side by side. Carrie already liked the look, with the frames having slightly different shapes but the same finish.

With Matthew's help, she could definitely increase the number of listings. She made him carefully wash the brush and clean up the supplies, and then they started a running tally of the money he was earning that they would keep at the front of the file she kept in the kitchen. He would only get paid when she sold a frame, but already he had earned $6, and he was keen to keep adding to his earnings. Maybe he would keep her motivated when she ran out of steam!

They went to bed at the same time, and Carrie figured they must have both fallen asleep right away. The next day was spent working on her projects and taking a long walk with the kids to look for cans and bottles. They came back with two grocery bags nearly full, and Katie quite worn out. Carrie let them spend the evening watching DVDs while she put the first coat of paint on the rocking chair and stool. The soft blue color was almost the exact same as the blue in the fabric she'd use to cover the cushions, and it was fun just watching the transformation as the paint went on.

After that she remembered she hadn't turned on her phone all day. There was a text from Jenny saying she'd love it if Carrie could fix up some furniture for the guest room, and could she come Tues-Thurs in the mornings? Carrie replied that she'd get the furniture done before Jonathan came, and she'd see Jenny on Tues. While she had her computer on, she checked her budgeting spreadsheet. With the pay from Jenny that she deposited on Friday, she was now up to $855 in her bank account, and $6,900 in her savings account! Now, she needed to figure out what to set aside for Christmas. And she needed to send off her application to the online university for completing her degree. There was lots happening all at once and Carrie couldn't be happier.

CHAPTER 24

Monday morning Carrie was up early to get a second coat of paint on the rocking chair and footstool. She woke up with the realization that it would need to be a few weeks of intense work to get the furniture done for Jenny's guest room and finish and sell enough picture frames before spending a week at her parent's for Christmas.

She had the chair nearly finished when it was time to wake up the kids, so she covered the paint and brush with plastic wrap so they wouldn't dry out and got started on her day. Matthew wondered if he should start getting up early to work on frames, but she declined. At least he was keen! Once he was off to school, she finished the chair before it was time to get Katie to preschool. They only found a few bottles along the way, and soon Katie was chattering away to Magnus and Angela. Kara left Magnus under Carrie's watchful eye and dashed off to the clinic where she had patients scheduled.

Max mentioned how nice it was to spend time with Matthew on Friday. He was hoping to add to the family one day, and Matthew had just proved that he needed a boy in the family! Without spilling her nasty past Carrie told him how impressed Matthew was with

Max's parenting skills, and she got the impression he could read between the lines that this was a new revelation to Matthew. "It would be nice to spend time with Matthew again. I have some time off over the holidays, so we'll have to plan something. Does he like watching football?"

"Actually Max, I have no idea! The poor boy's been stuck with a mom and a sister when it comes to entertainment so there's been no football or anything else like that!"

"Sounds like he needs rescuing! I'll see what's up during the holidays and text you some possible days." The preschool doors opened, and the kids all filed in after their goodbyes to moms and dads. Carrie said thank you again to Max for the offer over the holidays and quickly walked home. She was looking forward to two uninterrupted hours of work.

While the second coat of paint was still drying, she carefully used the cushions as a guide for cutting out covers from the beautiful flannel sheets Katie had discovered at the thrift store. She'd love to be able to put sheets like these on her own kids' beds one day. By the time she needed to head back out to pick up the kids the covers were sewn and on the cushions, and she just needed to hand stitch them closed.

Tomorrow she'd be ready to list the chair and stool, and as soon as it was out the door, she could bring in the dresser to start working on it. She realized she still needed to start getting some use out of the basement so she could have more than one project going at a time. The bedside table and shelf she had in mind for Jenny's guest room could be done downstairs while the dresser took up space in the living room.

After lunch, Carrie settled herself on the couch with the kids so she could finish hand stitching the closure on the cushions while they watched a movie. Her mind wandered while she was sewing, suddenly settling on the fact that it was Monday and she had totally forgotten to start the laundry. Deciding to leave the bedding for a week if she wanted the clothes dry before tomorrow, she quickly went upstairs to gather all the dirty clothes. They would literally have no underwear if she didn't get through the laundry. New underwear for the whole family! *That* would be the perfect Christmas gift for her!

Once the washer was running, she set the oven timer to remind her to switch the load over and settled back on the couch with her sewing. It was already feeling like a lot to keep up with everything. But she didn't want to be struggling for forever, so she had to do this. At least she could look forward to a relaxing week at her parents over Christmas.

When the older boys got home, Carrie had finished the cushions and was pleased to take a break, even if the break meant dealing with rowdy boys. They brought a football and Carrie played pass with the three boys while keeping an eye on Magnus and Katie. For a kid who was usually quiet, Matthew had a pretty good arm and kept up with the older boys no problem. But when Justin and Calvin turned it into a tackling version she and Matthew stepped back.

Hanging out on the swings with him helped to clear her head, and by the time they turned to go back home she was feeling refreshed and ready to do more work. The rocking chair was dry, so she set up the cushions and took some pictures while there was still natural light coming in the front window. Katie brought down her teddy bear to sit in the chair, and the result was adorable.

When Kara arrived, Carrie was proud to show off her newest project. One of the doctors in the clinic was expecting his first child, and Kara took some pictures of the chair and footstool to show him in the morning. Carrie was hoping to get $200 for it, but Kara suggested she try for $250. "It's one of a kind Carrie, and the colors are perfect for a boy or girl. And you can always go down a little in price if you have to… All right boys, let's leave this cute little family alone and get our crazy butts home!"

Carrie loved watching Kara with her boys. They were absolute terrors sometimes, but Kara never seemed phased by them, and she always managed to reign them in when they got carried away.

Maybe that came with growing up with brothers. After they left, Carrie listed the rocking chair online for $250 and then started supper. She figured it wouldn't hurt to list it even if Kara's doctor friend chose to buy it.

While Katie cleaned up supper and Carrie supervised, Matthew brought up the empty frames they bought on Saturday. These were smaller, and he was able to get five sanded and cleaned before Katie's bedtime. Carrie realized she should have set a different payment for the smaller frames but didn't want to change it now. He was so excited about the chance to earn money!

She got the last load out of the dryer and folded it in her bedroom while Katie got ready for bed. It was still a treat to tuck her daughter into a real bed, and not a mattress on the floor. She often mentally thanked Mr. Morris for that.

Back downstairs, she took out the sheet with Matthew's earnings and added $10 for cleaning the frames. Then she got out the two frames they primed the night before and set them out on the protected table while Matthew shook the can of orange paint for her. The paint was a high gloss and really made the frames stand out. Carrie couldn't wait to see the finished product with the scarves framed inside. She'd get up early again the next morning to put a second coat on that could dry while she was at Jenny's.

She tucked Matthew in and was grateful to head to her bed right after. Hopefully, she'd get used to this new busier pace and not feel quite so exhausted at the end of the day.

CHAPTER 25

Matthew and Katie woke up to the smell of fresh paint for the second morning in a row. The frames were too wet to move, so they all ate their oatmeal at the couch. It was fine for today, but Carrie didn't want to spend too many breakfasts eating in the living room.

Just before Matthew left for school, he remembered a notice about the class Christmas party and a permission slip for skating that started next week. Carrie breathed a sigh of gratitude that she could afford to buy a tray of baking for the party (no home baked goods allowed!) and pay the $25 for him to get skating lessons twice a week during December. At least equipment rental was included in the price.

There was just time to check emails before walking Katie to school. The online university had replied with a list of documents she needed for her application, and the free wills service confirmed her telephone appointment tomorrow at 1 pm. Things were moving along and Carrie needed to keep up!

By the time she got to Jenny's, Carrie was looking forward to a cup of tea. She hollered a hello up the stairs and then went down to start the laundry. A quick peek in the guest room confirmed that the furniture she had in mind would fit nicely. She would ask Jenny how she felt about everything being a glossy black. That would work well against the gray walls and could be used other places in the house if they wanted a change.

Jenny was looking fantastic. She said that getting out on Friday night made her feel like her old self, and she hoped she could get back to her usual work schedule soon. Her treatments had finished, but she still needed to go in every week for check-ups for a month. If her test results were good, she planned on starting work in January part-time. She was also hoping to be up to getting Angela from school but asked if Carrie could still come every Tuesday and Thursday in the new year to help her keep on top of the housework. Carrie was relieved to still have some regular income to rely on. She suggested they lower her rate if Jenny was going to pick up Angela, but Jenny wanted to wait and see how things went first.

They had a quick catch-up over tea, and then Jenny went to her office for the morning while Carrie took care of laundry and cleaning. By the time she left to get the kids the last load from the weekend laundry was in the dryer, and the kitchen and guest room bathroom were clean.

The kids spent the time walking to Angela's talking about all the things Santa might bring them. It was nice to listen to all their ideas, which gave Carrie a look into each of the kids' very different personalities. Katie was convinced Santa could make a pony farm in their backyard, Angela wondered if her Uncle Jonnie would ride with Santa because he was so far away, and Magnus said he hoped Santa would bring a baby sister because there were too many boys in the house. Carrie couldn't wait to tell Kara about that one!

On the way back home with Magnus and Katie, Carrie's phone buzzed with a text notification. Seeing that it was Kara, she opened the message. The doctor absolutely loved the rocking chair and wanted to come over that night after work to pick it up! She replied that they'd be home until 6:45 when she needed to take Matthew to Boys' Club. It would be nice to see the chair go to a happy couple.

The frames seemed dry, but Carrie didn't want to risk damaging them, so she took them downstairs before making lunch. They ate leftover spaghetti and sauce from the night before, and then Katie and Magnus asked for a Christmas movie. Carrie thought she had a few in the bin of Christmas things she had rescued from the old house and was happy to find three DVDs. She brought them up from the basement and settled the kids in before making a cup of coffee and starting up her laptop.

There was another email from the online university, asking if she could phone them, or leave her number for a call back. She had sent in her transcript only a few days ago and hoped everything was OK. When she called, the man on the other end identified himself as a career counselor. He confirmed their receipt of her transcript and her desired degree in Psychology. They had an opportunity for her to finish her degree in one semester if she could take four classes.

Carrie was delighted. With one less semester required, she'd pay less tuition and be that much closer to her goal. Then he dropped a bombshell. Was she interested in starting in January? "Hello? Ma'am?"

"I'm sorry, that's just quite unexpected. I need to think about it. How soon do you need an answer?"

"By the fifteenth of this month, please. Do you have any questions I can answer?"

"No, not at the moment. Well, how do I let you know whether I'd like to go ahead in January? And how much is tuition for the semester?"

"You can call me at this number. I work business hours Monday to Friday, and if you call after hours there's a call center that can take your call. As far as tuition, you've already paid the application fee, so the remaining balance for tuition and books is $2,200. That would need to be paid in full before the start date of January 7."

"Alright. I'll take a look at my situation and call you back before the fifteenth."

"You have a nice day then ma'am. Bye bye."

Carrie whispered a goodbye and hung up. Her mind was spinning. If she finished her degree next spring, she could start grad school in the fall. *If* she had the money. That was almost too good to be true... But there was no way she could be ready to start school next month! She needed to buy a new laptop and upgrade her internet... And she wouldn't have nearly enough time to work on furniture refinishing... But she could start her counseling business a whole year earlier than she planned... How much was that worth?

She finished her coffee and went into the living room. Cuddling up beside Katie to watch the end of the movie she kept on repeating the same questions in her head. Could she do it? Should she do it?

For the rest of the day, she felt like she was only half present. Even when the couple came to pick up the rocking chair and were so delighted with it, she struggled to focus on what they were saying. The $250 was given happily, and she at least had the presence of mind to put it in her wallet before helping them load the chair and footstool into their waiting SUV. Wishing them well with their new family she went back in to get ready to take Matthew to Boys' Club.

Back at home, she figured the only thing she could do was stop thinking about it. So, she went into the back yard to check the dresser she wanted to refinish for Jenny. It was a nice size for a guest room—just three drawers—and seemed well built. She took out the drawers first and carried them in, and then lugged the dresser inside. It had stayed dry and fairly clean under the tarp, but she gave the whole thing a gentle sanding before priming it. She wanted it to turn out perfect for the woman who had helped turn her life around.

Katie wanted to help too, so Carrie brought up one of the picture frames and gave her some sandpaper. She soon lost interest and brought her stuffed animals down instead. Carrie only got the drawers sanded before needing to vacuum up the mess and head out to pick up Matthew. He came home with a flyer detailing the different activities the church was offering for December. It would be nice to go out more as a little family. She put the schedule up on the fridge and got Katie ready for bed. Then, while Matthew did some homework, she sanded the rest of the dresser and vacuumed one more time.

After Matthew was in bed, Carrie enjoyed the mindless routine of priming the dresser. Slowly the horrid brown turned into a nice even gray. One of the books she got from the library suggested a gray primer for painting dark colors, so she picked up a can that she saw on sale. It would be nice to add some unique drawer pulls too. Maybe she'd find something at the thrift store... Leaving the newly primed dresser to dry she went up to bed, but her brain started spinning again about the future and it was a long time before she fell asleep.

The next few days Carrie kept busy but wasn't able to escape all the worries and thoughts spinning around in her brain. Start school now? Or wait until next September? The dresser was finished and looked sleek and glossy. She was just looking for something interesting to use as drawer pulls. When she was walking Katie and Magnus home on Thursday, with the check from Jenny for the three days' work in her wallet, she still felt like she didn't know what to do. Suddenly Katie darted into the bushes and came out with a handful of sticks. "Look Mommy! Aren't these beautiful?"

Carrie dutifully stopped to examine Katie's latest discovery. She had to admit, the sticks *were* interesting. And unique. "They *are* beautiful Katie! Can you see any more?" With Magnus' help, they found eight short sticks. When they got home, Carrie asked if the sticks could have a special job on a dresser for Angela's mom. Katie needed a bit of convincing until Carrie offered her $4 for the sticks. Now happy, she ran upstairs with Magnus to play until lunchtime. When lunch was over, Carrie joined the kids in the living room with her hot glue gun, and glued the new rustic drawer pulls right onto the old, plain handles. It was the perfect finish next to the glossy black, and she texted Jenny to say the dresser was ready. Max offered to pick it up since Carrie couldn't fit it into her car.

Sitting there looking at the finished product, Carrie finally felt like she had a plan. If she could figure out how to turn a free dresser into a cool new piece of furniture for a stylish couple, then she could figure out how to get her degree while still taking care of her kids and making money for grad school. She was resourceful, she knew how to buckle down and get things done, and she was proving to herself every week that she *was* good with money. Now it was the right time to take a big step towards something she really wanted — her degree.

She went into the kitchen and called her career counselor with the news. Not having a credit card was a problem, but she could send a bank draft as long as they received it before her start date. He would send the final paperwork in the mail since she didn't have a printer (yet), and she would send it along with the bank draft.

Suddenly it was almost time for the boys to arrive from school. Quickly she put away her computer and got a snack out for all the kids. She might be a university student now, but kids still needed to eat! Now that she had made her decision, she was feeling excited and ready to share with everyone. She sent a quick text to Kara and Jenny:

> *Do you have time for a glass of wine at my house tomorrow evening? I have something fun to talk about!*

Tonight, she'd talk to the kids and call her family. And get working on the rest of the furniture for Jenny's guest room! It occurred to her that this should be her last furniture project. There just wouldn't be time for big projects since she'd need to have space for studying. She was really looking forward to her courses. Her career counselor emailed her the list of courses she could choose from for her final semester as an undergrad student, and she wished she could take all of them.

When Kara arrived to pick up her boys, she tried to get Carrie to give her a clue about what she wanted to talk about, but Carrie wouldn't give. She wanted to tell both her friends at the same time.

Just before supper, Max came to pick up the dresser. He was more than impressed with the finished product, and Carrie and Matthew helped him carry the drawers and dresser to his vehicle. She promised the rest of the furniture would be ready as soon as possible.

While they ate supper, Carrie told them that she had an opportunity to start university early and be able to graduate with her first degree in May. They were both excited for her, while not totally realizing what it involved. That was fine. She would try to minimize the impact on them. Matthew cleaned up and took a minute to look at the flyer from Boys' Club on the fridge.

"Can we go to their Christmas play Mom? It's on Sunday night and it says it's for families."

"Sure, that would be fun! I'm going to work on some more furniture tonight. Would you like to help?"

"No, I want to finish my homework after we go to the library."

Sometimes Matthew seemed a bit too serious. Carrie needed to talk to Kara about some suggestions for helping him lighten up. Even though it was nice that he didn't need reminding to do his school work. When they got back from the library (with Christmas CDs and DVDs) she called her parents and sister and told them her big plans after the kids had each talked. It was nice to have such a supportive family who believed in her and she couldn't wait for a week of resting at her parent's place over Christmas before starting school in January.

Late that night, Carrie put a coat of primer on both the nightstand and the small shelf she brought up from the basement. At least she could work upstairs since Max had picked up the dresser. Playing off the idea of the wood pulls that Katie found, she wondered if she could find some interesting pieces of wood that could be turned into hooks for the guest bedroom. Without a closet they needed something for guests to hang a few things up. She'd put Katie and Magnus on the hunt tomorrow while they were looking for drink containers.

As she started to fall asleep later, she remembered she still had the $250 from the rocking chair and the $150 from Jenny in her wallet. She'd stop at the bank after dropping off Katie at school. It had shaped up to be a fantastic week, and it wasn't over yet!

CHAPTER 26

Friday Carrie hurried through her day. Although her plan had been to get up early enough to get the first coat of black paint on both the shelf and the night table before the kids woke up, it all took longer than she expected. By the time the kids were up, just the shelf was done. Taking a break to sit with them at breakfast, they all ate their oatmeal together and talked about the weekend. She promised they could go swimming on Saturday after checking the thrift stores for frames and fabric, and the hardware store for interesting mis-tints. Matthew told Katie about the Christmas play they would see on Sunday night, and Katie thought they should tell Magnus and Angela's families too. "If they go, I'm sitting beside Max, not Justin and Calvin!" Matthew stated.

With that thought, Matthew went to get his things ready and leave for school. He had made a poster on the solar system for his project, and Carrie was glad the weather was decent so it wasn't at risk of being wrecked on the short walk to school. After saying goodbye to him, she quickly cleaned the bathroom before getting Katie ready for school. Other than Mr. Morris, tonight would be the first time she had people over to her house for a visit. She couldn't do anything about the shabby look to her place, but at least she could have it clean!

Stopping at the bank after dropping off Katie, Carrie deposited $300. She was keeping the other $100 for supplies, swimming, and Christmas gifts. It gave her a thrill to see her bank balance at over $1,000, even after all her expenses for December were paid. This would be her buffer, and she would try to always have at least this amount in her account. From now on, any extra money would go to her savings account for grad school.

The same teller helped her again. Carrie told her about finishing her undergrad degree while the lady printed up the bank draft to pay for her tuition. Again, Carrie heard that there was a big need for good counselors, and she encouraged Carrie in her career plans. If all the people she talked to really knew of future clients, Carrie would have a full workload from day one!

When she got home, Carrie updated the numbers on her spreadsheet before getting started on painting the night table: $1,155 bank account, $4,700 savings, $150 emergency cash. Then she put on some Christmas music while she worked on her projects. The black paint went on beautifully, and Carrie was glad Katie and Magnus found enough sticks that she could use one for the drawer pull on the night table too.

While waiting with the other parents at the preschool later, Max asked her if he could take Matthew to the football game next Saturday. It was a charity game, with the ticket sales going to the winning team's chosen charity, so the game would be lots of fun. Carrie thought it was the perfect thing to help Matthew lighten up, and she thanked Max for including him. He was happy to have someone to go with.

"My dad and brother and I used to go to every game. Jenny has tolerated games with me a few times, but it's a lot more fun to go with some guys. I think we'll have fun!"

When the kids came out, they all said goodbye to Max and Angela and made their way home. Carrie tasked the two children with finding L-shaped sticks that could be used as hooks on the wall. Magnus immediately caught on to the idea, looking for just the right sticks, and Katie grabbed just about every stick she could see, holding them up for Carrie's inspection before they were discarded. By the time they arrived home (with a detour through a wooded walking path nearby), they had five good options and a bag half full of cans for recycling.

Carrie still needed to get groceries and a bottle of wine for the evening, so she made peanut butter sandwiches for lunch, and then bundled the kids into the car. It was her first time taking two four year olds to the store and took way longer than she expected. She splurged on chips and cookies for an after school snack for the kids, as well as some cheese and fruit for later on when Kara and Jenny came over. Katie decided they should have meat lovers pizza for their own supper after trying it at Angela's the week before, and Carrie was more than happy for a change from their usual cheese pizza.

They got back in time for Carrie to move the furniture she was working on further into the corner of her living room before the boys came in. All three of them were rambunctious, and she could barely wait for them to eat so she could get them outside. While the other kids played, Matthew walked around the edges of the park with the bottle bag, looking for more containers. He was more determined than ever to get a Nintendo Switch. Carrie figured they should at least look at them in a store over the weekend since she had no idea what one might cost. By the time they were ready to head back home the bag was so full he had to step on the cans to make them fit. Justin and Calvin were intrigued with the idea of buying something all on their own and spent most of the walk home making huge plans for the money they could make.

When Kara and Jenny showed up that evening, Carrie had cheese and fruit ready along with the wine. Jenny came with a bouquet of flowers for her. "I don't know what you have to say, but I figured some flowers were in order!"

Carrie thanked her, and then had to admit she didn't own a vase to put them in! The flowers went into a plastic juice jug for now, and she said she'd buy a vase tomorrow at the thrift store. She also hadn't realized until just before they came that she didn't have wine glasses anymore. They were left at the old house when she moved.

Matthew and Katie were settled in the living room with a Christmas movie and chips, and the ladies sat in the kitchen and drank out of Carrie's 'stemless wine glasses' which were her only non-plastic water glasses.

"OK Carrie, no small talk until you tell us why you called this meeting!" Kara loved to know everything about the people in her life and wasn't about to wait another minute to hear from her.

"A few days ago, I got a call from a career counselor at the online university I applied to. With all the courses I have already, I only need one more semester to finish my degree. And…I start January 7!"

"Oh Carrie, that's amazing! And way to save a whole semester's tuition without even trying!"

"I knew you'd tune in to that Jenny! It makes a big difference to cut out that semester, for the cost, and also because now I can start grad school in the fall."

"That's so fantastic! I can't say I envy you, because I am SO glad to be done with school, but I am so so very happy for you! Oh, and I know you're not counseling anybody yet, but I met a lady at the clinic today and gave her your number. She's about our age, single, and her mom is now living with her after her dad's sudden death. Her mom has rheumatoid arthritis and I think she's struggling to cope with the new demands of caring for her. I thought with what you've been through with your mom you'd be a good support to her."

"Yeah, I'm happy to talk to her. I know how challenging it is to be the one caring for a parent. Poor girl!"

The conversation shifted to their parents, and how things can change without warning. Jenny shared that Max's parents had died in a car accident last fall, and Christmas would be hard again for Max and Jonathan. Jenny's parents lived too far away to come at Christmas when flights were so much more expensive, so it was extra special that Jonathan was coming all the way back for a few weeks.

When Katie started to bug her brother, Carrie brought her in for a snack and a little visit before bedtime. Katie sat on Kara's lap to have some of the cheese and fruit that was still left, and solemnly told them that she'd have to take care of the house when her mommy started school soon. Carrie promised her she would still have time for lots of her mommy jobs like taking care of the house, but she'd take all the help from Katie that she could. After letting her say goodnight, she took Katie upstairs for bed.

Sitting on her bed ready to be tucked in, Katie had one more thing to say, "Mommy, I can't get Magnus and Angela a present anymore. Teacher said the best gifts come from the heart, not from the store. But I don't know what my heart can give them!"

"Well... spending time together is a gift from the heart. What if we have Magnus and Angela over for an afternoon to build gingerbread houses as a gift? Would your heart like to do that?"

"Yes Mommy, that's EXACTLY what my heart wants!"

Carrie said a prayer and kissed her goodnight before heading downstairs to her friends. Matthew had taken Carrie's place at the table and was talking to the ladies about his jobs and how he was saving for a Nintendo Switch. Kara mentioned that he had inspired Justin and Calvin to start saving for something too! Seeing the note on the fridge, he invited them to come to the Christmas play with them. They both said they'd try to be there.

Just before the ladies left, Carrie asked when Magnus and Angela might be free for an afternoon making gingerbread houses as a Christmas gift. They agreed that they would plan it for the last day of school before the holidays.

Saturday Carrie was up early to get a second coat of black paint on the furniture for Jenny's guest room. When she was about halfway through Matthew came down and sat beside her. "If you want, I can give you back the money I'm earning. I want you to finish school."

She reassured him that they were going to be just fine, and he could keep all the money he made. In truth, Carrie wasn't sure how she'd pay for all of grad school, but she had a good start with her savings. Another chat with Jenny about finances would be in order soon. Once the furniture was all drying, she sat down with her coffee before remembering the orange frames she and Matthew had been working on. There was so much going on they were still sitting in the basement waiting to be finished!

When Katie was up and awake enough to help, she brought the frames up along with the scarves. Together they picked one scarf that was big enough to be cut in half and put in each frame. Carrie carefully folded the edges and used a thin line of hot glue to finish them against the frame backing before covering them with the glass and replacing the frames. The final effect was striking. Certainly not everyone's taste, but for someone who loved bright colors and an abstract design, they'd be perfect.

She hung them on the wall behind her couch to photograph them and wished she could leave them there. But it was more important to build up her savings. After sending a quick email to Eleanor with the pics, she cleaned up the table and got breakfast out. Now she was ready for a fun Saturday with the kids.

Later that afternoon after shopping and swimming the kids were happy to watch another Christmas DVD. Carrie grabbed a much needed coffee and checked her emails. Eleanor replied that the framed prints looked fantastic, but she didn't have a client for them at the moment. She did need more of the empty frames, but painted silver if Carrie could do that. Carrie sent back a reply that she could have ten ready in about a week.

Checking the bookshelf and night table, she put the final touch on the night table—the found stick drawer pull. Then she cleaned off the bigger sticks that would become wall hooks. Matthew joined her, and together they sanded the ends of each stick until they were rounded and made sure the rest of the curved edges were completely smooth. There were more than Carrie thought the room needed, so they sanded two more that Carrie would put up in Matthew's room. Her last task was to carefully drill holes into each stick so they could be screwed into the wall. She'd have to remember to tell her dad how much all his tools and supplies helped her out!

After supper, they played *Snakes and Ladders* while listening to more Christmas music. Carrie ignored the impulse to start another project. She'd work on the frames for Eleanor tomorrow, but she really didn't want all her time with the kids to be taken up with projects.

The next day Carrie slept in, and then got working on the frames. She had five more frames ready for Matthew to sand and prime before realizing she'd need to buy silver paint before she could do anything else. They ate a quick breakfast and then went to the hardware store for paint. The kitchen table would now be a workspace until the frames were all finished.

By the time they were ready to head to the Christmas play, all the frames were cleaned and primed, and five of them had their first coat of silver paint. Matthew had added another $20 to his savings and was hoping the frames would sell soon so he could have the cash.

They met the other families by the church entrance and all went in to the main area together. Matthew was happy to be sitting with Max on one side, and Carrie and Katie on the other. The play was a hilarious adaptation of a modern-day Nativity with all the characters (including a few of the animals) texting and posting on social media as the story developed. Carrie loved being able to laugh so often in one night with people she loved and trusted around her.

Afterwards there was hot chocolate and cookies for everyone in the lobby. Max and Kara's husband Ken decided that *all* the guys should go together to the charity football game in two weeks' time. Carrie could see how pleased Matthew was to be included in the planning. They all finally said their goodbyes and went to put tired kids to bed.

CHAPTER 27

The week seemed to fly by for Carrie. While at Jenny's, she brought in the rest of the furniture for the guest room. Max ordered a mattress and black bedframe for the room, and they all agreed that the wood drawer pulls and hooks were a perfect balance to the shiny black furniture. Carrie and Jenny had fun looking through bedding online before choosing a set with cozy rustic tones. By Wednesday the guest room and bathroom were ready for Jonathan, who was scheduled to arrive just before Christmas.

The set of orange framed prints sold for $75, and Carrie immediately turned around and paid Matthew the $36 in total he had earned so far. Tuesday evening was the family Christmas party at the Boys' Club. Carrie enjoyed visiting with other families and being able to personally thank the leaders who made Tuesdays so fun for Matthew.

Confirmation of her course enrolment arrived in the mail, and Carrie jokingly put it up inside one of the finished frames. One day it would be her diploma hanging on the wall. By Friday she had all ten silver frames ready for Eleanor, who was happy to come by and pick them up.

SWEET, SMART, AND STRUGGLING

Saturday, they took all the cans and bottles they had collected to the recycling depot where they got $27.45. After putting aside 10% for charity and 10% for savings, Katie got $4 and Matthew got $18. Then they stopped at the bank where Matthew opened his first bank account (separate from the savings accounts Carrie started for the kids) and deposited $50 from the total money he had earned. He explained to Carrie that he needed the rest of his money for Christmas gifts.

Carrie received her usual check from Jenny for her work, plus another $300 for the furniture. Jenny had tried to give her more, but Carrie refused. She hadn't even expected any payment in the first place for the furniture, so the extra $300 they agreed on was a nice bonus. Matthew wasn't the only one keeping money aside for Christmas, but Carrie could still increase her bank account funds by another $50 and put another $350 into savings. Her bank account now had a buffer of a full month's expenses and she had $5,050 in savings!

Next week, Jenny wanted her from Tuesday to Thursday, but the real focus was on the football game coming up that Saturday. Matthew could hardly wait! Carrie offered to pay Max for his ticket, but Max was adamant that Matthew was his guest. And Kara had suggested that Katie come over for the afternoon to give Carrie time to do some solo Christmas shopping. It was going to be a fantastic week with a very happy ending, and then it was just one more week of school before Christmas holidays started and they went to her parent's house.

Tuesday morning Carrie walked over to Jenny's place, happy for a change. She had worked all Monday on getting her own house clean, catching up on laundry, and finishing the lucky side table. It was nice to work on a piece she knew she could keep, but she was getting tired of her own four walls and looking forward to seeing Jenny. She called up a hello to Jenny after letting herself in and went down to start a load of laundry.

When she got to the bottom of the stairs, the door to the guest bathroom unexpectedly opened and Carrie found herself face to face with a man dressed only in a towel wrapped around his waist. For a moment her brain completely went blank and her heart beat faster. He was a slightly older version of Max, but with wavy blond hair wet from the shower, and intense blue eyes. Carries eyes started to travel down his body before her brain kicked in and shut her down. Giving a quick smile, she said a cheerful "Hello!" and turned to go to the laundry.

Jonathan walked into the guest room and closed the door behind him. Leaning against it, he looked up at the ceiling. *What was that?* He had stepped out of the bathroom and looked down into the kindest set of brown eyes he had ever seen. For a moment, he was sure he had just experienced love at first sight. Her curly brown hair was up in a ponytail, but wisps were escaping around her face. The faded t-shirt and blue jeans she wore were nothing special and yet seemed completely perfect. He was just about to say something to this person he felt an instant connection with, when he felt a total shift and a sudden distance from her. A quick hello and she turned and walked away without waiting for a reply. He was completely baffled.

After starting the laundry and giving her head a shake for almost feeling interested in a guy, Carrie went up to join Jenny for their usual cup of tea. She realized as she walked up the stairs that he had to be Max's brother. Thanking Jenny for her tea, she added, "I think I just met your brother-in-law."

"He's up already? I didn't realize that, or I would have warned you! Yeah, he completely surprised us by arriving yesterday! Thank goodness you had the room ready! Max could hardly make himself leave for work today, but we figured Jonathan would spend the day catching up on sleep after his long trip. Oh, Jonathan, good morning! This is Carrie, my new best friend and savior!"

Now that he had his ability to speak back, Jonathan walked over to Carrie and held out his hand. "Hello! Nice to meet you. Sorry, I'm a bit jet lagged and my brain wasn't working a few minutes ago."

Carrie stood up and shook his hand. "No worries. Can I get you a coffee or tea?"

"Coffee would be great, thanks."

Jonathan sat down and watched Carrie go into the kitchen and start the coffee. He looked at Jenny with a questioning glance. She filled him in, "Just after we moved in, the housekeeper I hired bailed on me. Carrie came to my rescue a few days later and has been fantastic with getting the house in order and helping with Angela. I don't know what I would have done otherwise."

Carrie brought the coffee, cream, and sugar to the table. After thanking her, Jonathan took his first sip of coffee since arriving the night before. It tasted like heaven. He had gotten Max hooked on quality coffee years ago, and it was nice to know the house still stocked a good coffee.

Finishing her tea, Carrie asked Jenny what she wanted to do today. Jenny was ready, "Now that Jonathan is here, we need to switch to Christmas mode. Max hates all that decorating stuff, so we can get it all done and surprise him when he gets back. You know where everything is in the basement. Do you need help bringing anything up?"

"Not from you!" Carrie smiled, "Why don't I vacuum the living room first, and then if Jonathan is awake enough it would be nice to have some help bringing the tree up. Everything else I can do on my own. And you can sit on the couch with your feet up and tell me where you want it all to go."

Jonathan smiled, "I can see why you're so happy to have Carrie around! Just show me what to bring up."

Carrie told him to relax and enjoy his coffee first while she vacuumed. It was hard to believe she was getting paid to put up Christmas decorations. Katie would be impressed with that idea! And Carrie was looking forward to seeing all the Christmas things out. She had moved quite a few boxes of Christmas things into one place when she was helping unpack, so she knew it would be a big job.

After vacuuming, Jonathan followed her into the basement, and they carried the tree up together. He insisted on helping with all the other boxes too, and in no time the living room resembled a festive tornado. There was a small bag of ornaments that they set aside for Angela to help with, and Jenny would wait for Max to be home before setting up the nativity. Carrie set up the tree and started decorating it, only stopping once to switch over the laundry. Jonathan wanted to go with Carrie to pick up Angela, so when it was time to leave, they left together.

He had that same easy approach to life that Max had, and Carrie enjoyed chatting with him as they walked. At the preschool, Angela squealed with delight when she saw him. "Uncle Jonnie!!! Did Santa bring you early?"

"He sure did Angel! He knew I couldn't wait one more day to see you, so he brought me last night when you were sleeping!"

With his prompting, Angela introduced him to Magnus and Katie, and then they all walked back together. Carrie explained that she wanted to take the load of laundry out of the dryer, otherwise she would have left them to have time together without any extra people.

Jonathan, who was carrying all the kids' backpacks, smiled. "Oh, I'll have lots of time to spend with Angela, no worries there!" Carrie still made sure to be quick back at Jenny's so they could have time together without her and the kids interrupting. She thanked the stars that she had worked so hard to get the furniture for the guest room ready early.

On the walk back home with Katie and Magnus, Carrie thought about how nice it would be for Jenny to have Jonathan around. She knew Jenny was really missing her parents as Christmas approached. Plane tickets were out of her parent's budget during the expensive Christmas travel season, but Jenny was hoping to feel up to going to see them in the spring. At home, she made sure to text Jenny that she could be completely flexible in the next few weeks if Jenny didn't need her. Almost instantly Jenny texted back

I still need you desperately! Keep coming!

It was so nice to have someone that wanted her around. She wondered if Max would still want to go to the football game now that his brother was here. But he seemed like the type of guy who wouldn't change plans when there were kids involved.

When Kara picked up the kids, Carrie laughingly told her about meeting Jenny's brother-in-law with just a towel on. "He clearly wasn't expecting to see a strange woman right outside the bathroom door! I hope he didn't feel too awkward!"

"Seems like he surprised more than just Jenny, Max, and Angela! I'm happy that she has family over."

"Me too. Well, the boys have been talking all afternoon about the football game. I think it's passed Christmas as the main topic of conversation! Sounds like they'll have lots of fun."

Kara agreed, and wrangled her boys out of the house. When she left, Katie asked when they could set up their Christmas decorations because Angela already had decorations up. Carrie hadn't planned on putting up a tree since they were going to her parents' for Christmas, but seeing how excited the kids were at seeing Jenny's tree, she changed her mind. "We can do it this weekend! Thank goodness Mr. Morris let me take the tree and all the decorations. It will be fun to have them all out!"

The next morning Jonathan was at the preschool with Angela. She was clearly enamored with her uncle, and reluctant to leave him when it was time to go into preschool. Katie saved the day by reminding Angela it was their turn for painting that day, and she needed to stand beside her when they painted.

As they walked home, Carrie asked how long he was staying. "Forever!" He replied.

"That sounds permanent!"

"It is. I've been staying away for a while, but when Jenny was diagnosed with cancer, I knew it was time to be close to them. It's taken a bit of time to close up my life in Singapore, but now I'm here to stay. I dropped the bombshell on them last night and told them they'd never get rid of me now!"

"I'll be that was a pretty good early Christmas present."

"I think it's me who benefits the most. Max is a great brother and my best friend, Jenny's the sister I've always wanted, and Angela, she's just perfect. It's been hard talking to her online instead of face to face. I want to be here for everything now. I'll start looking for a place nearby as soon as my place in Singapore sells. I'd probably outlive my welcome if I stayed at their house too long!"

From what Carrie had seen already, she thought they'd love to have him in their house permanently. It was nice that he'd still be close by. At the house, she went down to start the laundry right away, and when she came back up there was a cup of coffee for her, instead of the usual tea. She gave Jenny a questioning look.

"Jonathan said he could tell you preferred coffee over tea, so he made you a cup."

"Oh, well I like tea too..." Both Jonathan and Jenny laughed. "OK, you're right, I prefer coffee. But I did find that I really like tea when it comes with good conversation!"

"From now on you can have coffee with good conversation! Thanks for setting up the tree yesterday. Angela loved putting on her decorations with Jon's help. I'd love to finish putting up the decorations today."

Carrie agreed, but suggested Jenny take time to rest before Angela came home from school. She could tell Jenny was happy to have

SWEET, SMART, AND STRUGGLING

Jonathan there, but she was looking a bit tired. Once the decorations were up Carrie gently sent Jenny to bed for a rest and cleaned the kitchen until it was time to get the kids. Jenny had called the preschool to add Jonathan to the names of people who could pick up Angela, so Carrie got the laundry out of the dryer and folded it before they left so she could go straight home from preschool.

Saturday morning Max and Jonathan both came to the door to pick up Matthew for the game. Carrie introduced Matthew to Jonathan but could see he was upset with the change in plans. She invited them both in and set Katie on them while asking Matthew to come upstairs for a minute. Reminding him of her promise to only let him spend time with men who were 'good guys' she assured him that Jonathan was super nice, and Matthew would be OK.

"But Mom, I was hoping to just hang out with Max today."

"Jonathan is like a second Max, so it's like you can hang out with him double! You'll have lots of fun today bud, OK?"

"OK." Carrie could tell he wasn't convinced, but she knew he'd be alright. She'd never get to meet Jonathan and Max's parents, but they had raised two of the nicest guys she'd ever met. And she was glad her son would get to know them too. Maybe it would even help him be less suspicious of men. She could hear Katie chatting away.

"You need to go rescue them from your sister now, or you'll miss the game!" Together they went back downstairs.

While listening to the very animated four year old in front of him, Jonathan was taking in the surroundings. It was obviously a budget property, miles from the exclusive condo he had for sale in Singapore. But there was something about this place that felt cozy and familiar. Looking up to see Carrie coming downstairs with Matthew, he knew it was her that made him want to be there. He had to come all the way around the world to find someone who made him have second thoughts about staying single for life. If only she was interested in him! Jonathan was used to discouraging women who were enamored with him, but the one woman he was finally interested in hadn't given *him* a single interested look since the first time their eyes had met.

Carrie was a bit surprised to find herself wishing she was going along. She didn't think of herself as a football fan, but the idea of hanging out with Jonathan appealed to her. Giving her head a little shake after she closed the door behind them, she told herself to put Jonathan out of her mind.

CHAPTER 28

Carrie's solo shopping trip on Saturday afternoon was productive. She found used skates for both kids and herself, and decided to give her parents and sister a framed picture of her and the kids for their main Christmas gift. Family pictures were something she had always wanted, and now she had the skills to make each frame unique too. She cleaned one thrift store out of frames, figuring what she didn't use for her family she'd fix up and sell.

At the third thrift store she went to, she finally lucked out on clothes for herself. Someone her size must have recently donated their whole wardrobe because she hadn't seen anything the last time she looked. Her favorite find was a sheer white blouse with gold accents through the ruffled neckline and cuffs. It was flashy compared to Carrie's usual clothes and she loved it. She also found a pretty gold tank top to wear underneath it, a black satin pencil skirt, and a few nice t-shirts in different colors. Remembering her promise to her friends, she also bought a vase. It would be nice to have fresh flowers in the house once in a while!

By the time she picked up Katie from Kara's, she was ready to put her feet up and have a coffee. Kara agreed to use her new phone to take family pictures of them tomorrow and email her the pictures so Katie could get prints made in time for Christmas.

Back at home she quickly took the bag with the skates and frames downstairs to be wrapped later. While Katie watched a DVD, Carrie cleaned the house and brought up the little artificial tree to put up in the corner of the living room. She decided not to do any more furniture projects before Christmas—at least ones that she worked on in the living room—so they would have room for the tree. It was quite small, so she found a nice little side table in her collection of furniture-in-waiting and stood the tree on it. Tonight, she'd decorate it with the kids. She put a pot of soup on, and then finally sat on the couch beside Katie with her laptop and a coffee. She needed to figure out what kind of computer and printer to get before school started.

When Matthew came in with Max and Jonathan, the house smelled like chicken soup and Carrie had Christmas music playing. Matthew was decked out in football fan gear, including a jersey that he was wearing over his jacket.

"What happened to you?" Carrie asked with a laugh.

"Mom, it was so awesome! We got to eat hot dogs and popcorn, and Max and Jonathan got me all this stuff so everyone would know what team I was cheering for!"

"Wow, that's incredibly generous. Thank you both! I haven't seen Matthew this excited in a long time."

"Yeah, Max and I probably had more fun than he did! We've never had a buddy to take to a football game before, so I hope we didn't overwhelm him. He was a great sport!"

"I'm pretty sure he'll survive. Thank you again!"

Matthew surprised Carrie by hugging both of the men and saying thank you before they left. It looked like he had decided Jonathan was one of the good guys too.

SWEET, SMART, AND STRUGGLING

They ate supper to the unusual sound of Matthew talking for the whole time. Carrie felt she hadn't missed a thing from the game by the time he finished. That alone was Christmas gift enough, to see Matthew so excited about something. She wished there was something she could do to thank Max and Jonathan.

It didn't take long to decorate the tree, but Carrie was glad they had done it. The living room felt much happier with the colorful lights and tree in the room.

Matthew was ready for bedtime after his busy day, and Carrie went back to the couch with her laptop. She updated her spreadsheet with her Friday bank deposit, bringing her account total to $1,200. Jenny encouraged her to continue adding a little bit to her savings every week, now that she had one month of expenses put aside. At the bank, Carrie also activated her very first credit card in her own name. Jenny repeated the teller's advice that Carrie needed to start building up her own credit rating, so Carrie applied for a card. She was uncomfortable with the $1,300 limit, but she was determined to use it carefully and always pay it off.

Before looking at Christmas sales for laptops, she went on the Buy and Sell site again. She wanted to try to get Matthew a guitar for Christmas so he could take lessons. They had done a few classes with ukuleles in school, and he really enjoyed it. Carrie asked the music teacher for advice and she recommended looking for a half size guitar, and also gave Carrie the name of a guitar teacher in their neighborhood.

There was only one listing for a child's guitar, so Carrie sent off an email asking for more info. Then she started looking for laptops. The store pages loaded slowly, reminding Carrie that she needed to upgrade her internet speed, too. Finally, she found a store that seemed to have a few good choices. She'd have to go on Monday when Katie was at school.

On Sunday they had fun dressing up in their Christmas outfits and going to Kara's for their first ever family pictures. Kara's dad had spent the summer landscaping their back yard, and it looked great, even in winter. They left the coats close by while she took a few different poses. Looking at the images on her phone, Carrie knew her family would love them. Ordering the pictures online would be her first job when she got her new computer.

CHAPTER 29

Monday morning Carrie made the biggest purchase she had ever made (aside from buying a used car) and bought both a new laptop and a printer. The total came to $1,100, which was $100 more than she planned, but she was confident it would serve her well for the next few years. She also upgraded their internet, adding another $25 to her monthly expenses. It seemed like a lot, but when she texted Kara to ask, she assured her that was pretty much standard for high speed.

Tuesday Carrie bought the used children's guitar for Matthew. She was grateful for the two mornings free to get her running around done without Katie. There's no way Katie could have kept something like a guitar a secret until Christmas. She had just enough time to gift wrap the skates and guitar before picking up the kids from preschool, but she kept the guitar in the basement so Matthew wouldn't be tipped off early about his gift. There was no way to disguise a guitar, even a gift-wrapped one!

By now Carrie was getting used to seeing Jonathan with the other parents dropping kids off at preschool. Together with Kara, there was always something for the adults to chat about, and he was good about giving his full attention to Katie whenever she had something to say to him.

While they walked to Jenny's after preschool started, he asked if she could help him. He had booked flights for Jenny's parents to join them for Christmas, and they'd be arriving on Friday. Could Carrie get things at the house ready for them without tipping Jenny and Max off? He wanted it to be a surprise.

"Are you kidding? What a perfect thing to do! Jenny has really been missing her parents."

Jonathan smiled, "They're the sweetest couple. After my parent's accident, they just sort of adopted me and her mom still calls me every week to check in. I thought it was the least I could do. They can stay in the guest room, and I'll sleep on the couch while they're here."

They agreed that Carrie would get the guest room and bathroom ready on Friday when Jonathan went to pick them up from the airport. Since Jenny usually ordered supper in, there wasn't much planning needed for groceries, but Carrie could take Magnus and Katie and pick anything up on Friday afternoon if Jenny needed. Jenny's mom was on a restricted diet, but Jonathan and Carrie weren't sure what she could and couldn't eat.

Friday morning while the three of them were at the table with their usual morning drinks, Jonathan casually asked Jenny if he could borrow her car to do some Christmas shopping. She teased him that he just needed to put a bow on his own head and they'd be good, but she agreed. As Jonathan turned to go out the door, he gave Carrie a conspiratorial wink. She smiled and got up to start the laundry.

Jenny had bought two sets of sheets and towels for the guestroom bed, so it was just a matter of quickly changing the linens and giving the bathroom a wipe down. Carrie noted that Jonathan was rather clean for a guy, and he had already packed all his things and set his suitcases by the guest room door. She paused at the suit hanging on one of the rustic hooks she had made. It was a gray pinstripe with a yellow tie draped around the neck. Matthew would love it. Ken had helped Matthew tie his festive necktie for their family pictures on Sunday, and Carrie noticed how much he liked being dressed up. Maybe one day she could get her son more dress clothes.

Jonathan wasn't back by the time Carrie was ready to go pick up the kids, so she told Jenny she'd get Angela. Jenny wanted to come with her, but Carrie pulled the 'you need to rest' story and insisted she'd get Angela. She wasn't sure what Jonathan's plans were and didn't want him to come home to an empty house.

The kids chattered happily on the way back to Angela's house. With only one more week of school left before the holidays, they were full of talk about Christmas. Angela told Katie and Magnus how lucky they were that they got to go to their grandparents' for Christmas. "My grammy and grampa are too far away so we can only have Facetime Christmas." Carrie couldn't keep her big smile away. Angela would get another Christmas surprise shortly!

Seeing Jenny's car in the driveway, Carrie pulled Katie and Magnus back a little, and let Angela go in first. "GRAMMY!!!! GRAMPA!!!!" she squealed. They were standing right at the entrance when Angela opened the door. Carrie felt her eyes mist up when she saw Jenny's face. She had a feeling Jenny's recovery would accelerate now that she had her parents with her.

Carrie stepped in and introduced herself and the kids and they all shared happy embraces. "Jenny's told us all about you. Thank you for taking such good care of our daughter and granddaughter!" her mom said into Carrie's ear while she hugged her.

"Carrie! You knew about this didn't you!" Jenny joined them in the crowded entryway.

"I might have heard something. The guest room is all ready for your parents." Carrie smiled. Jonathan was just moving his suitcase and suit out of the room.

"Before you go, can I get your number? I wanted to text you that I was running late but didn't have your info. And I thought Jenny might get suspicious if I asked her."

Carrie and Jonathan exchanged numbers, and then Carrie asked Jenny if she could grab some things at the grocery store for her. Jenny said she'd text her a list. Carrie said her goodbyes and gathered Magnus and Katie to go home and have lunch before grocery shopping.

Walking home she couldn't stop smiling. She'd love to surprise her family one day like that. Having money made a lot of things better, and Jonathan wasn't afraid to spend it on his family.

When she was married to Don, his family had been nothing but challenges to her. They seemed to spend all their time together drinking, and her mother-in-law did nothing but correct Carrie on her parenting and criticize the kids. It was nice to know there were families that got along so well.

When they got home, Carrie realized she had two texts. She'd have to pay more attention to her phone now that she actually had a bit of a social life. The first was from Jenny.

> *Mom brought her food for a few days so I don't need a grocery run, but thank you so much for helping Jonathan pull this off!!!! You are a FANTASTIC friend!*

Carrie smiled as she replied.

> *It was so fun to see your faces!!! Enjoy every minute and remember to rest.*

The second text was from Jonathan.

> *You make a great partner in crime. Thanks for your help!*

She didn't think she had done much, but it was so nice to be appreciated.

Anytime! That was such an amazing thing you did!!

Smiling, she got lunch ready. After, when the kids were relaxing, she went and chose the picture frames she wanted to paint for the family gifts. The pictures would be ready tomorrow for pick up. She had ordered 5 x 7 pictures of her and the kids, and then another one of just the kids for both her parents and Jessica and for her own wall, and then some 4 x 6's for each of her kids to put up. The leftover silver paint would be perfect for all the frames and she couldn't wait to get started.

The guitar teacher had gotten back to her to confirm lessons for Matthew beginning in January and Carrie stopped by the pool to book a set of swimming lessons for Katie. She'd have to bring Magnus with her since the lessons were after lunch on Tuesdays and Thursdays, but he was easy to have along. She and Kara hoped that being around the pool would help Magnus get over his fear of water. Kara said even the bath terrified Magnus, and it took both her and Ken working together to keep him calm once a week for bath time.

The kids had gotten some craft books out of the library the night before, and they were hoping to find something to make for their grandparents and auntie. Carrie would spend the next week doing Christmas baking to give to their teachers and friends and bring home to her parents. Her dad had learned to cook just about everything after her mom's accident, but he was still hopeless at baking, so Carrie promised to bring all their favorites. It would be an expensive trip to the grocery store to get all the baking ingredients, but she wouldn't need to buy groceries for the week she was at her parents.

Friday night they looked over all the crafts and decided to make 'World's Best' t-shirts for Grandma, Grandpa, and Auntie Jessica with their handprints on them. Carrie couldn't wait to make her little sister wear a t-shirt instead of the dress suits she was living in since graduating.

On Saturday they picked up supplies for the t-shirts and homemade cards from the craft store, and then picked up all the groceries, candy canes, and treats for gingerbread houses from the grocery store. By the time they got home both the kids were keen to get started on their gifts and soon the t-shirts were laying on the table in the basement to dry.

They spent the rest of the day making Christmas cards. As usual, Matthew was careful and thoughtful with the few cards he made for his teachers. He surprised Carrie by also making a card for Jonathan, explaining that Jonathan didn't have any kids, so he might not get a Christmas card otherwise.

Katie tore through her big list of school friends, and soon there was just as much glitter on the table and floor as there was on the cards. Once the cards were dry, they'd attach a candy cane to each one. Katie's class party was on Wednesday, since so many of the kids were going away early for the holidays and the teacher wanted to include as many as possible in the party. Then they would have their own special gingerbread house party on Friday with Angela and Magnus. Angela would come home with them after school for hot dogs, and then Jonathan would pick her up before the boys got home from school.

With her parents at the house, Jenny wouldn't need her this week, and Carrie was considering braving the basement to do one more round of furniture and frames. It would be nice to add a bit more to her account before taking Christmas off.

Carrie half expected a text from Don wanting to see the kids. She hadn't heard anything from him since the morning he had shoved them in her door when he was evicted, but it was hard to imagine not wanting to see the kids at Christmas. Although they hadn't asked for him at all.

The next morning they were up early and Matthew asked if they could go to church again. His notice on the fridge said there was a special children's service. At Katie's request, she sent a quick text to Kara and Jenny inviting them but told Katie they probably had plans for the day.

She was glad it was a casual church, and they could wear their regular clothes instead of needing to dress up. Although Katie could spruce up any outfit with her scarves and necklaces, Matthew and Carrie only had their Christmas outfits for going out.

As they were walking in Carrie was surprised to see both families there. It was nice to sit with people they knew, and the service was fun and happy. Afterward, Ken suggested everyone go to their place for lunch and they'd order pizza. Jenny and her mom declined, so Max dropped them off at home before the rest of them went to Kara and Ken's.

Kara was the opposite of Carrie with her house. As long as the kids were fed and dressed, nothing else mattered. Carrie helped her clean off the table so there was room for pizzas, and Ken grabbed a packet of paper plates. Matthew and Jonathan joined Calvin and Justin playing the Nintendo Switch, and the three preschoolers were happy to play in Magnus' room. Carrie enjoyed visiting with the other adults while happy shouts came from the TV room. Eventually, Jonathan came and joined them too.

Just before they left, Jenny sent a text to Max that he shared with the group, "Jenny and her mom have decided to have a Christmas party for everyone and their kids on Saturday night. Is everyone OK to come?"

Carrie had planned to go to her parents Saturday morning, but she could postpone it by a day so she could take the kids to Jenny and Max's. Kara and Ken weren't going to her parents until the Monday after, so it was set. Carrie offered to bring baking, and Kara offered to bring wine. Max mentioned he'd probably invite some families from his workplace as well.

CHAPTER 30

The last week before Christmas holidays seemed to fly by. Carrie almost missed the notice she received in the mail confirming her 'no contest' divorce would be finalized in January. It seemed perfect that she'd be free from Don just when she was going back to school. She would always remember how trapped she had felt in a marriage full of control, criticism, and hurt, but it was time for her to pay attention to the good life she had now, and the great life she was creating.

As if to confirm her decision to focus on the future, she also received her textbooks for the coming semester and she spent the evenings browsing through them after Katie was in bed.

When Katie was at school she worked in the basement, completing two end tables and another cute little corner shelf. The rest of the time she did all of the usual Christmas baking, and the house was full of the smells of sugar cookies, gingerbread, and all sorts of squares and treats. On Wednesday Katie was proud to bring her cards for all her friends, plus a special package of Christmas baking for her teacher and the teacher's assistant. Jonathan took one look at the baking and begged Katie to let him be the teacher. It took her a minute to realize he was teasing her. Carrie promised to bring extra baking to the party on Saturday for him.

Friday Carrie walked the three preschoolers home from school, and after lunch they all had fun decorating their gingerbread houses. She debated letting them try to assemble the houses as well as decorating them but was glad she had let Matthew help her put them together the night before instead. As it was, Katie broke hers because she was so enthusiastic about decorating, but Carrie set a water glass inside her house and used it to help hold everything up.

It was the first time she had spent with Angela away from Jenny, and Carrie could see how she needed a lot of reassurance and encouragement. Her mom's illness had been hard on her, and Carrie just wanted to make it all better. Katie picked up on Carrie's tone and became Angela's personal cheerleader. By the time Jonathan showed up, Angela was glowing with pride over her very decorated gingerbread house. He seemed reluctant to leave, but Carrie had seen how overwhelmed Angela was whenever she was around Calvin and Justin over the weekend, and she sent them on their way instead of inviting Jonathan in for a coffee. She sent a follow-up text:

> *Sorry to push you out the door, but I wanted Angela to head out on a good note. When Calvin and Justin come the house gets a little (a lot) crazy, and I don't think she's used to busy boys tearing around the house.*

> *Ah, that explains it. Thought maybe it was me! Thanks for taking such good care of Angela. She chatted all the way home about how fun it was. Reminded me of my Mom — she was always doing stuff like that with Max and I.*

Saturday Carrie got everything ready for heading to her parents the next day. The framed pictures turned out beautifully, and she had wrapped up Matthew and Katie's pictures as well. All the gifts and baking were by the front door, except for Matthew's guitar which she had already put in the trunk. Matthew and Katie unpacked their school bags so they could pack up for the week at their grandparent's. They stayed in, waiting for the buyers who were coming for the furniture Carrie finished earlier in the week. After they came, Carrie put aside the $120 to deposit when she got back home. Then they got ready for the party.

Matthew was happy to be wearing his dress shirt and tie again, and Carrie could barely stop Katie from twirling in her sparkly dress long enough to coax her hair into ringlets after her bath. Carrie quickly threw her own hair up into a ponytail and put on the blouse and skirt she had found at the thrift store. She was looking forward to a glass of wine at Jenny's and explained to the kids that they would walk there and back because of that. Matthew had enough memories of Don being drunk to worry about adults drinking, but Carrie was determined to show him that adults could drink and still be nice to kids.

They arrived just when another couple came, and Jenny greeted them all, looking beautiful in a red dress that was perfectly styled to hide her weight loss. Max was at the top of the stairs bringing everyone in and getting drinks. Matthew and Katie went up right away, but Carrie realized her phone was ringing. Excusing herself she handed the loaded tray of baking to Jenny and slipped into the basement, hoping everything was OK with her parents. She didn't get many phone calls. Jonathan was on his way downstairs to get more ice from the freezer and stepped back when he saw her answering her phone so as not to disturb her.

"Hello?... Sorry, who is this... Don, this isn't a good... wait, what?... Is everyone OK?... Oh my goodness, that's terrible!... You want me to what?... (Jonathan heard a distinct change in her voice from worry to anger.) Seriously? You have got to be kidding! No way!... You were drinking and driving, that's on you. You're lucky no one was killed!... How can you need bail?... Your third time, huh? Is that where our savings disappeared to? Your last bail?... How dare you! You blame your kids and me for all your problems and then you expect me to bail you out with money I don't have? Not a chance!... No, I will NOT bring them to see you for Christmas!... I don't care.

If you want your kids to visit you in jail get a court order... No, Don. I don't owe you *anything*! Goodbye!"

She hung up the phone and slumped against the door frame. Jonathan walked over and put a hand on her arm. He could feel her shaking. "Hey, you OK?" She looked up at him, and for a moment he felt that same connection he felt the first time their eyes had met. Then, she looked to the side and shook her head.

"I'll be OK. Sorry you had to hear that."

"Sounds like you handled it pretty good. Are you sure you're OK?"

"Yep! I'm going to go check on the kids."

Jonathan watched her walk away before remembering he was supposed to get ice. He wanted nothing more than to make everything better for Carrie, but she hardly noticed he was there except for those brief moments when she let her guard down.

Walking upstairs, Carrie took some deep breaths. She had suspected Don was drinking and driving, but except for one time when Katie was a baby and he nearly crashed into the house after a night out, she hadn't known for sure. Now the kids' dad was in jail, and the lady he hit was in the hospital. She'd do everything she could to protect the kids from him. But right now, she was surrounded by nice people who liked her, and she was going to enjoy the night.

Jonathan watched her check on each of her kids and give them a little hug before accepting a glass of wine from Max. She seemed to be perfectly fine, but he was starting to get the idea that she was used to putting aside her own feelings. Maybe she didn't need him, but he was going to stick around, just in case.

Carrie thoroughly enjoyed the evening. Everyone was so nice, and the kids were all getting along really well. When it was time to go, she could only find Matthew, until Jenny quietly called her over. She had set up Magnus, Angela, and Katie in her bed to watch a Christmas movie on an iPad, and all three had fallen asleep. After Kara took a picture and promised to email it to her, she stood there for a minute. Normally she'd carry Katie home, but in the heels she was wearing there's no way she'd make it! Turning around, she saw Jonathan standing right behind her.

"Um, is there any way you could lend me your arms? There's no way I can get her home in these shoes!"

"Absolutely! Let me get my coat while you get her coat and shoes on."

It was nice walking home with Jonathan carrying Katie, and Matthew holding her hand. When they got to the house, Jonathan followed Carrie upstairs and laid Katie down in her bed. He gently pushed her hair off her forehead before turning and looking at the room. Carrie stepped out and directed Matthew to get ready for bed, and Jonathan followed her.

Being in such an intimate area of her home, he wanted nothing more than to stay there with her and the two kids. It was a family he longed to be a part of, but he wasn't about to push himself on her. He understood a lot more about what she was dealing with after overhearing her phone conversation earlier in the evening. He couldn't help himself from asking about the one glaring problem in her little home though.

"So, I'm guessing that's your bed on the floor?"

"Yep, welcome to my home sweet home! I was really fortunate to find this place."

"But Carrie, you're sleeping on the floor! That can't be comfortable!"

"Actually, every night I get to fall asleep listening to my kids breathing and I know that no one will bother me—or them. It's perfect!"

He resisted the urge to reach out to her. "You're pretty amazing, you know that?" he asked softly.

She smiled, but it seemed like a sad smile. "Thanks! I keep all compliments! And thanks so much for carrying Katie home. She won't believe me tomorrow when I tell her she slept all the way home."

"You're heading to your parents tomorrow?"

"Yeah, a whole week of someone else running after the kids. It will be pure bliss!"

"I'll, uh, I'll see you when you're back then?"

"Sure thing. Thanks again Jonathan."

After letting him out and locking up, Carrie went to get Katie into her pajamas and kiss her forehead. Matthew was almost asleep when she got to him. "Mom, were all the grown-ups drinking tonight?"

"Pretty much bud, why?"

"Well, they were nice, that's all. And Jonathan helped you with Katie. Dad used to just yell at you when he drank."

"He's what we call a mean drunk. Most adults aren't like that. These people we're friends with are good people that make smart choices. You don't need to worry about them, even when they're drinking OK?"

"OK Mom. It was fun tonight. I love you."

"Love you too bud. Night."

She kissed his forehead and hung up everyone's party clothes before getting ready for bed. Despite Don's call, it had been a really good night. She lay in bed thinking about all the good things that had happened in the past few months. The year was closing on a perfect note.

Her last thought before she drifted off was about how nice it was to have Jonathan here for those few minutes before he went home.

CHAPTER 31

Despite the late night, the kids were up early and keen to get to Grandpa and Grandma's. Carrie quickly packed up, and they were on their way before 8 am. Both kids fell asleep before the next town and Carrie enjoyed the quiet time to think about everything. It was only the middle of August when she had made her great escape from her marriage. To be in the position she was in now—with her kids safe and happy, money in the bank, jobs, a little business, and now going back to school to finish her degree—took some time to accept. She was really starting to believe that she could turn her life into something good, no matter how bad the past had been. By the time she was pulling into her parent's driveway feeling sentimental and ridiculously grateful for her life, the kids had woken up and were raring to go.

In the few days before Jessica arrived, Carrie spent lots of time resting and visiting with her parents. Although she was tempted to bring her textbooks with her, she opted instead to bring two of the books she had from her old school days. She vaguely remembered reading Choice Theory and Reality Therapy as extra material for a counseling course she took, and she wanted to get a refresher while she still had time for her own reading.

When Jessica showed up, she slept for almost an entire day, and then declared herself ready for Auntie duty. She took the kids to the local pool, the sledding hill that had just received enough snow to be extra fun, and even to a Christmas tree farm that was hosting activities for kids. Carrie enjoyed the breaks from the kids and the chance to spend time with her parents. They were both slowing down, but still very much in love with each other and enjoying her dad's retirement.

She talked to them about Don's phone call, and her dad called a friend of his who had been a police officer in the city to see if he could get more information. A day later they found out that Don was being held without bail until a court hearing in April. It was his fourth time being caught drunk driving, and his second time driving with a suspended license. He was facing a certain prison sentence and was lucky the lady he hit did not have any lasting injuries or it would be longer.

Carrie was disgusted by his choices, and not at all surprised that he had lied about needing bail. He was just trying to drag Carrie into his mess. She sent off an email to the legal aid lawyer who had helped her with her divorce to see if she could get sole custody. She was more determined than ever to keep the kids away from him. Her dad's friend said there were cases when inmates got court orders forcing their kids to visit, but most judges were careful to keep the children's best interests in mind. Even if Don tried to get a court order, he might not be successful.

It was nice to get a phone call later that day from the lady Kara had told her about from her clinic so Carrie could focus on someone else's challenges, and put Don's problems behind her. Lisa was in her 20's, and unexpectedly caring for a mom with severe arthritis. Carrie had a long chat with her on the phone, encouraging her to get help with caring for her mom, and to make sure she kept time for herself. It sounded like Lisa spent more time working than anything else. They planned for Lisa to come over to Carrie's for coffee when Carrie got back home.

On Christmas Day Carrie was as excited as the kids. She had felt terrible about borrowing money from her parents and was excited for them to open the gift bag with the $2,000 in it. And for the first time, she was really excited about her gifts to the kids. On her last trip to the thrift stores without the kids, she had found some adorable dresses for Katie to go with the skates, and she had wrapped up a rubber ducky to represent the swim lessons Katie would be getting. Matthew's guitar had been snuck in and tucked behind the tree, and Jessica came out of her room the day before with an armload of gifts to put under the tree.

Drinking her coffee, with her family around her opening gifts Carrie felt perfectly content. Everyone was so happy with their gifts. Her dad tried to give her back the money, but she refused. Jessica surprised her with a nearly new iPhone, along with two LEGO sets for Matthew and a complete baby doll set for Katie. She had just received her first work phone and was happy to finally bring her big sister into the 21st century with her 'old' smartphone that was barely used.

Her parents had bought much-needed clothes for the kids, including brand new winter jackets. Their mom assured them that she had become quite the online deal finder and they didn't need to worry about how much she spent.

Together Carrie and Jessica made Christmas dinner—a tradition they had started when Carrie was old enough to take a turkey out of the oven by herself. Carrie got festive texts from all her friends from home, even Jonathan. It was nice to look forward to going back and seeing everyone again.

The last night Jessica was home, Carrie treated her to dinner and a movie out. It was something she hadn't been able to do for a long time, and she was surprised at how proud she felt to do it. As sisters do, they chatted about their lives over Mexican food at their favorite childhood restaurant. Jessica listed a few eligible men at the firm who seemed nice and were making good money.

"With the right guy in your life, you can do whatever you want, and not have to worry about money!"

"Jess, that's the last thing I want! I need to do this on my own to prove that I can take care of the kids and myself. I want to look back and say, 'I did it' not 'my rich husband did it'."

"I know Carrie. I just want to make things easier for you. You're doing amazing, but life has been really hard for you for a really long time… Tell you what, when I make partner, I'll treat us to the most fantastic all-inclusive luxury vacation you've ever seen! We'll leave the kids at Mom and Dad's and spend a whole week drinking and sun tanning."

"As long as you add in lots of sleep, I'm in!"

"You got it! I guess we should head over to the theater. Thanks again for treating me. I'm *so* proud of you, big sister!"

CHAPTER 32

Although she only planned on staying for a week and then heading back home to get ready for the new year, Carrie stayed until the first of January. Her parents couldn't visit her at her home until she lived in a place that was wheelchair accessible, and she was enjoying the time with them over the holidays. The day before Carrie was ready to head home, her dad went out with Matthew to do some 'guy stuff'. He asked if he could take Matthew with him and take Carrie's car so he could wash it for her. She happily gave him the keys. While she *could* wash her car herself, it was nice to have her dad do it for her.

She sat at the table with her mom and Katie, coloring with the new set of crayons that had been in Katie's stocking. Suddenly a horn honking interrupted their visiting. Her mom looked up, "You'd better see what that's about Care Bear."

Carrie went outside and stopped short. There, instead of her very well-used 1994 Ford Taurus was a newer looking Honda Accord. She was totally confused. Her dad and Matthew had grins that were nearly splitting their faces.

"Happy New Year Carrie!" her dad shouted after rolling down the driver's window. Then he turned off the car, got out, and brought her the keys. "I have a friend who was looking for an old car and traded him for this one. It's all yours!"

"Dad!" Carrie protested. "There's no way you traded this car for my car! What's going on?"

"Well, we got a bit of a windfall this Christmas. It may have helped."

"You used the cash I gave you? Dad! But still, there's no way…"

"Just take it, Carrie. This car will last you for a long time. It's way better on gas too, so it'll help you make ends meet when you go back to school."

Carrie was completely overwhelmed. She knew her parents were careful with their money and would only do this if they could. But it was still an amazing gift. Between this, going back to school, and her new little business she was a new woman!

That night she sat with her parents in the living room, enjoying a glass of wine in front of the fireplace after they had all gone to the early New Year's fireworks in town. Spending the last ten days with her parents had given her exactly what she needed to start the new year and her new life with excitement. Now, she couldn't wait to get back home!

Her dad had also visited all the local thrift stores with Matthew, and Carrie was bringing back almost two boxes of picture frames he had picked up for her to work on. Not having to run around looking for frames would give her more time to 'upcycle' and sell them. It was Jessica who had taught her about upcycling. Apparently it was all the rage in her city, and people were going a bit crazy paying top dollar for things, just because they were 'upcycled'!

The next morning, they had one more breakfast together before she got in her 'new' car with her kids and all their gifts for the ride home. It had been fun to give meaningful gifts to her parents and sister too.

She promised to get new pictures done in six months so they could begin a new wall of family pictures to sit beside the old ones of Carrie and Jessica that would probably be up forever.

They stopped to get groceries and then unloaded everything at home. Carrie spent the rest of the day putting things away, doing laundry, and making soup. She officially started school in five days (one day after the kids went back), and she wanted to be ready. After sending a quick 'We're home!' text to Kara and Jenny, she was happy to call it a day.

Carrie was up early the next morning to go over all her course outlines. Since she would be responsible for setting the pace for her schoolwork, she wanted to make sure she understood what was required so she didn't go over her self-imposed four-month time frame for finishing her classes. The online university gave up to six months to complete the courses, but if she took that long it would be tight to apply for grad school for the fall. She sent off a friendly introductory email to each of her professors and used the calendar app in her new phone to set out due dates and benchmarks for each class.

Over the holidays, Jessica spent some time helping Carrie get her phone set up and teaching her how to use it. She was already enjoying the ease of getting a notification on her phone every time she got an email, and she downloaded an app for the Buy and Sell site so she could post listings from her phone. By her calculations, she needed to make an additional $800 per month to pay in full for the first year of grad school by September.

Her monthly expenses were lower since she had qualified for an interest-free grace period on her student loan while she was attending school full time, but she expected to spend almost that much every month on extra groceries, guitar lessons, and maybe more swim lessons for Katie. It would be tricky, but Carrie thought she had a good chance of making it work if nothing unexpected happened.

When the kids woke up, they had a lazy breakfast together before Carrie started work on a new set of picture frames. Both she and Matthew had big plans for making money, and Katie had big plans for the new toys she had gotten at Christmas. Together they prepped and primed ten frames. Carrie did six, and Matthew did four. With the frames drying on and under the table, she got out the sheet where they were tracking Matthew's earnings. He added $8 to his credit account, and Carrie made sandwiches for lunch that they ate sitting on the couch.

They went for a walk with the bottle bag while the frames continued to dry and came back with another bag full of cans and bottles. It seemed like they were the only ones out there collecting containers that had piled up in all the usual places while they were away.

There was just enough time to tidy up before Lisa came over. Since the kitchen table was covered by frames drying, Carrie sent the kids to have play time in their rooms while she visited with Lisa. They had a lot in common.

Lisa had been entirely focused on getting on her own financial feet when her dad suddenly passed away. It sounded like they hadn't had a very good relationship, and Lisa had minimal contact with both her parents for the last few years. She thought that her dad would leave money for her mom to at least survive if he passed away, but he had accumulated a vast amount of debt that her mom hadn't known about. Liquidating nearly everything earned just enough to protect her mom from debt collectors.

Her mom had arthritis and her health had deteriorated after learning she had been left destitute. She was beginning to need a wheelchair much of the time. Lisa had been saving for years to buy a house, but she had to tap into her savings to move into an apartment for her mom to live with her and to adapt it for a wheelchair. Carrie couldn't imagine caring for someone all on your own. She had always had her dad there to do the heavier part of caregiving.

She encouraged Lisa to take time for herself, away from work and caregiving, and to look into hiring an aide to help with the more physical things like helping her mom shower. It also seemed like her mom may need time to heal from living with such a controlling man. It would be good to develop a friendship with Lisa and her mom. She suggested they all meet in a few days at the soft play area, and the ladies could visit while the kids played. It should be easy to get a wheelchair in, since so many moms showed up with strollers. Just before Lisa left, Carrie called the kids down to say hello to Lisa. Carrie liked the way she treated the kids—as if they were her equals.

Lisa walked down the steps from Carrie's house feeling strangely at peace. Nothing had really changed. She was still the full-time caregiver for a parent she had barely spoken to for four years, and she was still further away from her dream of buying a house than she had been six months ago, but she felt like she had genuinely connected with someone who understood how challenging her life had become. Not that she hadn't seen challenges before, but this was a whole new level of challenges.

After Lisa left, they took a quick trip to the library to get out some books and movies for the rest of their holiday. Carrie planned a movie night with the kids, so together they made nachos for supper and settled in to watch a movie.

In the morning Carrie got the first coat of black paint on the picture frames before the kids got up. After oatmeal for breakfast, they all left for much-needed eye check-ups for the kids. Although she knew they should go every year, she had delayed in the past because she didn't want to have to ask Don for money if the kids needed glasses. Now she was free to do what was right for the kids. It was nice that the exam itself was free, and she would only need to pay if the kids needed glasses.

As she suspected, Matthew's vision was fine, and Katie definitely needed glasses. She had astigmatisms in both eyes, but the doctor assured her that getting glasses at this age would help her eyes work better together and improve her overall quality of life. The optometrist's office sold glasses, but Carrie confided in the salesman that she was on a tight budget, and he recommended a discount eyeglass store that provided excellent service. They spent a fun ½ hour at the Eye Glass Warehouse looking at different frames before they all agreed on a pair of pink frames with sparkles. The glasses should be ready in a week.

Just as they were getting ready to leave, Carrie got a text from Jenny.

> *Can you all come for supper tonight? It's my parent's last night and Mom's making a HUGE lasagna! (And I'm suffering from Carrie withdrawal!)*

Carrie jokingly asked the kids if there was any chance she could drag them to Angela's house for supper. They both shouted "YES!" at the same time.

> *That would be nice, we'd love to come. Can I bring anything?*

> *Nope, just you three.*

It would be nice to spend the evening with friends and get to know Jenny's parents a bit. Of course, Katie was excited to see Angela, and Matthew was looking forward to seeing Max and Jonathan. They stopped to get a little bouquet of flowers for Jenny, and then went home for lunch.

The picture frames were dry enough to get the last coat of paint on after lunch, and Carrie was pleased with the result. She'd leave them to dry for a day before sanding off some of the gold to show the black underneath. Carrie also decided to refinish and sell the remaining furniture in her backyard and basement. It was there for free, and she needed all the income she could make. After the furniture was sold, she'd focus on the empty decorator frames, and the framed scarves.

With Matthew's help, she reorganized the basement so they could move the remaining furniture from the back yard down to the basement. Carrie wanted to keep her front and backyard looking tidy, even though hardly anyone else in the complex seemed to care about things like that. A quick inventory showed that she had a dresser, a tall bookshelf, three small bookshelves, a small desk, and two side tables waiting for a makeover. Hopefully, the creative outlet would be a nice break from her studies.

CHAPTER 33

Dinner at Jenny's was fun! All the adults kept up a relaxed conversation and were great at including Matthew. Katie and Angela went straight to the playroom, stating they had 'lots to play'. The house smelled amazing with lasagna and garlic bread competing for everyone's attention. Jenny looked better than Carrie had ever seen her. She claimed that two weeks of her mom's cooking had been a magical cure.

Max and Jonathan had spent the day looking at houses for sale for Jonathan, and the conversation soon turned to real estate. Jenny's parents weren't shy in talking about how Jenny helped them get their finances in order so they could buy their first house. Jonathan chimed in that Jenny's advice had helped him get his own finances figured out and he was looking forward to making a good profit when he sold his apartment. Now he was looking for a house that needed some work.

Carrie didn't know much about what he did, except that he was now doing freelance work and would divide his time between working at home and traveling for work. She mentioned meeting Lisa, and how hard she had worked to buy a house before suddenly having a mom relying on her for everything. Jenny asked if she was able to give Lisa any advice since her own mom was disabled. This led to them asking questions about Carrie's parents and family.

They all talked about how hard it must have been for Carrie to care for her mom at such a young age. Looking at Max and Jonathan, Carrie said the biggest blessing was still having her parents around, and she mentioned how Jenny's parents seemed to bring everyone into their family.

"We always hoped to have a big family" her dad, Tom said, "So we've just taken advantage of Jenny's friends to grow our family! Like it or not, you belong to us now!"

Carrie smiled, "I can't have enough good parents!"

Jenny's mom, Martha declared that supper was ready, and together they all sat around the big dining table. Carrie loved the friendly, easy banter that went around the table as they ate. This was exactly the type of family interactions she wanted her kids to get used to, and she felt so lucky that she had met Jenny.

Near the end of dinner, Angela started complaining about eating the rest of her food. She pushed her plate away, and it caught her juice cup and tipped it over. Carrie watched Matthew and Katie both sit back in fear while Max quickly came over. He set his napkin over the spill and reached to pick up Angela. "Hey baby girl," he said gently, "Are you OK?" Angela turned and buried her head into his shoulder. He went back to his chair and sat down with her in his lap, stroking her hair, and Martha went to the kitchen to get a cloth.

Katie broke the spell, "Is she in big trouble?"

Max looked over at her and smiled, "I think she needs a little snuggle right now, she's not in trouble."

"Well, my daddy would get really mad if we spilled. I like you better."

SWEET, SMART, AND STRUGGLING

"I like you too Katie. And you can spill at my house whenever you want!"

Katie giggled, and Martha quickly cleaned up the spill. "See Katie, it's all gone now. No trouble at all!"

The adults all went back to their dinner and their conversation, and Carrie could see Matthew slowly relaxing again. After dessert, Angela was ready to play with Katie again, and Max asked Matthew if he wanted to play chess. The rest of the adults insisted that Martha and Jenny relax while they cleaned up supper.

A bit later Carrie was ready to walk home with the kids. With school starting for them soon it was time to get back to earlier bedtimes. They said their goodbyes, and Jonathan joined her at the door. "I'll walk you all over."

On the way home, Katie found some pop cans on the side of the road, and Carrie promised they'd come for a walk in the morning to collect them. She hadn't thought to bring their drink container bag.

"Are you really into recycling?" Jonathan asked.

"Sort of," Matthew answered. "We used to collect cans and bottles so Mom could buy groceries, but now she has enough money for groceries, so Katie and I get to keep the money. I'm going to buy my own Nintendo Switch!"

Carrie wondered what Jonathan thought of her parenting. All the other kids they knew had received gaming systems as gifts from their parents. She was probably the only one who hadn't been able to. But at least now he knew how broke she really was!

"Good for you! It's a big deal for a nine year old to buy his own things you know."

"Yep! And I make money helping Mom with painting too!"

Carrie loved hearing the pride in Matthew's voice. She needed to make sure he had lots of chances to earn the money for his goal. It was a good reminder to focus on how the kids were doing, not what other people might think of her parenting. They said goodbye to Jonathan at the door, and Carrie got Katie straight into bed.

Later, she had Matthew help her take down the Christmas tree and decorations and pack them up. Then they brought the small desk upstairs for Carrie to start working on in the morning. It made the living room crowded, but she knew it would be temporary.

While Matthew watched a movie, Carrie began reading one of her university textbooks. For her semester she was taking Advanced Developmental Psychology, Cognition and Emotion, Clinical Psychology, and Rehabilitating the Brain. Really, *this* was the best Christmas present she could get this year: the chance to learn more about what she had always been passionate about while setting herself up for a better future. She completely lost track of time and looked up only when Matthew's head dropped onto her shoulder. It was way past both of their bedtimes! She got him to bed, set up her morning coffee, and then tucked herself in.

CHAPTER 34

The next morning Carrie was up early to finish the frames. As soon as they were done, she emailed Eleanor, wishing her a Happy New Year and offering her first chance at the frames. Then she had her coffee while reading her textbook again. It was hard to stop and get working on the desk, but as she sanded down rough edges and pen marks from the desk, she reviewed what she had read so far. She hoped her brain could keep up with all the new learning after so many years of trying to hide her intelligence.

The kids both came downstairs at the same time and finished waking up on the couch while Carrie cleaned up from sanding the desk. By the time they were ready for breakfast, she was set up to prime the desk later.

After breakfast they got dressed, and she had the kids finish unpacking their backpacks from visiting Grandma and Grandpa so they could get ready for school the next day. They were both excited to see their friends again and to start their new activities. Matthew had his first guitar lesson on Thursday after school, and Katie would start swimming lessons in a week.

Then they went for a long walk to collect drink containers before coming home and loading all of them into the car to go to the recycling depot. Carrie bumped up the $34.50 they earned to $35, and had Matthew figure out how to separate the money using the percentages they agreed on. $3.50 would be deposited into the kids' bank accounts, they took $3.50 to the collection jar at the corner store that was raising money for a little girl's cancer treatments, and the remainder was divided with $22 to Matthew and $6 to Katie.

Over the holidays, Carrie's mom had encouraged them to play games together, and now they were starting to sit and play a game instead of just watching a DVD. She sent the kids to entertain themselves while she got to work priming the desk. It was dark wood, with black handles. She had already removed the handles and decided it would look best with a white glossy finish. Hopefully, inspiration would come to her about what to do with the handles. The inside of one of the drawers was quite stained, so Carrie painted the insides of all the drawers a teal blue paint that she bought for $1 at the thrift store.

Matthew came down asking for something to eat, and Carrie realized she had been painting for almost two hours. Going up to check on Katie, she found her sound asleep with her new toys around her. While it was tempting to let her sleep, she needed her awake now so she'd get to sleep at a decent time tonight. A promise of dessert after supper got her up. They had an easy pasta supper and ate the last of their gingerbread houses for dessert. While Matthew cleaned up, Carrie practiced letters and sounds using flashcards with Katie. Then she settled the kids on the couch with books and music while she got out the textbook she had started reading. This time she was smart and set a timer for Katie's bedtime.

Later that night, with the kids both sleeping, Carrie lay in bed and thought about what it would be like to be back in school. The next two-and-a-half years would be hard work, but nothing like the hard times she had gone through with Don before she managed to escape. Now, everything was up to her, and she would take advantage of it.

The first day back at school in January was always exciting for the kids. Carrie had planned to get the first coat of paint inside the drawers right away, but it was too hard to do anything with the kids hopping around. With Matthew off to school she managed to get Katie ready and then tidied up the house before they left. It was also her first day of the new schedule with Jenny; she was torn between being happy to still see Jenny and wanting to get working on everything she had going on at her own house.

Jonathan walked Angela to preschool, and together they walked back after dropping off the kids. He would be renting a desk at a local workspace company until he had his own home office but wanted to be available to help out with Angela whenever he was needed. When they got in, he thanked Jenny for lending him the car, kissed her on the cheek, and wished the ladies well before driving off to get to work.

Carrie watched him go, feeling a little sad that he would no longer be around the house every day when she was there. It's not like they were best friends or anything, but she found it strangely comforting to have him nearby.

Jenny already had a coffee made for Carrie, along with her own tea. They talked about the holidays and Jenny explained that she had client calls scheduled for Tuesdays between 11 and 12, so she'd still need Carrie to bring Angela home. Thursdays were open for now but could change at any time. When they finished their drinks, Jenny went to her office and Carrie got started on laundry and cleaning. Again, the time went quickly and she nearly missed leaving in time to pick up the kids. When they got back Jenny was off her call and getting lunch ready for her and Angela. With a promise to see her on Thursday, Carrie, Magnus, and Katie all went home for their own lunch.

The kids were tired after their first day back at school and were happy to watch a DVD in the afternoon while Carrie got the first coat of paint on the insides of the drawers. She loved the look and couldn't wait to get the white paint on the outside.

By Friday Carrie was exhausted, but happy. Her first week of school as an adult student had gone well. She had figured out that it was easiest to study when Katie was at school or asleep, so she was using her early mornings to study, as well as the mornings when she didn't go to Jenny's. After lunch she tried to work on projects. The final coat of paint on the desk was almost dry. The old drawer pulls looked great next to the white paint, so she would list it tomorrow when it was all assembled for pictures.

Friday afternoon she took Katie and Magnus with her to the bank and to get groceries, and by the time Kara picked up the boys later, Carrie was ready for a break. She made pizza, and they sat and watched one of the DVDs she picked up from the library the evening before. When Matthew went to bed Carrie was right behind him. She promised they would work on more picture frames the next morning so he could continue to earn money.

CHAPTER 35

Saturday morning Carrie took a quick look at her budget spreadsheet before she started on her day. After paying for Katie's glasses she only had $121 to go into her grad school fund. She needed to work hard to get to her $800/month goal. If she made any more than $800 in a month, she would put the first $50 into her bank account and set aside the rest for birthdays.

Matthew would turn ten on February 10th, and Katie would turn five on March 19th. Carrie wanted to make these birthdays as special as possible. Her own birthday was coming up on January 15th, and her parents had already made reservations for them all at a restaurant on the outside of the city. It was about a 45-minute drive for each of them, which would be manageable for her mom, and the restaurant had received good reviews for being wheelchair accessible.

Carrie updated her spreadsheet and shut her computer down. It was time to get moving on her day. She was just getting ready to take pictures of the desk and list it when an email popped up from Eleanor. Was there any chance Carrie had a small desk for sale? She had a client who wanted only one-of-a-kind pieces and needed a desk. Carrie laughed out loud at the coincidence while she emailed her pictures of the desk and reminded Eleanor that she had frames available too. Almost immediately she got a reply back. The desk was perfect, especially with the bright color inside the drawers. How much did Carrie want for it? And she didn't need any more frames right now but would be interested in buying them to keep as stock if they could do a deal with them and the desk.

It took Carrie a few minutes to figure out a price. She wanted to give Eleanor enough of a deal to sell everything to her. Finally, she decided on $300 and sent off a reply. *Deal! Can I pick up this morning?* Eleanor answered. Carrie responded positively and went up to get dressed. She didn't mind if the kids were still in their pajamas but she needed to look decent.

Eleanor showed up shortly after. "My accountant got after me for not getting receipts. You know I hadn't planned on coming back here until I saw the beautiful things you were making. Otherwise I would have asked for receipts right away. Are you OK to sign receipts for the things I buy from you?"

Carrie thought that would be fine. Fortunately, Eleanor had a receipt book in her purse, and she wrote up a receipt for the day's purchase. Carrie made a mental note to buy her own receipt book the next time she was at the dollar store. When she went to sign the receipt, she saw that Eleanor had set the price paid at $375. She tried to correct her, but Eleanor wouldn't have it. "I wanted to see the desk in person before I said anything. You do quality work, and the finish on this desk is excellent. I think it's worth it and I won't change my mind."

After thanking her profusely, Carrie took the check and then helped Eleanor load everything into her SUV. She was delighted with the sale, and so grateful she had connected with Eleanor. She needed money for the admission to the indoor activity center this afternoon to meet Lisa and her mom, and about $25 for more supplies. Oh, and $8 for Matthew's work. But that still left over $300 to put into her bank account!

The kids were up by then and excited with Carrie's big sale, plus the prospect of going to the indoor playground in the afternoon. They had a relaxing breakfast before Carrie realized she would need to buy more paint before they could do any projects. She also needed to make a quick stop at the bank to deposit the check and get cash. Already she was more than halfway past her January goal!

At the hardware store she got a can of white primer, some new paintbrushes, and a can of fantastic bright green paint from the mis-tints. Then, they made one more important stop to pick up Katie's new glasses. She looked adorable and was very proud of her new look. Carrie knew she'd catch Katie staring at herself in mirrors more than a few times until she got used to seeing herself with glasses.

Back at home, Matthew brought up one of the boxes of frames that Carrie's dad found for her. There were a few that were mirrors of different sizes, and Carrie decided to make a mismatched set of mirrors and empty frames, all in the bright green paint. It wasn't everyone's taste, but she'd be happy to put them up in her own place if they never sold.

They got all thirteen frames sanded and primed before it was time to leave for the soft play. Matthew earned $24 for his contribution. After entertaining herself while her brother and mom worked, Katie was more than happy to have something fun to do.

Once they arrived at the indoor play center, the kids quickly tore off to play, and the ladies moved to the viewing area. Carrie enjoyed meeting Lisa's mom, Maria, and talking to them both. Lisa had hired a caregiver to come in twice a week and help with her bathing and personal care, and they both thanked Carrie for the suggestion. After some time talking about a variety of things, Carrie asked Maria what she planned to do now that she was in a new place.

Maria seemed surprised by the question and sat drinking her coffee for a minute before answering. "I'm just not used to thinking about things like that. Robert was in charge of everything, and I did what he told me to do. I've wanted to get a job for a long time, but I don't know if there's anything left that I can do. I need to sit, and I can't do anything that requires much strength. I never went to college or anything..."

"What do you like doing?"

Again Maria struggled to answer. Carrie understood how hard it was for her, after living with a domineering man for so long. She wanted to encourage her to face the future, not the past. "Maria, you did what you had to do to survive during your marriage. But from here forward you get to have a new start. The thing is, you'll need to practice a new way of thinking. I can tell that Lisa accepts you just where you are, so you don't need to worry about pleasing her. This is a wonderful opportunity you have! So, what do you like?"

Maria smiled. "I like this right here. I like talking to people and having conversations. I like looking around and seeing happy children playing. I've been so lonely. I want to be around people now!"

Now Lisa was smiling too. "Wow, Mom! That's the first time I've seen your face light up like that! All we need is to find a job where you can hang out with people!"

Carrie agreed that it was a great start and encouraged them to keep their eyes open for something that would be a good fit. At this point, every little success would be a big step towards healing for Maria and Lisa. It would be neat to see what they figured out. By the time they were ready to go, Lisa, Maria, and Carrie had brainstormed a list of options for Maria. Some of them were just fun, but others might work well. They promised to keep in touch, and update Carrie.

Back at home, picture frames were covering nearly every surface in the kitchen, so Carrie made sandwiches for supper that they ate at the couch. Then she set the kids up with a DVD while she tried to get some studying done.

CHAPTER 36

By the end of January, Carrie had fully settled into her new, very busy life. Every morning she studied for about an hour before the kids got up. On Tuesdays and Thursdays, she enjoyed the break that going to Jenny's gave her, and on the other days she took advantage of the time when Katie was in preschool to get heavy schoolwork done. She was learning to force herself to focus intensely during these times and was getting a lot done.

In the afternoons she worked on furniture or picture frames until the older boys came in, and Saturdays she and Matthew worked together for as long as possible before Katie got too bored.

Carrie sold both side tables for $60 each, and the dresser for $125. She was a little disappointed to say goodbye to the green frames, but the $150 she got for the set was nice. She had also done a set of framed scarves, which Matthew did almost all the work on. They sold for $50. With the money she received from Jenny and the furniture, she made a total of $1,083 extra in January. After paying Matthew $44 for his work, spending $45 on supplies, putting $50 into her bank account, and $800 into her grad school account, she had $94 for Matthew's birthday. It was the most she ever had to spend on one of her children's birthdays.

The kids were both enjoying their lessons, and Carrie loved seeing them already improving. They had adjusted well to the new family schedule and were Carrie's biggest cheerleaders as she got high marks on her papers and quizzes. Her birthday was a welcome break from the busyness, and Carrie enjoyed the dinner out that her parents had paid for. They also gave her a beautiful bouquet of flowers that she happily placed in her one and only vase when she got home.

When she looked at her spreadsheet on the last Saturday in January, she couldn't help but feel proud of herself. Her grad school savings were at $6,288, her bank account was at $1,250 extra, and Matthew had $145 saved after cashing in cans and bottles last week and getting paid from his mom for his work on the picture frames.

February started off with a freak snow storm and three days off school for the kids. Carrie didn't mind having a few days straight with the kids. At least the electricity stayed on, so they could stay warm. After the first day, the blowing snow stopped, and they all enjoyed playing in the snow together and building a small family of snowmen in their little backyard. They called Carrie's parents to say a special thank you for the kids' new winter coats, which made playtime that much more fun.

Carrie also took advantage of extra time to work on school and her projects. It was surprising how much time she already spent taking kids to and from their activities and preschool and so she made the most of having a break from those tasks.

She also found that when she was able to schedule in the intense study times, it gave her a complete mental break from all the worries that sometimes overwhelmed her. There just wasn't enough brain power to worry *and* get good grades. At times she was shocked to see how fast time had flown by while she was studying. The kids were especially cute in their support of her, loudly whispering to each other that 'Mommy's studying' and then going off to keep themselves occupied.

With Matthew's help she got three pairs of framed scarves finished, and one set of three pictures where she divided a gorgeous sunset-colored scarf between three frames painted in leftover bright orange paint. They also dragged the tall bookshelf upstairs and Carrie got the entire bookshelf primed and ready for some fun accents. She was planning on using either wallpaper or an accent color paint on the back of the bookshelf and adding some wooden decorative accents to the corners of the bookshelf before painting it all a cream color. She did need some supplies to finish it, but getting it this far, she hoped she could finish and list it by the weekend.

The only drawback to the snow days was missing her time with Jenny, and the day's pay. Kara messaged her that she still got paid when the clinic was closed due to weather, and she would still pay Carrie for the days of childcare that were missed. It was very helpful to know the income would still be there for the week.

By Thursday the roads and walkways were cleared enough for the city to get back to normal and Carrie and the kids were more than happy to get back to their usual routine. Matthew's 10th birthday was now just over a week away, and he wanted to invite a few friends over for pizza, cake, and a movie. They decided the boys would all make their own personal pizzas, and part of his birthday gift would be the new release DVD he'd watch with his friends. He had five invitations to hand out to his friends.

Carrie had been watching the Buy and Sell site for a full LEGO set that she could get for Matthew at a discount. With her small budget, it wouldn't go far unless she could get some deals. She lucked out that morning, finding a listing for a set where the box was opened, but the packages inside were still sealed. At $20, it was a third of the new price and she'd pick it up Friday after she dropped off Katie at school.

After dropping Katie off on Thursday, she was happy to go see Jenny. The walk was a bit quieter without Jonathan, who was out looking at houses for the morning. Kara had dropped off Angela with Magnus. There was lots to do at Jenny's and Carrie found the routine she had established was relaxing and gave her time to review everything she was studying while she worked.

By the weekend, two of the pairs of frames sold for $60 and $70, and the bookshelf was ready to list. She hoped it would sell quickly so she would have room to work on the last three smaller bookshelves left in her 'furniture' line. Then she could focus on the frames and have more room to move around the living room.

Only three of Matthew's friends could attend his party, which gave Carrie enough room in the budget to let him make up goody bags with some things from the dollar store. He was counting the days to his party the next Saturday. There was just enough left in the birthday budget for Carrie to also take him out to a cheap movie on the Sunday afternoon following his party. She was taking the big step of hiring a babysitter whom Kara often used to come and stay with Katie so she and Matthew could watch a more mature movie. Then they'd go home for hotdogs and birthday cake with Katie.

On Friday afternoon a buyer finally came for the tall bookshelf. That, along with a full week's pay from Jenny got her earning back on track after the snow storm.

Carrie's parents sent Matthew a birthday card with $30, and Auntie Jessica sent $20 which he happily added to his savings. Adding in the $24 he earned working on frames brought his grand total to $219. He was now only $100 away from being the proud owner of a Nintendo Switch. His ability to stick to his goal was certainly impressing all the adults in his life, although Katie felt sure he was missing out on buying a lot of candy like she always did with her money.

The boys who attended Matthew's party were a lot like him. Fairly quiet, and all seemed a bit older than their years. Carrie was actually relieved when two of them got silly making their pizzas and ended up with goofy faces made of pepperoni and ham slices on their pizzas. She was also relieved none of them had seen the movie Matthew had chosen. Afterwards, they had cake, and Matthew was excited to get another $20 in birthday money, a small LEGO set, and a new football.

But by the time Carrie sat down at the end of the month and looked at her spreadsheet, she was ready to give it all up. The high from Matthew's 'best birthday ever' (his words) was followed by some difficult weeks. Katie spent a weekend sick, and then missed Monday of school, forcing Carrie to have to drive a very miserable little girl to preschool to pick up Magnus and watch her friends go by. Tuesday she had bounced back to her usual self, but the extra attention she had needed left Carrie behind in her school work. It was just too hard to study when someone was calling 'Mommy' every few minutes for three days straight.

She had only sold $185 in the last two weeks. Adding that to her extra earnings working for Jenny and she was close to her target, but not on it. That worried her, as she already didn't know how she would pay for all of grad school. In February she earned an extra $845 but deposited only $760 so she'd have money for Katie's birthday on March 19. Katie desperately wanted a birthday party at McDonald's for all her friends, but Carrie knew that would be out of her $85 budget.

Carrie was tired and discouraged. She knew she needed to keep up a consistent and aggressive pace with her schoolwork and her sales. Slowing down would lead to delaying her goal, or maybe even never getting her masters. It was one of the first times she wished she had a supportive partner who would give her a pep talk, make her another cup of coffee, and then offer to take the kids out for the day so she could catch up on studying. She put her arms on the table and laid her head down, just for a minute.

The sound of the TV woke Carrie up. Now she had a sore neck, *and* she had missed out on an hour of studying time by falling asleep. She went into the living room and saw her kids, both with bedheads and sleepy eyes, totally relaxed on the couch. Their visible peacefulness made her smile. A year ago, they would have never turned on the TV on a Saturday morning, out of fear they might wake up Don. Now, they were all safe, and no one would be yelling at them today. Even if she didn't ever get her degree, Carrie knew her escape from Don was one of the best things she could do, both for her future and the kids. She'd try to focus on that, and just do what she could.

CHAPTER 37

During the first few weeks in March, Carrie slowly got back on track with her schoolwork. She was now more than halfway through the semester, and almost able to see the light at the end of the tunnel. Again, Matthew was a big help with the frames and she sold another $60, plus $45 for one of the small bookshelves. She was running low on frames and would need to add to her stock soon.

Jonathan was back in Singapore, finalizing the sale of his apartment, and doing some things for his job. It seemed like everyone missed having him around, including Carrie and her kids.

Kara and Jenny had helped Carrie figure out a solution for Katie's birthday. Katie invited five friends to meet her at McDonald's for a birthday lunch (with Jenny and Matthew helping out). Then, Carrie borrowed Kara's minivan to drive the kids back to her house for cake and ice cream before their parents picked them up. While it wasn't an official McDonald's party, Carrie provided birthday hats and a helium balloon for decorations, and the kids all had great fun pretending to eat their food and playing in the play place before Carrie took them back to her house for cake and presents.

Katie received the usual mix of craft kits, stuffed animals, and sparkly accessories as gifts and squealed with pure delight each time she opened a gift. Carrie bought her a playdough McDonald's set that she found on a good sale, and all the kids went home with a little goody bag. Katie was thrilled with her party, her friends, her gifts, and her new elevated status as a five year old.

The kids had the fourth week in March off school for spring break and were excited to go to Grandma and Grandpa's. Kara's kids would also all go to their grandparents since Kara and Ken both had to work, and Jenny and Angela were flying to Jenny's parents, so Carrie had the week 'off'. She was hoping to use her parents to occupy the kids so she could get ahead in her schoolwork and then work on frames when she got back. The week of no income from Kara and Jenny would hurt, but Carrie was trying not to worry too much about it.

Jenny encouraged Carrie to ask her school guidance counselor if there were any scholarships she might access for grad school. Carrie's plan was to attend the same online university to do her masters, so it made sense to see if there was anything they might offer. The first thing she did after the kids were settled at her parents was send him an email. Then she enjoyed a quick chat with her parents before getting to work on a term paper she had due at the end of the month. Her parents were extremely supportive when she asked if she could spend the week studying, and her dad offered to take the kids out each day for an activity if the weather permitted.

Again, Carrie got completely absorbed in what she was doing, especially since she didn't need to keep an ear out for the kids. By the time she needed to stop and get supper going, she was well on her way to completing the first draft. Her mom offered to help by reading and editing her paper as soon as she was done.

They all took one day off to go to the local zoo, which was a birthday gift for Katie from Grandma and Grandpa. Auntie Jessica sent them money so Katie could choose a stuffed animal from the gift shop. Carrie had to laugh when Katie choose a ridiculous looking monkey. She'd probably smile every time she saw it on Katie's bed.

At the end of the week, Carrie had one completed term paper, and two more nearly completed. She had gotten ahead of schedule in all four classes and was looking forward to final exams when she could prove to herself that she was still just as smart as she used to be.

Her dad and the kids had enjoyed going to thrift stores and even answering classified ads for picture frames and Carrie was well supplied for at least the next month of projects. She tried to explain to her dad how much pressure it took off of her to have his help. He got a little teary eyed in response, "Carrie, you've made me so proud this past year. You're just charging into your future making everything work all on your own. I'm happy to do anything that helps you get where you're going. Never forget what a wonderful woman you are!"

One more long hug from each of her parents and Carrie and the kids headed home for what she felt was the last home stretch to getting her bachelor's degree. It was only four weeks away now, and she could handle anything for four weeks.

When Carrie went to open her spreadsheet on the last Saturday morning in March, she was interrupted by an email notification. Seeing it was from her guidance counselor, she opened it.

Dear Mrs. Bennet,

I apologize for the delay in replying to your inquiry about scholarships for the Masters in Counseling program. I was away on holidays and then waiting to hear from your professors about your current progress. They all speak well of your progress, and you are on track to receive high marks.

If you can achieve a minimum 86% average in all of your courses, you will qualify for the J. Arthur memorial scholarship. This is a $2,000 scholarship for each of the two years of the program, provided you maintain the 86% average throughout your studies.

I'm attaching the application form for the scholarship, as well as for two smaller bursaries you may be interested in. Please note there is a personal essay required for this and the application deadline is April 15.

There are numerous other scholarships available outside of our university system that you can use towards any programs you might attend here. I encourage you to search online for these, and in particular those that apply to mature students.

Good luck!

Carrie opened the attachments and smiled. After the term papers she had been working on, a 1,500-word personal essay on How Higher Education Will Change My Future was pretty easy stuff. And as long as she did as well on her final exams as she had done in her courses so far, she'd meet the minimum requirements.

The bursaries were short online applications which Carrie filled out immediately and sent off. Receiving even a little bit of financial help would make her goals that much more achievable. Her March total was only $185 going into her grad school account since she had to make up for the missed week of earnings that she normally used for her monthly expenses. But it still brought her total up to $6,500. *If* she got that scholarship, she would only be $1,000 short of paying for her first year of grad school, and she knew she could earn that before September.

Matthew's finances were also looking good. He earned another $24 for helping with picture frames, and $27 for pop cans. With $290 saved, he just needed a little more to be able to make his big purchase. Carrie was tempted to top off his account herself, but she didn't want to take away from him the pride in saying he had earned it all himself. Plus, she was well aware that the world could be a tough place and she wanted him to have some confidence in his ability to reach goals. He had been watching the flyers every week when they came in and was happy that either there would be a sale, or that in just a few more weeks he'd be able to pay full price (plus tax) for a system.

CHAPTER 38

April! One more month until Carrie could sleep in on a Saturday and do nothing all day if she wanted. But with the prospect of a scholarship in her near future, she was determined to keep up the pace for the month and graduate with top marks. Plus, Carrie loved everything she was learning. The only hard parts were having less time to spend with the kids, less time sleeping, and still worrying about money. In four weeks, two of those would be over until September.

In the meantime, there was coffee. Carrie had designated part of her more flexible grocery budget to make sure she always had enough coffee. Often the morning started with two cups while she studied and the kids slept, and then another cup in the afternoon before the boys came in from school.

Over the weekend she sold a set of framed scarves for $75, and a little bookshelf for $45. It was a good way to start the month. After not working for Eleanor for quite a while she got an email asking if Carrie could do a set of 11 frames using a specific paint that Eleanor would drop off. It would be nice to have a guaranteed sale again, and she happily agreed.

Katie finished Level 1 of swimming and moved on to Level 2. Magnus surprised all of them by agreeing to take Level 1, so now Carrie had to juggle both kid's lessons on Tuesday and Thursday afternoons. They overlapped a bit, giving Carrie time to send Magnus to his lesson before having to dry off Katie and getting her dressed, and then getting Magnus dried and dressed. Kara had bought Carrie a bouquet of flowers as a thank you for helping Magnus get over his fear of the water, but Carrie was pretty sure that it was watching Katie for a whole session from the viewing area that helped him the most. He just needed to do things in his own time.

Jenny was now working almost full-time, and Carrie found her days there were even busier than they had been before. When she worked, Jenny left a bit of a tornado behind her throughout the house, and Carrie laughingly claimed it was no problem since Katie was the same way. It was nice to see Jenny so happy and fulfilled again.

Jenny also asked her to watch Angela after school until just before the older boys would arrive. Jonathan would be over to pick her up just before 3 and keep her with him for the rest of the day. Carrie was happy to help out, but only once she finished school for the semester. Angela was becoming more outgoing almost every day, but she was still an easy child who wouldn't be much more work for Carrie. And the extra $100/week, on top of the $100 Jenny paid her each week for housecleaning would be a great help.

Until then, every minute Carrie could spare was used for studying or for getting the frames done for Eleanor. Again, Matthew was a huge help, and they both noticed the difference when using the very expensive primer and paint that Eleanor had brought. By the middle of April, the frames were ready to be picked up. Carrie paid Matthew $40 for his help and promised him a shopping trip as soon as her exams were done. The other $180 would go in her grad school account as soon as she had time to stop at the bank. She kept having ideas for different ways of doing frames. Once her exams were over, she'd only be working on frames for projects and she had a feeling her earnings were going to increase without much extra effort on her part.

At the end of April, Carrie's dad came and spent two days and one night with them to watch all the kids while Carrie wrote her final exams. As a 4th year student, she didn't have any midterms (just term papers) so this was her first time going into the university exam center. She had been struggling to figure out how to manage everything while being away during the day until her dad offered to come in. A friend of theirs would stay with her mom during that time.

Matthew moved to the floor in his bedroom, leaving Grandpa the bed. He was quite pleased to be sharing his room. Carrie felt strange leaving the first morning of exams. She'd be driving to the transit station and taking the train into the city—something she had never done before. Plus, she realized she had never missed taking Katie to preschool or picking her up! Fortunately, Katie was very excited about Grandpa taking her, and was happy to say good-bye to Carrie the night before, since Carrie was planning on leaving before Katie was up. She didn't want to risk being late for her first exam.

As it was, Carrie was almost an hour early, so she treated herself to a latte at a nearby coffee shop while she waited. Looking around at all the tired and stressed-looking customers, she was glad her future career plan did not involve fighting strangers for a place on a train into the city center every day. She still didn't know how she'd set up an office for sessions in her tiny rented townhouse, but she'd figure it out when the time came.

By 2 pm Carrie was on her way home with two exams complete. She was confident that all her hours of studying, especially in the past month, had paid off. Now she'd give her brain a break for the rest of the day and enjoy time with her kids and dad before going back and doing the same thing tomorrow. It was an hour and a half before Carrie walked in the door at home, and she was greeted by Katie as if she had been gone for months. Her dad was looking a little tired, so Carrie insisted on taking all the kids to the park for a while so he could have a few minutes to catch his breath.

The next morning Carrie left at the same time, even though it was a bit too early. Some sort of trouble along the line delayed all the trains, and she was grateful she left when she did. There was just time to put her things into a locker before her first exam of the day started. On her way home that afternoon she could hardly believe she had done it. All the build-up, the planning and saving, the months of studying and missing sleep suddenly seemed to have passed too quickly. It felt like she should have one more thing to do. One more paper to write or test to take. It would probably take a few days to sink in. She took a minute to send a group text to Kara and Jenny:

It's over!!! I can hardly believe it!

Kara was the first to reply.

It's about darn time. Congratulations!!! Can you have a social life now?

Before Carrie could answer, Jenny joined in.

Congratulations!!! I think a girls' night out is long overdue. Can we go tomorrow night?

Carrie could already feel herself relaxing. She was so grateful for her friends.

Ohhhh, that would be perfect. Let me see if I can get a babysitter.

Jenny was quick with a reply.

There's always Max!

She laughed when she read Kara's addition to the message.

> *And Ken! Although he'd have no idea what to do with Katie! LOL I'll book somewhere for 7. Let's meet at Carrie's and go from there.*

Carrie was already looking forward to spending time with her friends, almost as much as she was looking forward to sleeping in on Saturday morning. She had just enough time to send off a text to her newly-discovered babysitter to see if she was free tomorrow night before she got into her car for the short drive home from the station.

After thanking her dad for taking care of the kids for the past few days he was off for the drive back home. He had enjoyed the chance to be Grandpa on duty but admitted it was a lot more work than he expected. They would see him and Grandma at the end of May when they came up for Carrie's convocation ceremony. She was excited to finally be walking across the platform to get her degree!

When Kara came to pick up her boys at 5:30, she was carrying a bouquet of helium balloons that said Congratulations. She hugged Carrie and told her how proud she was of her, and what a good role model she was. The boys all told her congratulations too, and after hugging her, Magnus looked up and said quietly, "You're my favorite friend mom."

Carrie hugged him back and replied, "And you're my favorite Magnus!" When Kara and the boys left, Carrie reluctantly packed the kids up to go get groceries. As she expected, Friday at supper time was the worst time to go grocery shopping. Everyone was tired and in a rush. Finally, they were back home, and Carrie put the frozen pizza in the oven for supper. They hadn't made it to the library the day before, so there was no new DVD to watch. She'd have to take them tomorrow and pay late fees for missing the one-week due date.

After Katie was in bed Carrie sat facing Matthew on the couch and they played UNO together. He had been very understanding all the times she had been studying, but she had missed the one-on-one times with him. Tomorrow they would go buy his very own

Nintendo Switch, so who knew if he'd even want to play cards with her anymore when he had something so fun to do!

When he went to bed Carrie was right behind him. Suddenly it felt like the past four months had caught up to her, and she could barely keep her eyes open.

Saturday morning found Carrie wide awake at 7 am. Maybe it would take a while to get used to not needing to get up early to study. She went to get a coffee and opened up her spreadsheet. With Eleanor's extra order, April was a decent month. She was still off her old goal of putting $800 a month into her grad school savings, but she made an extra $650 even with missing a day of work with Jenny when she had her exams. Just over $500 would go into her savings, bringing the grand total to $7,000. The rest she was keeping aside for going out with Kara and Jenny tonight, paying the babysitter who confirmed she was available, and picking up more picture frames and supplies.

When Matthew came downstairs Carrie put away her computer, made another cup of coffee, and hung out with him on the couch until Katie came and joined them. They sat like that for almost an hour, and it felt like bliss to have nothing to do except be with her kids. Finally, she got up for a quick shower before they all had breakfast and set out for the library, then the thrift stores, and then the games store.

It was a big moment for Matthew *and* Carrie when he used his very own money to buy the Nintendo Switch. Matthew was so proud of being able to buy it all by himself, especially after waiting and saving for so long. The lingering guilt Carrie had felt about not being able to buy him a gaming system herself disappeared when she watched him give the cashier his money. Now he knew he could make a goal and stick to it until he made it happen.

By the afternoon Matthew was well-settled on the couch gaming with the hand-held part of the Nintendo Switch, Katie was watching a 'new' DVD from the library, and Carrie was catching up on her house cleaning. She had been doing as little as possible for the month and it felt really good to finally get everything cleaned properly. Then they took a long family walk together with their bottle bags. It was a perfect spring day, with tulips showing their colors in many of the yards they walked past. Carrie allowed herself to dream of a time when she would have her own yard to brighten up with things like tulips. In two more years, she'd be ready to start her career, and get going on things like saving for a house, and maybe even taking the kids on a proper vacation.

But for now, she was happy to have a whole day free to spend with her kids, an evening out with her favorite friends, and four whole months of working, making beautiful frames, and earning money before starting school as a grad student. She had come further in the past year than she could have ever imagined. A year ago, she had been struggling to hide enough cash from Don so she could get out of a horrible marriage. Now, she had enough money to go out with the girls, hire a babysitter, and know that she and the kids were safe and happy.

The next four months would be her last as a mom of a preschooler. It was going to be quite a shift for Katie to be attending school every day. Of course, she was already talking about everything she would do in school!

In the meantime, Carrie's fingers were itching to start doing more frames. She had gotten so many new ideas when she was studying and had only been able to write herself quick notes on her phone and then turn her focus back to her studies. Now she had time and energy to make all those ideas happen and build up an even bigger savings account.

Matthew's successful purchase of a Nintendo Switch with his own money had been a big boost to his confidence. He decided his next big purchase would be a truck when he turned sixteen. Already he had reminded his mom that he could help with picture frames whenever she wanted. Carrie was so proud of him for the way he could work towards big goals.

She could see how much she had changed in the past few months too. It felt like her own spirit was starting to thrive. Whenever insecure thoughts tried to bring her down, she would remind herself that she was a university graduate on her way to grad school with two kind and loving children, wonderful friends, and a talent for making frames destined for the dumpster into something people would pay big money to hang on their walls! From where she was standing, the future looked amazing.

A NOTE FROM THE AUTHOR

Thank you for taking the time to read *Sweet, Smart, and Struggling*! If you enjoyed it, please consider telling your friends or posting a short review. Word of mouth is an author's best friend and much appreciated! Thank you again!

To be one of the first to hear when my next book comes out, and for a chance to win bookish prizes, sign-up for my newsletter:

www.carmenklassen.com

And you can like my Facebook author page:

fb.me/CarmenKlassen.Author

May all your days be full of good books, nice people, and happy endings.

Sincerely,

Carmen

Read on for a sneak preview to Book 2:
The Cost of Caring
(Author's Note: Yes! Carrie is in Book 2!)

Lisa sat beside her mom in the front row of the funeral home chapel, still wearing her gray dress coat—she didn't plan on staying very long. She faced her dad's coffin with a strange mixture of distaste, anger, and sadness. The picture of him on the coffin was from his early twenties. Long before he met her mom and became saddled with a child he never wanted. Like someone she should have known, but never did.

They had waited an extra twenty minutes before starting the service in case anyone else showed up. There was nobody besides the two of them. Finally, Lisa leaned over to her mom, "Should the officiant start, Mom?"

Her mom looked at her in surprise. Maria was wearing a dark skirt with a cream top that Lisa helped her put on that morning. It was a shock to see how much arthritis had debilitated her in the past four years—she looked much older than forty-four. She supposed her dad had been the one to help her mom until now. But it was probably the only thing he had ever done for her. He liked his women quiet and obedient and hadn't let her or her mom have a say in anything. Maybe that was why Maria didn't realize it was up to her to begin the service. She turned and gave the officiant waiting at the corner of the stage an apologetic nod. He took her cue and stepped forward.

"We are gathered here to remember Robert Naylor, husband to Maria Naylor and father to Lisa Naylor..."

As the officiant's voice droned on, giving meaningless trivia about a man who had been nothing in his life except cheap and mean, Lisa's thoughts drifted back to the last time she was in the same town as her dad...

From her place on the stage, Lisa looked out on the sea of parents, friends, and family. At last, she had made it to her high school graduation. She knew her dad wouldn't come, but she had hoped her mom would stand up to him for once and come to support her. Obviously she had caved, again. That morning when she asked her mom one more time to come to her graduation, her dad had interrupted, "It's no big deal. Everyone graduates. You're nothing special, and your mom won't waste her time coming to see you."

She had looked at her mom, trying to communicate to her how important it was to have *somebody* at her graduation. But she refused to make eye contact. Now, Lisa would walk across the podium, accept the diploma that she had worked so hard to get, and then turn around and walk out of this town for good.

There was polite applause when Lisa went up to collect her diploma, but nobody really knew the girl walking across the stage. She had done her best to blend in at school. At 5'5 she wasn't tall or short, and in her 'uniform' of dark straight-leg jeans, plain black sneakers, and gray t-shirts and sweatshirts over her average-sized body, people seemed to look right through her. Her dark brown hair was in a single French braid, and if anyone had gotten a closer look, they would have seen sad brown eyes and a light coat of mascara—the only makeup she could put on that her dad didn't notice.

After trying to dodge all the proud families taking pictures of their children in caps and gowns, Lisa left her own cap and gown at the registration table and went to the café where she had worked and avoided her parents for the last two years. The owners were sad to see her go. She was the only employee who was willing to work evenings, weekends, and holidays, come in on a moment's notice, and do any job without complaining. Her last paycheck was waiting for her.

Mr. Shoud, her 10th grade accounting teacher, had helped her get the job, and then went with her to the bank to open her own account when she turned sixteen. He was one of the few people in her life she had asked for help. As an old timer in the town, he knew about her dad, and had encouraged Lisa to create her own future by getting a job and protecting her earnings. For two years she had lied to her dad every time she went to work, claiming she was 'hanging out'. He saw little value in her, and believed she was a waste of life, so it was easy to let him think she wasn't doing anything useful. The café she worked at served a trendy crowd who preferred organic, natural ingredients for their meals, and her dad had never gotten wind of his daughter's secret life.

She picked up her final paycheck, deposited it in her bank account, and withdrew enough cash for a bus ticket. The past year she had spent any free hours when she wasn't working or studying in the library at the public computers researching jobs in the city, and the cost of everything from bus tickets to rent. Her escape was a dream she clung to as she struggled alone to pass her classes and work as many hours as she could. She was as ready as she'd ever be.

Back at home, she went straight to her room. Nobody asked her how the ceremony had gone or congratulated her. Nobody even said hello. She quickly packed her work outfits, a few changes of clothes, a blanket, some toiletries, and a picture of her grandparents. It was a tight squeeze in her backpack, but she didn't want it to be obvious that she was leaving. Her dad's big plans for her involved getting a full-time job and paying him back for all the "years of bleeding me dry" that he claimed she owed him. She walked out of the house without saying goodbye and never looked back.

Lisa was suddenly brought back to the present by her mom struggling to stand up. The service was over. She tucked her arm under her mom's and helped her get to her feet. It seemed like she was shorter than Lisa remembered, but she still wore her thin brown hair in a braid and her dark brown eyes still stood out against her pale cream skin. With Lisa's support, she walked to the coffin and stood there. "I don't know what I'll do without him" she whispered.

ALSO BY CARMEN KLASSEN

SUCCESS ON HER TERMS SERIES

Book 1: Sweet, Smart, and Struggling

Book 2: The Cost of Caring

Book 3: Life Upcycled

Book 4: Heartwarming Designs

Book 5: A Roof Over Their Heads (Preorder)

Success on Her Terms: Boxed Set 1 to 3

* * *

NON-FICTION TITLES

Love Your Clutter Away

Before Your Parents Move In

Made in the USA
Lexington, KY
01 September 2019